Weirdbook

VOL. 2, NO. 7   **ISSUE 37**

Features

Stories

Poetry

Artwork

From the Editor's Tower

It's been a good year for *Weirdbook*, our contributors, and of course you, the reader.

We published five issues this year! Four quarterlies and one themed annual. The Annual will be a yearly event if the sales justify it.

This is the fifth and final issue for 2017 and to be honest probably our strongest issue of the year.

We'll be back in February 2018 with even more weirdness than ever before!

And before I go I have a small favor to ask of all of you. We sell the magazine online and nothing helps sales more than a review. So help us out and go to either (or both) Amazon and/or Good Reads and leave us a short review or rating. It only takes a moment and will help to insure the magazines continuing success.

It's my deepest wish that 2017 has been a good (or at the very worst, tolerable) year for all of you. Remember to keep the important things close to your heart this upcoming holiday season.

Those would be Family, Friends, and *Weirdbook* (which by the way, makes a wonderful gift).

Happy Holidays, God bless, and may the Weird flow into your life!

—Doug Draa

Staff

PUBLISHER & EXECUTIVE EDITOR

John Gregory Betancourt

EDITOR

Doug Draa

CONSULTING EDITOR

W. Paul Ganley

WILDSIDE PRESS SUBSCRIPTION SERVICES

Carla Coupe

PRODUCTION TEAM

Steve Coupe
Ben Geyer
Helen McGee
Karl Würf

SEA GLASS HARVEST
by Bear Kiosk

Sonia Vadera never considered herself any different than anyone else. No one who knew her thought she was different either. Yes, her skin was a bit darker than the other children's, but in southern Vermont any color other than pale whitish-pink was darker. Her playmates spent so much time outdoors in the warmer months that some of them became and stayed just as brown well into the fall. Despite the limited palette of skin tones in Londonderry and its environs, falling outside the majority on this characteristic was no different than being Roman Catholic instead of Congregationalist.

Having a medical doctor father from India and a linguistics Ph.D. mother from Nicaragua whose father was Russian might have made Sonia different. However, in Londonderry, Sonia's parents and parentage were merely interesting, not different. The population in Vermont is always in flux. Young Vermonters leave for college or military service. They find someplace with less snow or more snow. They find someone they never would have met at home. Other people move to Vermont for college or to escape urbanized regions for a place renowned for each of its distinctive seasons. While many people spend their entire lives as residents of Vermont, many others come and go, creating a hotch-potch of backgrounds. It is only polite to ask someone how they ended up in the Green Mountains. It would be rude and inaccurate to say they are different.

The Vaderas enjoyed participating in uniquely American holidays their children learned about in school. There was no harm in encouraging the practices of going to see fireworks or dressing up for trick-or-treating. What little their parents gleaned from colleagues, patients, students, and neighbors was compensated for by the materials their eldest daughter brought home from school and her eager research into any means of having fun.

Sonia's two siblings were among the Vermonters who looked elsewhere for education and stayed where they landed. Her parents retired to Costa Rica soon after her thirtieth birthday. Aside from leaving her the house, they also provided her with an annuity that provided an above-average income for the area. Their goal had been to allow their daughter to live any life she wanted. While she enjoyed drawing, painting, and photography, her favorite pursuit was fashioning jewelry using stones she collected along streams and in old quarries. Even when she went away, walks took her to places where she would be scanning the ground for just the right specimens.

While on vacation at Hampton Beach, New Hampshire, she was looking around for interesting materials. Just as it was getting dark, she discovered a smooth, milky green stone. A woman walked up behind her. The stranger said it was sea glass and if she liked it, she should visit Misquamicut Beach in Rhode Island where a lot of pieces wash up. The woman told her the best time to go was around November 1, when it is quiet and before it got too cold.

Sonia created an intricate design for a pendant to hold the one piece of sea glass she had found. At the Bennington Garlic and Herb Festival in early September, customers fought over the pendant, bidding up the price. Sonia decided to take the woman's advice since the sea glass seemed to be so popular. She never liked staying at home anyway around Halloween. Trick or treating as a child, Sonia had gotten candy at houses that she learned later had been unoccupied. As much as she wanted to understand what had actually happened, she preferred to simply avoid the holiday as much as possible. So, she booked a room in Westerly, Rhode Island, within walking distance of the beach, for October 30 to November 2.

October 30 came soon enough, just a week or two after the last leaf peepers had evacuated Vermont with their weight in cheese and syrup. Sonia packed a light bag and took a canvas tote to hold the promised treasures. The drive would be part interstate, part state routes. However, on her way to the coast, her GPS malfunctioned and told her to exit into a small Connecticut town miles before she was supposed to leave the highway.

Figuring the universe was telling her take a break before making the final lap, Sonia stopped at an inviting café in the triangle where the main street split. Despite it being the dinner hour, there were no customers. The proprietor, at an age somewhere between senior and elder, welcomed her and asked whether she was heading for Misquamicut Beach. Sonia asked how he knew this. He replied that about once a month people ended up in his town asking for directions because their GPS rerouted them. They typically wound up at the café because it was the first business they saw after exiting the highway.

Sonia was surprised when the gentleman asked whether she was going to look for sea glass. However, he saw the disturbed look in her face and quickly added that everyone who got lost here seemed to be going to the beach to look for sea glass. Sonia expressed concern that there wouldn't be any sea glass if it was so popular, but the man reassured her that the currents provided a steady supply. He gave her simple directions to get to Westerly by continuing on the part of Main Street that split to the right. His directions were perfect. Within half an hour, Sonia arrived at the inn and settled down for the night.

Sonia spent the next day exploring Westerly and the nearby nature reserve. She went out late in the afternoon combing the beach for sea glass. Sonia found nothing, but wasn't too disappointed because the location was so pretty and peaceful. No storms were forecast during her stay, so she knew she could just take each moment without concern. She felt happy Halloween had been so relaxing and slept soundly.

At lunch the next day, Sonia stopped in a Mexican restaurant. She remarked to the manager on the colorful Halloween decorations. The manager told her that Mexicans celebrate November 1 as the Day of the Dead. Now that she knew about this second day of ghosts, Sonia was relieved she wasn't going home until the next day. At least the Mexican decorations were much cheerier than black, white, and orange. She celebrated with cinnamon churros and vanilla ice cream.

That afternoon on the beach, she still couldn't find any sea glass. She remembered the café owner saying the currents were always dropping it on the beach. Perhaps the currents had shifted in the weeks before her arrival. She was halfway through a second pass along the beach and thinking of just heading back to town for dinner.

As the sun set a group of six or seven casually-dressed people came up to her and asked her what she was looking for. Sonia told them. One man in the group wearing a hoodie said, "We thought so." They all held out their palms full of sea glass and offered their bounty to her. Sonia refused, but the young man insisted they didn't want it; they had been collecting it to pass the time and hoped someone might want it. As they deposited the opaque nuggets and shards into her canvas bag, she offered to go back to her room and get some maple syrup she brought as gifts for the staff at the inn. The man told her that wasn't necessary and the group continued walking down the beach.

Sonia took the glass back to her room. It struck her that the man on the beach had the same distant way of speaking as the café owner. However, she was so relieved she had such a large collection of sea glass now she had little trouble forgetting the idea by the time she went to dinner.

Just before dawn, Sonia dreamt about a ship going down in a storm. Thinking that her dream was real, Sonia jumped out of bed. She raced to the beach, not even noticing that the weather was not stormy as in the dream. Just as the sun began to break the horizon she spotted the same group of people from the day before. As she rushed to catch them they seemed to evaporate in the sun's rays. Reaching where they were, she found a small pile of sea glass on the sand. Sonia picked up the sea glass and walked back to the inn.

After breakfast, Sonia checked out. She asked the inn's owner whether many boats go down off the coast. The owner told her that it happened now and then when boaters foolishly went out without checking the weather forecast first. She went on to mention that many people claimed the boaters who drowned off the coast as a result of egotistical decisions did penance by helping the living.

Leaving Westerly, Sonia wondered about the helpful dead. She had begun to believe that seeing the group on the beach that morning was just part of the dream. Now, she wasn't sure. Without thinking, Sonia retraced her route and wound up in the same small town in Connecticut where she had detoured before. She decided she would stop at the café and ask the owner what he knew on the subject of the dead helping the living.

Sonia spotted the café. As she pulled up she discovered it was closed and appeared to have been closed for years. Instead of freaking out, Sonia suddenly realized what had been going on since she was a girl. She had no need to fear Halloween. If there had been ghosts in her life, they all had been benevolent. She thought about how many pieces of jewelry she would be able to make from the sea glass provided to her by the strangers at Misquamicut Beach. Sonia really didn't need the money. Maybe the point was to use the proceeds from selling what she would make to be helpful to others. For the rest of the drive back to Londonderry, more at peace than ever before, Sonia thought about the ways she could pay forward her sea glass harvest.

✗

THE CHANGELING
by R. Rozakis

As soon as she looked in the cradle, Abigail knew it was not her baby.

She had had her suspicions when she woke up gradually instead of being yanked from sleep by a wail. Her first thought as she drifted into wakefulness was a sleepy appreciation of comfort. She listened to the fire crackling soothingly on the hearth of the cottage. Then the bottom of her stomach fell out as she realized that Madeline wasn't crying. It had finally come, as everyone had been predicting for days. She wanted to curl in a tight ball around the knot of despair, but she forced herself to open her eyes. And then she realized she could hear the tiny breath of the newborn sleeping peacefully.

But when she peered into the cradle, the second wave of nausea washed over her. The baby resembled her daughter, it was true. The same tiny snub nose, the nearly translucent eyelids, the lashes as fine as the silk thread she had seen once in a fancy shop in London. But the cheeks had rosiness that her sallow baby had never boasted. The sweet lips, gently parted, held none of Maddy's peevishness. And even in sleep, her daughter had pinched her eyebrows together in infant distress at the cruelty of the world.

Nathaniel padded up behind her and Abigail braced herself for his dismay. He wrapped his arms around her bare shoulders and looked down. His breath caught.

"She turned the corner," he whispered, his voice filled with awe.

Abigail whipped her head around. Could he not see? "That's not Maddy," she said harshly, not caring if she woke the interloper.

He blinked at her. "Abby, of course it's Maddy. Who else would it be?"

"I don't know," she said, her voice thick with the grief she had staved off ever since Maddy was born. "It's a changeling."

He almost laughed and caught himself. "I thought the legend was that fairies take healthy babies and create changelings out of twigs that they leave to sicken and die. They don't take sick ones and leave healthy ones in their place."

"Anything would look healthy, compared to Maddy." She already knew she had lost him. Nathaniel didn't believe in fairies. He had always been more interested in newfangled ideas and had, in better days, laughed at what he called her little superstitions.

"But why would they even take a sick baby in the first place?" he tried to reason.

She didn't bother to answer that one. Everyone knew the fairies thought differently from humans—who could say why they did anything? Spite, amusement, because they couldn't have children of their own, because the vitality of a mortal soul was entertaining to an immortal—how could she guess what went through their heads? "I don't care, that's what happened. That's not my daughter."

"Abigail. Dear heart." Nathaniel held her at arms' length. "You haven't been sleeping. It's natural. The midwife, the doctor, they all said she would die, but you wouldn't give up. And now, it's a miracle, thanks to you. Our daughter—she's going to live, Abby, I know it. You were right. She's going to live."

"But that's not her," Abigail wailed.

Its eyelids fluttered. Both parents braced themselves instinctively for the thin shriek that was sure to follow. But the baby just looked up at them, placid.

Abigail collapsed on the floor, weeping.

* * * *

The changeling whimpered softly to itself in the cradle. Abigail rocked absently next to it. She was too exhausted to move, but the idea of picking it up was revolting. The midwife had been feeding it goats' milk since Abigail refused to nurse. Her own breasts ached with unreleased milk. It leaked through, staining her dress. Nursing the changeling would be a relief of sorts, but it seemed a desecration, a betrayal of her own child to feed the interloper. Soon enough, the flow would stop.

Someone in the next room was talking.

She had ignored them, choosing to stare at the wall vacantly. But the sound of her own name caught her attention again, and she finally listened.

"It's just the shock of relief," Nathaniel was saying. His voice had an odd pleading tone.

"Don't look like relief to me," someone else grumbled. Abigail thought she recognized the midwife's voice. "Looks something closer to madness. Is she still insisting the child isn't hers?"

"She just needs time," Nathaniel said.

"She needs to nurse her babe," replied the doctor. "It's unnatural. All this talk of fairies and changelings…we're past the point of superstition. This isn' t a matter of leaving a dish of milk out for brownies anymore."

Abigail waited for her husband to defend her again, but all she could hear was silence.

"Unnatural," the midwife echoed.

"I know you want only to protect them," the doctor continued, "but you may be harming one by protecting the other."

Yes! thought Abigail. *Stop protecting the fairy thing.*

But he continued speaking. "If she does not give up these fanciful notions of hers, you may have to confront the idea that your wife is no longer sane."

Now Nathaniel broke in. "There must be a way to save her. I can't lose Abby, not when we just got Maddy back! Isn't there anything you can do?"

"Well," the doctor said slowly. "I would have recommended the madhouse to keep her from harming the child. But I have heard of some remarkable results from experiments with electrcity up in London these days…"

Abby bent over in the rocker, clutching her stomach. Madness? Electricity? What had she done to deserve this?

Maybe they were right. Maybe it was just alienation brought on by exhaustion, and there was nothing wrong with her daughter. No one else could see it. But when she looked into the cradle, she felt another wave of revulsion. No one else could see it, but she could. She knew her own child, and that wasn't it, no matter how identical they looked.

But electrical experiments. Surely even the madhouse was preferable to that.

Could she pretend? Act as if everything were normal? She wanted to throw up. But if they took her away, if something happened to her, then no one would be here if Maddy ever came home. She had to survive, no matter what it took, for Maddy's sake.

She picked up the changeling, and held it numbly to her breast. It immediately stopped mewling and latched on with enthusiasm. It ate steadily, easily, nothing like the epic battles she had had with Maddy. It had her daughter's face, but not her ferocity, that ruthless desire to live that had awed Abigail even in her exhaustion.

Her cracked nipples had begun to heal. She'd prayed for that, but now she welcomed the pain, longed for it even. She wanted nursing this creature to hurt.

Nathanial peered in. Seeing her nursing the little thing, his face lit up. He nearly bounded into the room, and then remembered not to disturb the baby and tiptoed. He needn't have bothered. Nothing could distract the changeling, whose hands opened and closed in contentment.

The doctor and the midwife hovered in the door. She did not miss the look of relief they exchanged. Abigail kept her features carefully neutral while they all exclaimed how much better she was looking, how much more like herself. Her husband admired the changeling, proudly pointing out various features to the receptive audience.

Nathanial's coos nauseated her. She could not find any of the joy he obviously felt over the waving baby fists, the fattening little feet. Yes, this baby was healthy and cheerful and…easy. But she didn't want an easy baby, she wanted her daughter.

* * * *

But she could fake it. She fed it, changed it, rocked it off to sleep. Day after day, numb to the world. She dared not let her true feelings show.

One day, as she changed the nappy by rote, the little thing smiled up at her, a first real smile of heart-breaking sweetness. Abigail stared back as the smile slowly faded in disappointed confusion. She was such a tiny creature, Abigail realized. And she was trying so hard.

"If you're not mine," she said slowly, "then you don't have a mother at all, do you?"

The little eyes looked up at her solemnly. Abigail felt a rush of pity. Even if it wasn't Maddy, she was still a baby. She still wanted to be loved by someone. And it wasn't her fault the fairies had left her, was it?

"Oh, little one," Abigail sighed. "Perhaps we can be lonely together."

She tried a hesitant smile, the first she could remember since they had laid Madeline in her arms. Her face felt stiff. But the returning smile was dazzling. The changeling—the baby—the baby changeling grinned, tooth-lessly ecstatic, and kicked her feet in delight at her success. Abigail felt the muscles in her face relax as her own smile became more genuine.

"You don't ask for much, do you?" Abigail picked up the child, who burrowed into her shoulder. Somewhere, she hoped someone else would do the same for Maddy. Silently, she made a deal with the universe. She would take care of this child if someone would take care of hers.

It wasn't hard to take care of this one. With Abigail's smiles in response, the baby grew radiant. She smiled at everyone, gurgling and laughing at the slightest provocation.

"Sunny little thing," commented Nathaniel.

"That she is," Abigail agreed. The name stuck, much to Abigail's relief, as she had never been able to bring herself to call the creature Madeline.

* * * *

She had insisted that any celebration would be on the day of Sunny's getting well, not on the day that Abigail had given birth. Nathaniel was all too willing to humor her. It was the day, after all, that he had begun to hope they might keep his firstborn. So the cottage was quiet on Madeline's birthday when Abigail slipped out before dawn.

She gathered handfuls of flowers from the pasture. Without a grave to lay them on, she finally settled on scattering them by the handful into the creek.

"She's still here," Abigail told her absent daughter. "I kept waiting for whatever magic animated her to wear off and for Sunny to waste away. At least no one thought me mad for that. I suppose, after such a beginning, it was only natural for a mother to watch so closely for any sign of sickness." She laughed bitterly. "As if any of this was natural."

Some of the petals swirled, trapped in an eddy. She fetched a stick and, without knowing why she did so, prodded the flowers until they bobbed on to follow the rest down the creek.

"But she hasn't shown any signs of turning back into wood, or whatever she was made from. So I'm beginning to think that I'll be allowed to keep her. Maybe your father is halfway right, and not everything they say about the fairies is true. Maybe changelings aren't sickly at all, maybe they're just different. I don't know. But I'm glad," she confessed. "I don't know if I could have lost another one. She's a delightful baby. Smiles all the time. Maybe you would have played together." She thought about her daughter's stubbornness. "Maybe not."

The flowers had all but disappeared from sight, and the horizon was lightening. She needed to get back before someone noticed she was gone.

"I still love you," she whispered. "I always will."

* * * *

From that day, though, she set aside the thought of her real daughter. The tug on Abigail's heart never eased, but she learned to live with it. A part of her never forgave Nathaniel, but she hid it away. Except for that one morning a year, she tried not to think of the tiny newborn she had barely gotten to know. As the years passed, she had increasing trouble recalling the few details she had. They had no more children, for which Abigail was secretly glad.

She cheered when the girl took her first wobbly steps, helped her learn to feed and dress herself, even teared up a bit when Sunny's first word was "Mama". She could not help but love the girl. It felt like a betrayal, but her heart melted every time she saw that smile. And Sunny was a good child— sweet, helpful, as even tempered as she had been as a baby. Even as a toddler, she insisted on doing chores. Abigail and Nathaniel smothered their smiles as the girl solemnly set the table, a single plate or fork at a time, tongue sticking out of the corner of her mouth in concentration. If Sunny's first oatcakes were lumpy and strange (and choked down with smiles and compliments), they rapidly improved.

She and Sunny were nearly inseparable, the child following her everywhere. Others noted that she treated the child more as a companion than a daughter, but the girl was looked after well enough even if the mother was a bit odd. Abigail was careful never to breathe a word that might indicate she still longed for the only girl she thought of in her heart as Maddy.

Sometimes she even found herself wondering if they were right, if she had been mad. Everyone else seemed so sure that Sunny was her daughter. And the girl's unquestioning trust sometimes shook Abigail to the core. But for the most part, she tried to forget.

And so she thought little of it when she and Sunny went mushroom hunting in the woods and Sunny ran off a bit too far ahead. The girl was seven now, already a beauty with hair like eiderdown and upturned, laughing eyes. Abigail took no notice of the mist curling through the wood.

"Mama? Mama!" The voice echoed through the mist.

"I'm here, darling," she called absently, focused on the pile of mushrooms she held in her apron.

"Mama?" The voice wasn't right.

She looked up. For a moment, the sallow, pinch-faced creature was unfamiliar. Then, somehow, she knew.

"Maddy?" she whispered. The apron corners fell from her nerveless fingers. Mushrooms bounced along the ground.

"Mama, I'm home." That plaintive whine Maddy had had as a baby had never disappeared. The face was the same as Sunny's, but thinner and with the rosy glow and good humor stripped out. Her eyes burned with the fierce determination to live and be loved.

Abigail took a hesitant step towards her daughter, and then another. But before she could break into a run, Sunny appeared on the other side of the clearing, her arms full of wildflowers.

"Mama?" she asked. She looked at the other girl and then back to Abigail, confused, trusting.

"No," Maddy shrieked, her face contorted in sudden anger. "You're my mother. They left her for you so you wouldn't complain, but I escaped and came home and you don't need her anymore. You can't have her. You have to choose!"

Abigail's breath caught in her throat at the force of that rage. Her head whipped back and forth, between the child of her body and the child of her heart. Which was really hers? The one she had borne for nine months and pushed out into the world after two days of agony? Who she had sobbed over, desperately trying to get her to latch, certain that she would die in Abigail's arms? Or the one she had raised, who she had taught to walk? Whose sleeping head she had kissed and whose smiles she had delighted in?

Maddy saw the indecision in her mother's face, and her own face fell.

"It's not fair," she sobbed, all of her rage deflating. "She isn't really yours, she isn't real. You were mine first. You used to be mine!"

She turned and ran into the forest.

Abigail chased after her, hands outstretched. After all this time, to have been so close! But the sounds of weeping disappeared almost immediately into the mist. Only after a few minutes of stumbling blindly did she remember the other girl.

She raced back towards the clearing. But in the darkening wood, every way seemed unfamiliar. The shadows taunted her. Time and again, she saw what she thought was the shadow of a little girl. Her heart would pause a beat. She would crash through the underbrush in her haste, hoping, praying, trying somehow not to think about what she would do if it were the wrong one, about which one would be the wrong one. Each time, when she reached it, she found only rocks or bushes or tricks of the light. Her head spun and her breath came in gasps. She stumbled, skinning a knee like she hadn't since childhood. She called out into the mist.

"Darling? Where are you? Stay put, I'll find you." She wasn't sure which one she called.

When every thundering heartbeat felt like eternity, it became impossible to tell how long she wandered. Finally, she burst back out into the clearing. The sun was setting beyond the cloud cover. But no little girl waited for her. There was no one to clutch to her breast, no hysterics to soothe but her own. She looked around frantically, searching for some clue, some trace of her daughter in the gathering gloom.

But all she could find were a handful of scattered flowers, a pile of twigs, and a wisp of eiderdown.

THE MAIDEN VOYAGE OF THE "ARIONA"

by Dale W. Glaser

How did I come to be here? I imagine that in the broadest outlines my tale would not be entirely dissimilar from your own, or any of the other unfortunates all around us. But perhaps in the particular details lies a story worth telling. In deference to the assured commonalities in our respective tales, and with no desire to insult your intelligence, I shall endeavor toward succinct brevity.

I suppose I should begin with the fortunate happenstance of my being offered employment as part of Mister Edmond Stonington's latest venture. Fortunate may be an understatement, of course, as it rescued me from penury after a prolonged period wherein I had no means of earning a living whatsoever. Some no doubt felt that it was foolhardy at best to sign on as paid labor for one of Mister Stonington's ventures, and that a debtor's prison would be preferable, but I put little stock in the opinions of such wilting spirits. Far better, to my mind, to risk my very life to secure a livelihood, to risk and fail, even to die, than to eke out a pale imitation of life as the wretches in such bondage. I have not yet lost my life, but neither do I doubt that those same skeptics would consider themselves validated and proven right in their distrust of Mister Stonington.

But can it be, as the lack of any recognition in your eyes seems to indicate, that you do not know who Edmond Stonington is? How long have you been so isolated here? Mister Stonington is a captain of industry, a man who has enjoyed a meteoric rise to fame and fortune in the last ten years. He is also a man of peculiar passions, perhaps none greater than his fascination, his obsession, with the sea. That much, at the very least, you no doubt already would have guessed. But moreover, this obsession takes not as its focus the sea as most men think of it, the surface waters spreading out to the horizon, the rising swell and crashing fall of waves and tides, the shipping lanes and trawling shoals which, true enough, were the source of much of Mister Stonington's wealth. No, Mister Stonington dreamed of the hidden, unknown depths of the ocean, the world untrodden by foot, untouched by keel, unfamiliar even with the sun itself. The deepest waters, Mister Stonington believed, hold mysteries all their own, and represent a crucially important new frontier to be conquered and claimed by those willing to risk all.

Mister Stonington's latest project was to be his masterpiece and his legacy. In his grand vision, he foresaw a railroad that crossed the Pacific Ocean, not on a bridge in the open air but rather underwater. Can you imagine it? Safe below the turbulent surface, immune to storms, invisible to pirates, a locomotive running through the deep, dark waters from San Francisco to Shanghai, faster than any seagoing ship or wind-riding dirigible could make the same journey. I admit that at first I had trouble believing in such a fantastic promise myself, but Mister Stonington's conviction was both absolute and infectious.

I was brought in on the locomotive frame assembly team, after the engine had already been constructed, based on a truly remarkable design formulated by a brilliant inventor, Doctor Terrence Abercrombie. Are you familiar with the principles of electrolysis, and the use of anodes and cathodes in oxidising brine? Perhaps none can claim the same depth of understanding on the subject as Dr. Abercrombie, and I assure you, I know far more now after having worked aboard the ocean train than I knew on the first day I reported to the roundhouse where it was given material shape. Suffice to say that Dr. Abercrombie had conceptualized a wondrous alchemical engine which consumed seawater and transmuted it into various chemical components: hydrogen gas to fuel a combustion engine, and sodium hydroxide and chlorine gas as byproducts. This chloralkali process enabled the train to move through ocean waters in much the same way an earthworm might burrow through soil, gulping down what lies in its path in order to create energy and expel waste.

The superstructure was designed and built from scratch utilizing customized components cast at a foundry which Mister Stonington had converted expressly for the task. To both accommodate the chloralkali engine and withstand the crushing pressures of the depths of the ocean, the locomotive was flatter and wider than any chassis produced anywhere else in the world, and reinforced with novel arrangements of undergirdings. It was backbreaking work, positioning the plates and bars one by one with no guidance save for the strokes of a draftsman's pen, yet every protest of my overtaxed muscles, every abrasion of my knuckles and even the sting of sweat in my eyes was in its own way a pleasure to me, for there is no true glory without tangible sacrifice.

As monumental an undertaking as the locomotive itself represented, the rails represented the greater challenge by orders of magnitude, as you may well imagine. Even as luminous a figure as Mister Stonington faced a daunting predicament in trying to rally investors to his cause in sufficient numbers to underwrite the creation of over six thousand miles of track, more than twice the length of the Transcontinental Rail! A demonstration of the viability of the chloralkali engine and the seaworthiness of the locomotive was in order, but how could such a thing be demonstrated before it was built, and how could it be built without the backing of those demanding a demonstration? You see the horns of the dilemma, I trust.

Mister Stonington's solution was to fund the prototype line himself, albeit on a smaller scale covering a much shorter distance beneath the ocean. Thus he mounted an immense expedition to lay tracks from a small Alaskan outpost called Wales to a remote village on the Chukotka peninsula of Siberia, a northerly route of dubious commercial value yet inarguably effective in proving the feasibility of the larger enterprise. If an underwater train line could span the one hundred and seventy miles from Alaska to Siberia, surely it could run anywhere beneath the seven seas.

Mister Stonington had initially announced the track engineering expedition with an estimated completion time of six months, before the first elements of the locomotive frame had ever been forged. Uncountable legions of detractors had dismissed such projections as wide-eyed optimism, even taking into account Mister Stonington's promise to spare no expense and hire as many laborers as the admittedly herculean task required. Some openly questioned whether or not such numbers of trained oceanographic surveyors and underwater welders even existed. Yet not only did Mister Stonington defy the odds, he thrashed them resoundingly. The prototype tracks were completed after a mere ten weeks, during the latter half of which I and the other workmen labored feverishly to construct the locomotive, even as new specifications for the gauge of the tracks the axles must match caused setbacks and duplications of effort.

Notwithstanding the great difficulties, less than three months after Mister Stonington's survey ships had steamed westward across the Bering Sea, a hastily erected train platform rose above the harbor in Wales, where the rails and ties for the eastern terminus had been laid down. Most of the workmen, including myself, were retained to serve as crew for the maiden voyage, and so I was afforded one last look at the resplendent marvel of engineering before boarding one of the full complement of train cars coupled one to the next behind the *Ariona*. Mister Stonington had christened her thus, concluding that his seafaring iron horse should take as her namesake the immortal stallion sired by Poseidon himself. The summer sunlight sparkled across the water of the bay and the ice and snow crusting the ground, and imbued the galvanized hide of the *Ariona* with a triumphal gleam. Crowning the locomotive was a half-globe of blue sapphire glass, providing a translucent window through which a lookout could observe the progress of the journey. Near the front was a powerful headlamp capable of piercing the darkness of the deepest trench in the ocean. The forward face of the *Ariona* was dominated by a cavernous mouth agape, a single enormous funnel intake like the jaws of a basking shark, ready to imbibe the brine which would be the lifeblood of her engines.

Once within the confines of the train, I could only speculate on the pageantry that would accompany her launch. Investors, now paying respectful attention to the details of the enterprise, no doubt crowded the platform to see the prototype depart, dressed in top hats and tails, accompanied by representatives of the fairer sex in their most fashionable finery. Mister Stonington I am sure gave an impassioned speech about the inevitable progress of future technology and commerce which would trace its origins back to this very moment. When the *Ariona* finally rolled forward under her own power, I imagined the assembled dignitaries and well-wishers waving, cheering heartily and fluttering handkerchiefs. The train pulled slowly out of the station, and almost immediately began to run downhill, along the sloping rails that disappeared into the surface of the water. Like a metallic leviathan, the locomotive submerged, flooding her intakes with brine. In a great churning of foam the *Ariona* dove along the tracks.

At first riding the train felt the way I imagine being trapped within a sinking steamship must, the sheer mass of a colossal aggregate of dense metals bearing inexorably down through the waters towards a final resting place of saturated darkness. But inexorably the *Ariona* began to pick up speed, imbuing us with a sense not only of descent but of forward motion. I tried to visualize the vortex of water being siphoned into the chloralkali chambers, while the train cut through the frigid coastal waters on its way to the floor of the Arctic Ocean.

The trip was uneventful for the first hour, during which the chief engineer estimated that we traversed at least seventy-five miles of the seabed track. Seventy-five miles in an hour! Mister Stonington had assured the entire crew, as well as the guests aboard the train, that he would celebrate with a complimentary champagne toast once the train had logged one hundred miles along its journey; at that stage, well beyond the midpoint, Mister Stonington conjectured that the proof of concept would be inarguable. A train that could run one hundred miles beneath the ocean could run a thousand, or ten thousand, or in circuits without end.

Unfortunately, scant minutes into the second hour of that maiden voyage, the locomotive was forced to decelerate, and stop. The lookout had called the halt from his perch atop the engine, sounding three dolorous chimes, the pre-arranged signal for an obstruction on the tracks which could potentially damage, or at worst derail, the train. Mister Stonington himself met with the lookout, the chief engineer, and the second engineer in order to determine the appropriate course of action. It was decided that the lookout would return to his observation dome, while a team of four men would climb into pressurized diving suits, exit the train, and clear the tracks so that the voyage might resume. Volunteers were requested from among the crew, and with no small amount of pride in my own ability to further repay Mister Stonington's generosity by contributing to his venture's success, I stepped forward.

The bulky suits required assistance to pull up over our bodies and seal, in which we were aided by other crewmembers. The helmets were connected via hoses to the interior of the train, where reagent tanks independent of the chloralkali cells were still maintaining a steady supply of breathable air. The second engineer, Mister Von Vock, was in a diving suit as the leader of the track-clearing detail, accompanied by myself, a grizzled old hand named John Hertford, and a quiet youth, barely more than a boy, whom I knew only as Gregory. When the four of us had been girded up in our sheaths of padded canvas, insulated against the cold, rubber seals and brass helmets, we were led into the car directly behind the locomotive, which was empty. Valves jutting from air pipes running along the walls were connected to the breathing hoses feeding our helmets; additionally, we were tethered together at the waist in pairs, Mister Von Vock to Mister Hertford, and myself to Gregory. Doubly secured and anchored, we were bid farewell and good luck by our crewmates, who departed the car and sealed the doorway. A hatch in the roof of the car opened, and icy dark seawater poured in. As the ocean enveloped us, we climbed up and out of the car.

Atop the train, we could make out the bright enclosure of the lookout's dome, and beyond that the pale cone of light shining from the *Ariona*'s headlamp ahead into the darkness engulfing the rails. The beam of light was interrupted along its lowermost arc by an irregular shape, sitting quite close to the intake funnel of the chloralkali engine.Led by Mister Von Vock, we walked the length of the locomotive, until we reached its front and floated down to the tracks below. A school of mercurial fish swam past, knife-like with slender chartreuse bodies and serrated dorsal fins, seemingly unmindful of us and unbothered by our presence. We continued toward the obstruction in our train's path, and upon reaching it discovered it to be a massive boulder, as large as an elephant and so heavy as to be nigh unmovable.

Mister Von Vock and Hertford crouched down to examine the boulder more closely, in order to determine how best to shift it off the rails. For my part, I looked around at the area in which we had been forced to pause in our journey. I could barely see beyond the halo of the *Ariona*'s headlamp, certainly nothing in any detail. Yet the character of the ocean floor was severe enough to differentiate the largest shapes in their subtle variations of dark green and deep brown. The tracks were running along a ledge traversing the side of an undersea mountain. To the starboard side of the train, the surface ran up, and to port, it dropped away. If we could move the boulder even halfway, levering it onto the portside rail, our job might well be nearly done, as the stone could simply roll the rest of the way down the oceanic peak once its center of gravity was appropriately shifted.

I presume even now that Mister Von Vock and Hertford were discussing that very approach to the dilemma, although I was not privy to their exchanges. The tethers connecting us in pairs were hollow, such that sound could carry freely from one diving suit to the next. As such, I had only Gregory to speak with, and as I mentioned he was not known to be particularly talkative. Nonetheless, I was about to ask him if he thought it at all feasible that the four of us could nudge the boulder up onto and over the port rail, when I realized he was no longer standing beside me. Startled, I jerked my entire body round in surprise, and felt the tug of our tether assuring me that our connection had not been severed. I was forced to pivot and bend my waist to properly look around, only to apprehend at last that Gregory had lowered himself to his hands and knees. He was closely examining the tracks themselves, the front plate of his diving helmet nearly scraping the starboard rail. I inquired as to what, exactly, he thought he was doing.

"Looking at the rails," he answered, as though I could not have ascertained as much on my own. "It's so dark down here. They're hard to see."

"Are you worried that the tracks were damaged by the falling boulder?" I asked him. "I think it unlikely myself, given the rigorous strength of materials Mister Stonington has wisely insisted upon throughout the entire manufacturing process. If the rails are half as sturdy as the *Ariona*, whose creation I witnessed with my own eyes, then they should be all but impervious."

"But ..." Gregory began to interject.

Unfortunately, I had just begun to warm to the topic. I admit, I may have preferred the sound of my own voice to the chilling, tomblike stillness of the undersea mountainside. "Furthermore, in my opinion, if there is any damage whatsoever to the rails, it will only be found at the impact site itself. Although I doubt very much there is any to be discovered."

"But these ..."

"Whether or not you share my faith in the durability of our employer's infrastructure, if you prefer that our voyage continue expeditiously, the task at hand is to assist Mister Von Vock and Mister Hertford in moving that stone off Mister Stonington's tracks!" I finished in a rhetorical crescendo.

"But that's just it, sir," Gregory insisted in a small, pitiful voice. "I don't think these are Mister Stonington's tracks."

"What?" I was agog. "What a preposterous thing to say! Gregory, are you feeling quite all right?" I had heard that the increased pressure of the deepest waters could cause something like temporary madness in men, and presumably boys, of a certain constitution.

"Feel fine, sir," was Gregory's reply, and I was forced to admit that he sounded lucid by any reasonable measure.

"Then what do you think we are standing upon, if not the tracks of Mister Stonington's train line?" I demanded.

"It's not that I don't think these are tracks, sir," Gregory said, "Just not Mister Stonington's. Look, see for yourself."

Reluctantly, I lowered myself to the same position as Gregory, and peered closely at the rails. A queer and queasy feeling knotted my stomach as I began to comprehend what Gregory had been trying to tell me. The rails were not made of steel, nor any other metal forged by human hands. They had the luster, even in the pale indirect light of the headlamp shining its beam over our heads, of mother-of-pearl. Iridescent whorls of green, blue and violet were visible within their impossibly smooth depths. They did not seem to have been constructed so much as extruded by a living thing. I ran a hand over the surface, and cursed the heavy canvas for its muting effects on my sense of touch, but I could detect no seams or other signs of manufacture.

Disparate thoughts began to crystallize in my mind, the brilliance of epiphany illuminating various ideas which had puzzled me and yet which I had resolved, out of propriety and gratitude, to set aside. Without once impugning the honesty or industriousness of Mister Stonington, I had wondered how he had been able to construct and lay down the entirety of the undersea rail line in such a miraculously short time; here before me now was the miracle itself. Mister Stonington's first expedition must have fortuitously discovered this segment of the route already extant, and spent the remaining ten weeks merely building the terminal extensions to Alaska and Siberia. Even recognizing the duplicity of Mister Stonington's non-disclosure of the serendipitous nature of the project, I still could hardly fault the man. His foreshortened timeline of construction enabled him to silence his critics and attract widespread attention, interest and crucial investment, and in the end the results would be exactly the same: his prototype locomotive would prove his theory, and he would go on to apply the lessons learned to building the Trans-Pacific Railroad, the greatest undertaking of the century.

Nonetheless, a new and more disturbing question arose in my mind, like a single bubble in the cold seawater ready to burst on the surface: if Mister Stonington did not build the nacreous rails bridging the deep, dark midpoint of his tracks, who did?

Movement nearby drew my attention, and I looked up to see Mister Von Vock and Hertford had turned away from the problematic boulder.

Hertford was pointing agitatedly in the direction of the summit of the undersea mountain the rails encircled. I turned, slowly and awkwardly in my dive suit, to see for myself what had him so aroused, but from my crouching vantage point I could see nothing beyond the looming shadow of the *Ariona* herself.

Then one of the train cars rocked towards the abyss. Everything behind the locomotive was shrouded in brumous murk, but the movement of such a large object was noticeable even as a silhouette within shadows. The wheels closest to the mountainside lifted several inches off the weird, pearlescent rails, then lowered with a dolorous clang of its wheels. Lifted again, and lowered again. At first I attributed this to some unknown property of the strange material, but the more rational side of my mind observed that the engine of the train was moving in precisely the way I had anticipated we would move the boulder. It was rocking because someone, or something, was rocking it, trying to tilt it off the rails and into the chasm yawning beneath. Soon the fifth car began to lurch back and forth between the rails, joined by the second and third cars soon enough.

I looked up the slope of the undersea mountain, where I still could only hope to discern shades within the caliginosity if they seemed to be moving more purposefully than the currents. The headlamp, mounted above the empty frozen scream of the intake, shone a focused and precise beam away from the train, and shed no light on what might be immediately behind the locomotive. The lookout dome of blue glass cast a muted glow of its own, too scant to penetrate far into the icy waters at our present depth. Suddenly a monstrous silhouette emerged from the darkness, rearing above the sapphire hemisphere and revealing its underside in the bluish light. A pale banded body, long and slender, was surrounded by four pairs of bristled, segmented legs. Two pairs held fast to the top of the locomotive, while the others flexed upraised, brandishing long black claws at their distal tips. A tapered head between the front pair of waggling appendages was almost like the body in miniature: elongated and narrow, with blunted antennae and sturdier, limblike mouthparts that scissored menacingly.

The terrible sea spider seemed to be suspended weightless for an interminable moment, and then its forelegs crashed down on the lookout dome and shattered the panes with its claws. Spumes of air bubbles rushed upwards from the holes as frigid seawater poured into the locomotive. I watched in mute horror as the monstrosity climbed over the dome, proceeding towards the front of the engine, while behind it nearly every car in the train was rocking back and forth on the rails. I could feel the awful reverberations even through the boots of my diving suit, like the ringing of a carillon of bells as played by a riot of madmen.

From that point onward, events unfolded with alarming swiftness, as a horde of giant sea spiders charged down the side of the mountain. Most of them joined the ones which had already braced themselves near the tracks in order to lend their eight-legged strength to the efforts of rocking the train cars over the side of the ledge. A few of the creatures descended to the rails in front of the engine, and there in the light of the headlamp I was finally able to see that the sea spiders were not merely wild animals attacking the train mindlessly. Each of the pantopods had been mounted by a rider seated athwart its thorax. I do not know if you have seen these fearsome steeds for yourself, which is why I described the sea spiders in such detail, to conjure the image in your mind should you lack firsthand knowledge of your own. And in truth, it eases my mind somewhat to hear my own account, and to remember my own first sense of awe and dread in their presence.

Regardless, I allow that you know perfectly well what form their riders took, their troglodytic profiles and sepulchral colorations. Yet, I beg of you, understand that when I first saw those creatures who had tamed the sea spiders and rode atop them, I looked into their black bulbous fisheyes and in an instant understood the folly of a man such as Mister Stonington. Those eyes were inhuman, perhaps altogether unnatural, yet they were cunning. Not merely clever, in the way that a rodent might evince some instinctual ability to escape a trap, or the way that a dog might seek approval from its master for performing a trick. Not even in the way that a circus monkey might make sport of human foibles in its imitation of man. No, the deep-dwelling creatures are something more than animals. They are capable of thoughts, of feelings, of setting goals and putting plans into motion to achieve them. One need only catch the faintest glimmer of the inner light in their ink-pearl eyes to know that.

Or, one need only ruminate on the works of the deep-dwellers, their undersea rails so similar to the train tracks mankind had built on dry land. One need not know the exact aim of those shimmering lines of chiton frilling the mountains of the ocean floor to surmise that they must serve some constructive and intentional purpose inspiring the hands, or clawed fins, which wrought them. Granted, such thoughts did not immediately press upon my consciousness when young Gregory first drew my attention to the strange rails, but I had only moments between that initial discovery and the siege of the sea spiders. Mister Stonington had understood the implications of the rails as well, he must have, and yet he saw them first and foremost as a miraculous boon to his enterprise. He seized the opportunity to wed his own undersea railroad to the pre-existing path his diving surveyors had discovered. Over the weeks, the months that the project required for completion, not once had Mister Stonington considered that the ancient line of rails were still being used, being watched by nubilous eyes, or that a conflict arising from his usurpation of them might be one he could not win. I wondered then, as I wonder even now, if Mister Stonington ever suspected that the boulder which blocked the maiden voyage of his *Ariona* had been deliberately placed in our path, or if he had assumed up to the very end that it was a naturally-occurring phenomenon, an accidental lapse of Providential oversight.

Whatever Mister Stonington suspected or assumed, I now saw the truth all too plainly before my eyes. A sea spider positioned itself between the locomotive and Gregory and myself. The deep-dweller atop its carapace braced itself with one arm, and with the other raised a black spear, limned by the light of the headlamp behind it. For a moment I believed that some time remained to attempt to reason with the rider or appeal to its mercy, before it could dismount and threaten us with its weapon more directly. Then the spear hurtled through the water and struck Gregory in the chest, emerging through his back with its velocity barely diminished, driving the gore-smeared blade of its head into the igneous surface between the rails. As crimson ribbons of blood unfurled in the icy water from the ragged perforations in Gregory's diving suit, the deep-dweller reached behind and produced another identical spear, this one clearly intended to pierce my heart. I finally perceived the conical shape in the deep-dweller's hand, as it guided the spear into a nest of delicate tentacles emerging from the wider end, clearly a specialized mollusc which provided the propulsion necessary to drive a spear through the water like an arrow.

Before the deep-dweller could induce the shellbound creature to launch the second spear, however, the many sea spiders arrayed against the line of coupled cars finally succeeded in overturning the train. The *Ariona* bucked and rattled jerkily as the weight of the cars pulled it from the rails, down into the abyss. The goliath sea spider had splayed its rearmost pair of legs to span the width of the wedge-shaped pilot at the front of the locomotive. As the train derailed, the pilot jolted the beast's appendages in passing. This prodded the sea spider to scuttle away from the rails and rejoin the others as they ascended the mountainside.

I was compelled to act quickly in order to save my own life, with no time to spare for pitying poor Gregory's regrettable fate. I genuflected beside his lifeless form and grasped the spearhead, turning it awkwardly as the shaft still ran through Gregory's ribcage. I braced the blade against my knee and pulled taut across its lethal edge the tubing which conjoined my diving suit to Gregory's. With a tug, the material parted, and in a heartbeat, so had we. My gloved fingers were too clumsy to tie the tubing remnant into a knot, but I wadded the rubbery mass in upon itself to plug the opening of my suit's valve plate, and the ingress of seawater was slowed to a trickle.

I then took as deep a breath as I could and similarly severed the air hose connecting my suit to the train, pinching the end closed in my quivering fist. Although it meant forsaking my only supply of breathable air, my reason for doing so became self-evident soon enough. Gregory, and the spear that impaled him, were yanked away by the plummeting car to which his air hose was attached. A moment later, the bodies of Mister Von Vock and Hertford went flying past me, also tethered to the train. Like Gregory, they were already dead. Hertford's diving suit had been gored to grisly shreds, to all appearances by the trampling claws of a sea spider. Mister Von Vock's bell helmet bobbed loosely against his chest, held fast to the diving suit by a single rivet; I presume that the helmet contained Mister Von Vock's head, but can only say for certain that nothing emerged from the neck seal of his suit except for a few ragged strips of flesh trailed by rapidly dissolving blood-red pennons.

The dwindling illumination from the headlamp shone up from below as the engine was pulled down by the weight of the rear cars. Then the locomotive struck an outcropping of rock which smashed the lamp, plunging me into darkness. I was cold, and growing colder. My diving suit no longer supplied with warmed air from the train, the arctic waters inexorably leached the heat from my paltry insulation. The decreasing oxygen available to me similarly sapped the heat from my very bones, while the grievous thought of the horrible deaths of every man aboard Mister Stonington's train froze my heart in my chest. The lucky ones would die quickly from injuries sustained as the train rolled out of control down the underwater cliffside, while the less fortunate would drown in their steel tomb.

I sat down between the nacreous rails to await my own demise. I comforted myself with tales I had heard about the peacefulness of asphyxiation, how my body would grow numb with cold as I gently fell asleep, never to awaken. I closed my eyes, since I could see nothing in the lightless undersea ridge, leaning forward to rest my brow against the glass plate of my diving helmet.

But of course I did not die. The deep-dwellers presumably decided that I was a prize worth salvaging, as they must from time to time determine in regards to the many otherwise forsaken victims when shipwrecks occur in the waters above their mountain demesne, including the one which brought you here. It occurs to me to wonder how many of those shipwrecks are truly accidental happenstances, and how many the riders of the sea spiders induce themselves. Although, in the end, to ponder such questions changes nothing.

And that, at long last, is how I came to count myself among this company, the latest inductee into the ranks of those who toil beneath the very floor of the ocean itself in service of the deep-dwellers, mining the precious metals that course in liquid form through magma veins and dribble out of our boreholes into strings of ingots cooled by the currents, lading the carts that convey the lodes along the rails to their forbidden temples. You might wonder if I curse the day that I ever signed on to work for Mister Stonington's venture, but I tell you this: in truth I find the differences between the life of labor I expected under Mister Stonington and the strife here to be minimal. Perhaps even illusory. I would have worked my fingers to the bone in either case, for however long my strength could hold. Had I not taken employment in the Trans-Pacific venture, I surely would have died bereft of hope. Instead I swore fealty to an indifferent master in hopes that he might allow me to prolong the time I draw breath. One master or the other, I still breathe, and I must allow that I find the symbiotic polyps which the deep-dwellers have implanted in our nostrils to allow us to work here in their undersea mines far less cumbersome than a brass diving helmet.

✗

ONE MILLION & ONE
by Andre E. Harewood

Living machines taller than mountains float across the scorched ground below as I look at the stellar stream swirling around and through the dead spiral galaxy above.

Those who lived and died on this planet never became industrialized. They were an elongated, soft-bodied species that lived in the shallow methane ocean covering their world, writing their history on the sea bed with viscous secretions. Many civilizations have myths where a deluge wipes out almost all life but this one experienced a yearly fire from heaven that ignited their oceans, a fire they believed was destined to one day destroy them. I look at remains of dead comets about to rain down once again on schedule. Their destiny was fulfilled.

The methane oceans are gone along with the atmosphere and anything else biotic, only the secreted history of worms remains. They feared the galaxy that looms large overhead because its yearly rise in the sky heralded the rain fire. Their cosmology was quite intricate when it came to that galaxy. They believed the stellar stream, the Silver Sliver, in which their sun lay was at war with the spiral galaxy, the Butcher Vortex. They were closer to the truth than they would ever know. They lived in the remains of a small galaxy being pulled apart and absorbed by the dead spiral but they never developed the science to know the truth, to know they were partially correct. The galaxy's yearly rise had to do with their planet's rotation and axial tilt, and the cometary remnants just seemed to come from the radiant of the spiral. We call that barren expanse The Wane because its teeming life was wiped out by one race's extradimensional experiments. It is an example of why we do what we do, why we must find and protect all life. Why…they find and protect all life. My job is death: the many ways of it, the varied aftermaths of it, the methodical cataloguing of it. We are not always able to save a sentient species but we try to ensure none are ever forgotten. I ensure. While my million brothers and sisters do their duties across the billions of standard light-years of our megatruss, I sift through the rubble of extinct sentient civilizations to see how they lived, what they believed, and why they ended.

With recording here finished, my probes and I slowly ascend to Vessel in orbit. The Wane weighs on my mind, the thought of an entire galaxy wiped clean of life. The Shepherds surveyed its billions of dead worlds before my family's time so there is nothing of interest there for me. Its dimensional ruptures make it almost impossible to navigate while radiating energies and twisting reality in ways that can kill almost anything, including me. I contemplate its lifelessness for some time as Vessel's warm embrace envelops me; I stare into its nothing for so long that I find something staring back.

"Impossible."

Life.

The barest ember of sentience. I doubt any of my family could have felt it. After so many centuries in the wastes, my senses are fine tuned to anything living, especially here at the outer boundary of our dominion with desolation all around. This feels different, though. Slower, distorted, static. Vessel's sensors cannot see what I feel; only we can detect life. That is our first duty, our prime reason for existing. Vessel brings me to the Wane's halo of elder stars quickly but takes some time plotting a safe course to where I feel conscious minds. The ruptures are at their lowest density where we are headed but still pervert normal space-time hideously. We head in cautiously and slowly, stopping every few seconds for course corrections as a rupture expands or contracts or appears or disappears, warping the fundamental properties of reality for dozens of light-years around it. For one used to traversing galaxies in moments, the wait is an annoyance that compounds my nervousness. I have found wonders in the voids between galactic clusters: lost generational ships, hive mind aerosol nebulae, the occasional post-corporeal thing believing itself a god… Why am I feeling anxious now? Premonitions are sometimes the purview of the Shepherds, not we their servants, but I feel something pulling me uneasily forward. Is this the worms' destiny?

Vessel finally stops thirty thousand light-years from the galactic core at a safe distance from one of the rare metastable ruptures. It is a small wound, a purple puncture infected with the exotic matter and quixotic properties of a universe anathema to our own. This rupture has effectively stopped time near it, freezing everything in place including a small hexagonal cargo ship. Vessel's relativistic manifolds create a bubble of normal space-time around us so we can move beside the craft, and then grows an airlock to one of the ship's ports. Once open, I go aboard with an extension of Vessel's space-time field surrounding me. I think it best to investigate without having to deal with the occupants initially. Hull damage, the stationary sparks of blown relays, the crew lying down or flying or running… Vessel confirms the damage came from battle, not the rupture. They are raiders, most likely. I loathe to seem speciest but these Stylets are known for attacking weaker ships and isolated outposts for rare materials and juicy sentient delicacies to feed on. Someone must have fought back quite hard to make them enter the Wane.

As I walk, I realize these dozen aphid raiders are little more than background noise compared to a life force I feel a few decks below. Ten stasis tubes fill most of the small room, all but one is empty. A Stylet is frozen where it jumped up from sucking the fluids from a tripedal victim whose species I do not recognize. When I look into the occupied stasis tube, however, I recognize instantly and angrily.

I extend Vessel's space-time field around the aphid, grabbing its sucking mouthparts covered in the dying triped's copper-based blood.

<Human.> I think to it. <How do you have a Human?>

Its mind races from the pain of my grip to whether there is a weapon nearby to what is happening with the ship to wondering exactly what I am. It seems I have found a ship from before the Shepherds created us. I focus the sucker's thoughts for it.

<How do you have a Human?> I think again.

<Paid.> Its ordered thoughts are just what I command them to be: short and to the point. <Collect specimen. Take to buyer.>

<What buyer? Where?>

<Queen knows. Not I.>

I let go and it freezes in mid-air again. Its mind told me how to turn off the pod so I extend my space-time field again and I do. There is a momentary ripple as the stasis field shuts down and the transparent door slides open. I stare at the naked man before me. His skin is a beautiful shade of dark brown I have never seen on a Human before, his lovely hair so tightly coiled and so abundant all over his body, but his organs and bones are so worn, his genetics so flawed. Could he be one of our ancestors? The Shepherds said that they saved us from a dying world and made us better. Maybe this man was...

The ship rocks as a gravity wave washes over us. Vessel's manipulations must be affecting the rupture more than anticipated. Sparks fly in the corner of the room as normal space-time is restored and I know I do not have much time. The man starts to stir as I hear the murderous thoughts of the raider behind me.

* * * *

I feel groggy, almost hung over. There are smells in the air I can't describe. I try opening my eyes but they feel like I haven't opened them in forever. The sudden jolt and the sound of things exploding force me fully awake but I know I must be having one hell of a dream. I'm in some kind of crystal tube and there's a naked bald guy with gold skin standing before me looking very puzzled. He turns quickly and I see a man-sized insect holding some kind of mineral and goo stick in three of its…hands? Do insects have hands? The man stretches out his hands, points at the insect, says something that reverberates through the fucked up hive room or maybe just through my mind, and incinerates the bug in a wave of blue flame. Not flame, not really. More like… It's hard to think so I can't remember what I had for dinner last night but I'm going to try and remember not to have it and the resulting screwed up dreams again. Dinner? I remember having a romantic dinner with Valentin out on Coral Ridge to celebrate our anniversary. It was a beautiful night, not a cloud in the sky, just a half moon and stars and a light that kept getting bigger and brighter until…

Another tremor rocks me. It feels like its rippling through my body. Naked golden man looks back at me and I hear him in my head say that we have to get to his boat quickly. Why am I on the ocean? Why do man-bugs have a yacht? Like most of my dreams, I just roll with it and hope I remember enough to write down in the morning. This would make a great story. He looks sadly at some half-dead three-legged thing on a table before touching it gently and disintegrating it. Moving is difficult but his firm grip catches me before I fall and we start floating down exploding corridors. More of the bugs appear with their weapons. More strange words and blue not-flame from the nude gold dude cremate them. There's another strange smell, like ozone this time. Something hits me on the shoulder from behind, something so hot that my entire right side goes instantly numb. I see my whole arm lying on the ground but I can't scream. I know this isn't a dream now but I still can't scream. The man looks behind us then stretches out his arms again. I see small blue concentric circles swirling on various parts of his gold skin. Two violent vortices form on his palms then more of the blue not-fire. I can't look behind me. All I can do is look from him to my seared hand on the floor. Like my body, my memory of what happens next is in pieces.

I'm floating as well as drifting in and out of consciousness. I see a night sky through one of the ship's windows but the stars are below me, too. A huge purple thing that hurts my brain to look at is shooting off waves that threaten to tear the ship apart. The last thing I see is where the man is taking me: his ship. Vessel, I hear him correct me in my mind. It's huge, kilometres across, with a blinding white light at the center of a blue wheel within another blue wheel at right angles to each other with soft glows appearing and disappearing all across its surfaces.

Another wave hits me and I drown.

I open my eyes again and I'm floating upside down above a huge forest. Or am I right-side up? Like the stars before, the trees are above and below and all around me. I try to rub my eyes and yawn but can't move my right arm which I shouldn't have but is now reattached to me with several little glowing balls shooting thin beams of light into the almost gone wound.

<You will be healed very soon.>

The voice in my head comes from above…below me? Naked dude floats down or up or sideways to hover next to me. He's the most beautiful man I've ever seen.

<Thank you,> he thinks to me. <You are also beautiful and naked.>

I should be having the sudden urge to cup my jewels but I feel nothing but relaxed and at peace.

"Are you…doing that?"

<Yes. You must remain calm during healing.>

"What's going on?"

<I hoped you would tell me.>

"Those bug things…"

<The Stylets.>

"They abducted me? I was outside…with my boyfriend. There was…a flash…then I saw you."

<Outside where?>

"Coral Ridge. Best view of the valley."

<What planet?>

"Earth, duh."

<Urt'daa? I do not know that planet.>

"No. Earth. You're in my head, why not just find what you want?"

<That is not our way. If you allow me to go through your memories, I can get the answers I require more quickly.>

"With you already in my head making me remain calm and more likely to agree?"

<Yes, I understand the dubious moral concerns at play but it would be best.>

"All yours, big man."

<You may experience some of my memories, too. You may see what we are.>

And I see his gold people in ships like this flying through hundreds of thousands of galaxies across a billion light-years, seeking living beings and bringing them peace and science. I see asteroids being deflected, stars being stabilized, whole species moved to better worlds, knowledge and cultural exchanges facilitated, would-be interstellar invaders stripped of their technology and culture and denied space travel… I see him alone in the dark digging through dead world after dead world, forever cut off from the life he was created to experience and protect. Somewhere in the background of all this are tall, dark figures. I can't see them clearly but they are there and he is done.

<Your people are amazingly terrifying.>

"Your people, too."

<We find and protect life. It is why we were created.>

"By your…Elder Things?"

<The First Shepherds. It is the best way to describe them.>

"I saw your people neuter whole civilizations."

<That would have destabilized whole galaxies. They still live but they will not be allowed to subjugate others. Once you can move about your solar system or beyond it, there is no shortage of resources. To conquer or destroy others is borne from societal or religious perversion, not necessity. We do not permit that.>

"You don't permit it across half the universe."

<It may seem like that to you but we only watch what you call the Laniakea, the local supercluster of galaxies.>

"I call it that?"

<You read about it years ago. The information is buried in your memories.>

"Find anything else interesting in there?"

<Your species studied its history and that of its planet. You are undoubtedly native to your Earth…but you are almost genetically identical to us.>

"Distant cousins?"

<Our creators, the Shepherds, said that we Humans were saved from a dying world and reborn as their emissaries.>

"Global warming was a thing. We were always on the brink of nuclear or biological holocaust, too."

The gold man looks slightly perplexed.

<It is becoming increasingly difficult to keep you calm.>

"I've been abducted by two sets of aliens, it's the far future, everyone I love may be dead… I'd be on the floor rocking and crying but I'm floating here getting my arm reattached. So yeah, I'm getting a bit agitated."

<Vessel downloaded some records of the Stylet ship before it exploded. I do not know who hired them to take you or why but Vessel is returning to your Earth.>

"When?"

<Any second now.>

The balls of light stop their work on my arm then just disappear.

<Try moving it.>

I flex, extend, rotate, do anything I can think of right down to wiggling my fingers.

<Good. My name is Exu.>

"Ty. Ty Garvey. All this telepathy. Don't you ever speak? Vocal cords, tongue, lips, all that?"

<In private, yes. Vocalization is reserved for our most loved.>

"Moaning and screaming, too?"

<Yes. Oh, yes.>

"We still do…that?"

<For pleasure, yes, and for procreation when necessary. We are biologically immortal but we can still be killed.>

"How many of you are there?"

<One million and one.>

We descend or ascend until we land in the middle of the forest. A blue robe hangs from a branch.

<I saw that some of your people have taboos against nudity. I hope this will relax you a bit.>

"We all can't fly around with our big dicks swinging in the wind."

<I can begin genetic cleansing and optimization on you.>

"Let's see about Earth first, thanks."

<Look. See.>

As I put on the blue robe, a wall of silver rises from the grassy ground near us with a display showing the solar system.

<Standard hydrogen to helium fission star. Nine planets.>

"Eight planets."

He points to a dot far beyond all the others.

<Nine. You haven't discovered this one yet, obviously.>

"Wow."

<And here is the third planet from the star. Here is your Earth.>

The slightest hint of a gray atmosphere when the sun hits it just right. Hundreds of huge black craters. Arid purple and yellow plains. Red cracks that look like they go all the way down to the core. Not a hint of blue or green or life. Hell on Earth. Earth is Hell.

I'm only aware that I'm screaming after I've been rocking on the grass screaming for a while and Exu has mentally calmed me down again. I'm barely in any condition to tell but there is genuine concern and sadness in his thoughts.

<The…records from the Stylet ship, the metastable flux ratio of the rupture it was caught it, and the radioactive decay rates of several elements…down there all point to this having happened approximately two thousand seven hundred and thirty eight years ago. You were taken in your year 2017; this year would be 4755.>

I'm not even looking out a window. I don't know which way what's left of the Earth really is, not that it or anything matters anymore. Valentin, my family, everyone I knew has been dead for almost three thousand years.

<I am sorry. There was a spatial rupture near here not long after you

were taken. This would be the earliest evidence we have of them. The others across this galaxy occurred about two decades later, and my family was created one hundred years after…>

"Stop."

<Of course.>

"Is there anything alive?"

<No. Even I cannot feel anything living in this system.>

"Look again. Please."

<Vessel has initiated a full sensor scour from quantum indeterminacy to the higher dimensions. There is…an aberration.>

I sit up and look at the silver screen but I can't tell where Exu is pointing. It could be Canada, Australia, Barbados, Antarctica… Earth is now several lovely shades of dead. Even if I could pick out land masses, my eyes are far too red and tear-filled to be of any use.

<Our technology allows us to bend space-time in many ways. We can create wormholes for travel, manipulate the flow of time, or create pockets of folded space for concealment or imprisonment. There is an artificial space-time fold on the surface that Vessel can barely detect. This is beyond our technology but Vessel may be able to warp a hole through.>

My blue robe changes, enveloping me in a protective skin tight suit.

<There may not be an atmosphere you can breathe. I can survive in almost any…>

Exu doubles over and grabs his temples in pain as he screams out loud. I go to him and help him back upright once whatever it is stops.

<Thank you. There was a…noise like I'd never heard before…and a feeling like suicide tried to make my psyche…destroy itself.>

"What was it?!"

<A deterrent and alarm, I believe.>

"Did this suit protect me?"

<No, I do not think so. It was most likely fine-tuned to affect beings advanced enough to get through the warp. We don't have much time.>

Several small balls of light appear next to the screen wall before a circular portal into darkness appears and they fly through.

<Come.>

Exu takes my suited hand in his and we step through the portal onto the ground level of a black dome partially illuminated by the spheres. There are gray human-sized containers floating in the air as far as the eye can see all around us.

"Are they…?"

<I don't know. Each container is surrounded by its own warp field.>

"Can't you undo one like you did for me and to get into this place?"

<Space-time in here is normative. It is only the protective shell that we

have made a very temporary opening in, and Vessel is focused solely on keeping our small wormhole stable. The extreme counterforces make any other distortions inadvisable.>

"What could do this?"

<There are few powers that rival the Shepherds. We never discovered who created the ruptures that are destroying this galaxy, and there are the forces that move against us in shadow.>

"I saw them in your head, the dark clouds."

<Yes, they turn societies against us, destroy those loyal to us, and help those who would conquer other species to spite us. I...>

There is a ripple of darkness behind Exu, a solid piece of it slits his throat and tendrils expertly puncture then throw his body through the lattice of gray containers and out of sight. I don't know why but I'm amused that Exu's blood is still red. The darkness coalesces into a human form then dissipates slightly around the head to reveal the face of an impossibly pale, old, and scarred woman. Exu's calming influence is gone. The horror of all this is hitting me again. I can't breathe. I can't think.

"Are...that...it...you...Ty?" she struggles to ask in English.

I struggle to nod my head in disbelief.

"Katya. This...I...am Katya, Ty."

* * * *

"Katya?" she calls out into the darkness.

The aliens' ship with its dozens of wheels within wheels orbiting and turning in ways chaotic to human understanding no longer blocks the sun but I haven't felt warm since they arrived. At night, it blocks half the stars. Only the highest members of the contact taskforce have seen the aliens and none of them have given descriptions.

"Katya?!"

"I'm here, Dr. Vang."

I flick on the pool lights so she can see me lying on a deck chair staring at the night sky half blotted out by the twinkling chariot wheels of the gods and that damn blue light at their core. Dr. Gao Jer Vang is one of the socio-cultural liaisons between the aliens and the United Nations. I lucked out in being one of her current doctoral assistants and now I have higher clearance than eight billion other people but I haven't seen my family or boyfriend in months. I wonder if I still have a boyfriend. The community the UN has put us up in is pure American planned suburban hell with every house and every street perfectly identical but at least the one Dr. Vang and I are in has a nice pool. Thinking about the mundane is all that's keeping me sane. She rushes over as quickly as her little feet can bring her.

"Worst case, Katya."

I stand as she sits. The thought kept crossing my mind and taking up residence. The aliens demanded that we renounce our religions, our prejudices and intraspecies warfare, even our genetics which they would purify to make us ready to join the transgalactic community. They said it was for our own good. If we as a species didn't agree, they would leave us to either destroy ourselves or become the victims of whatever race might come across us next. Dr. Vang and a small group had been trying to negotiate with them for help advancing humanity without giving up what makes us human, self-destructive tendencies or not. The look in her watery eyes says that we failed.

"The diplomatic game is over. They have revealed their hands. Their… tentacles."

"And we lost?"

Dr. Vang fumbles to light a cigarette.

"We never had a chance. Human germline modification to their specifications will begin whether we agree or not. Our children will become what they want them to become. They say we possess a psychic force unseen in millions of years, one they will speed up our evolution to unlock. Future generations will be able to mentally locate and communicate with any sentient species, to move matter with thought alone, to live forever. Either we serve them in taming the galaxies or they will exterminate us."

She takes a drag and coughs a bit. I am speechless.

"You've never seen them, Katya, looming over you. You've never felt their slippery tentacles around your paralyzed body and their sickening thoughts ooze into your mind…and you never will."

A section of the starry sky not blocked by the alien wheels suddenly darkens.

"We call them visitors or the aliens but I've met others who've revealed what they call themselves: the Old Masters. Life is sacred to them in that it must be protected but the quality of that life is inconsequential. We will remain human in shape and perhaps name only. They will turn us into their dogs, sniffing out and guarding life across the galaxies while ripping their enemies to nothing, every shred of what we were and are modified away."

"What others?"

"They don't have tactile telepathy like the vi…like the Old Masters. They use computer interfaces for contact. They're called the Night Folk or the Invisibles, something like that. Their empire in Andromeda was dismantled, their people driven back to feudal conditions, all history of who they were destroyed. Some escaped thanks to their stealth technologies but they can't rebuild their society."

"And they want us to help them?"

"The Old Masters are stretched thin. They cannot hope to police a billion light-years or more by themselves, and they distrust fully sentient artificial intelligence. They need humanity."

I've been playing devil's advocate to Dr. Vang's enthusiast for so long that sliding back into that mind-set is the only way I can continue right now.

"The Night Folk need us, too, it seems."

"They have begun to save as many of us as they can."

"Save? As in abduct?"

The dark patch in the sky gets larger.

"The Folk take those who are worthy and willing, Katya. The best minds of Earth have slowly and quietly begun disappearing. I suggested you."

I can't move. I can't speak. I'm wrapped in darkness coming from the void in the sky.

"I'm sorry. The Night Folk have intermediaries, pirates and raiders, to take others but they came for you themselves. Only a few thousand can be saved but our knowledge, our art, who we are will live on in you. They chose you to be one of the leaders of humanity. A list of everyone being saved will be given to you once you are safely away from the solar system. Those of us left here who know will keep what is happening a secret for as long as we can."

The world starts to fade as does Vang's voice.

"I'm sorry, Katya. We have no choice but to trust the Folk. With the others, all that we are will die. Katya…"

* * * *

"Katya. This…I…am Katya, Ty."

I hear myself say the words and they hurt even more than my mind does from that alarm. Our languages and society have evolved so much over the million days since Earthloss but speaking English brings back all the horrible memories of that time. There is so much I want to tell Ty about how we've survived in secret with our genetics turned from connecting with anyone to staying hidden from everyone, how we and other species united to save who and what we can of cultures the Old Masters would erase. I can't tell him that we let his ship stay frozen in time as bait for a curious Human to find, hoping they would follow the trail back to Earth and give us access to this place. So many things to say but no time to say them.

My slavebots planted singularity bombs across the facility while Ty and the Human, Exu of Death, talked. The Old Masters cannot be allowed to keep original human stock. The transgalactic tyrants keep the numbers of live Humans low and give them technology not quite as powerful as their own so that the chances of rebellion are diminished. Their Humans believe themselves on equal footing with their lords in a quest to bring peace and protect life but genetic programming and social engineering can create the almost perfect slave race. Taking out this facility will damage the Old Masters' morale even if they have the genomes of all eight billion now dead humans stored elsewhere.

I never thought I would ever return to Earth, much less to destroy the last vestiges of original humanity, but this is war and we Unseen must do what is necessary to win by any means necessary. Obliterating the methane worms' biosphere was unfortunate but necessary to summon Exu of Death and have him within thinking distance of Ty. Exu will be regenerated fully any second now. I extend my hand to Ty, hoping he will take it quickly and come with me before this base and what is left of Earth implode. The only thing that makes contact with my shadow hand is a wave of focused ultramarine plasma.

* * * *

"Katya. This…I…am Katya, Ty."

The shadow woman's outstretched hand looks as maimed and decrepit as her face. I would step back in horror but I've already stepped in so much horror that it doesn't move me. She looks like she desperately wants to communicate so many things to me but cannot, as though the years have left her as cold as the umbra she's cloaked in. I hesitate, looking at her ancient hand as it is blasted off.

Exu is an avenging angel wreathed in wings and an aura of blue plasma. Being in his mind briefly told me what the not fire yet still fire is: a form of matter ionized and controlled by his mind called plasma. His gold skin shines, the blue circular tattoos blaze, his eyes burn with rage and power. Katya's scream is primal as the darkness covers her cauterized forearm stump and forms an oversized, misshapen claw. I scramble behind one of the space-time coffins as living shadow and zealous light battle to a stalemate, neither one gaining any further edge beyond the lost partial limb. I clutch my right shoulder and empathize with her. I have no horse in this race, no side to back. Exu's memories showed me what his people and their overlords do in the name of protecting life. They also showed me what these children of twilight do to stop them. Both powerful beyond my imagining, both utterly convinced of the truth of their fervent realities, both willing to do anything to anyone for their beliefs. So painfully human.

The black dome shimmers and the abhorrent galaxy appears above me, its festering purple sores exuding toxic ruin. Most of the dying sky is taken up by wheels within swirling and blinking and reversing wheels orbiting a blinding azure flare. Exu and Katya don't stop fighting so much as their fighting is stopped, frozen in place like the coffins I'm hiding behind.

That's when I met a First Shepherd: a red coral-like cylinder a few storeys tall that slowly floats down from its ship as though it has all the time in the universe. Considering what's all around me, that seems true. I rise, pulled up by a force much like Exu's to the being's midsection where there is a ring of small apertures. Out of one opening comes a transparent tentacle thicker than my body with all of the physical processes of pulsing flesh and pink pulp laid bare. It passes right through my space suit and envelops me in its cold, wet grip as its thoughts leak into mine.

<Beautiful mind. Poet. Dreamer. Last of your kind awake.>

Unlike Exu calming me, I feel light-headed and weak, and my whole body tingles but I can still barely talk despite the smothering.

"What are…?"

<Cnidoblast neurotoxin. Small amount, docile, communication. Large amount, dead.>

"You?"

<First Shepherds, keepers of sentient beings. Humans, seekers of sentient beings.>

"Billions of us…billions…"

<Dead. Painless.>

I mentally curse it but it doesn't care.

<Asexual. No mothers.>

Its thoughts drift down to Exu amd Katya frozen below us.

<Exu replaced. Unseen interrogated. You?>

"I have…a choice?"

<Sentience is self-determination.>

"You…took away our…choice."

<To find, save many more.>

"Did you…rip open this galaxy…to hide your…tracks? Or…did they?"

<Choose well, understand later.>

"What…are…my options?"

<Painless death. Sleep.>

"Like the…others here?"

<Yes. They sleep until all is safe.>

I start to cry.

<No sadness. Valentin sleeps.>

I don't know if it's lying or not.

<Truth. When we make all this safe, you wake to paradise, rise in glory.>

"When?"

<Fullness of time.>

"How many…humans sleep?"

<One million.>

"Make that one million and one."

WAR IS GRIMM
by Clifford Beal

He had liked the chocolate. Greasy American stuff and sickly sweet but almost better than a Lucky Strike for a pick-me-up—if you could manage to steal it off some kid. But now the Americans had left and the new masters had no chocolate, no gum, no cigarettes.

The soldier pulled at the cuffs of his overcoatthat dangled over his chapped hands. Cuffs so threadbare they resembled lampshade tassels. The year was beginning worse than the last, even if the Reich was now burned to ashes and with it most everyone he had known. Yesterday, Beltzer had taken the soldier's gloves along with ten cigarettes—the price to keep his mouth shut. The others in the work party were just as bad but Beltzer was the boss and all the swag went to him, to be divided as he saw fit. The six of them had stopped on the side of the logging road, huddling against the sharp January breeze that blew up little whirlwinds of icy snow, cutting the face like ground glass.

"I want the gloves," insisted the soldier. "I'm the one walking furthest off the road to find the wood so I'm the one who needs them."

Beltzer's laugh ended in a cough while his best mate, another black market chancer by night, broke into a yellow-toothed grin, his breath condensing in the wretched cold. "You know," said Belzer, "the Russians rounded up another four SS guys yesterday. You don't want to make it five do you?"

The soldier looked down at his feet and his boots, yawning without their laces. The bare birches were mocking him, squeaking and creaking with laughter. He *had* been SS and still had the tattoo on his inside bicep to prove it. Now a mark of Cain. He bucked up his courage a little. "Fuck you. They wouldn't be interested in me anyway. I was drafted into it for the Ardennes. None of us got a choice, we all got screwed."

Belzer poked the soldier's chest. "You want to bet your life on it? I hear the Russkies get a bounty for every one of you bastards they bring in."

Whether true or not he didn't care to find out. The Russians had taken over the Harz six months earlier, Wernigerode included. Some deal with the Yanks. Which had fucked anybody on the wrong side of the mountains. And the Russians did what they wanted. Took what they wanted. The soldier didn't answer Belzer but just turned to look at the sledge piled high with logs and brushwood.

One of the others piped up, a spotty kid with his hair so short you could see the scabs on his scalp. "Come on, Belzer, I'm freezing my balls off out here. Let's go trade this load for some coffee and cigs." Belzer gave the youth a glare and wiped some snot from under his nose. They'd been out for five hours and the temperature was dropping with the sun. Belzer's mind ran through the options: give some wood to the commissar's office and brown-nose a bit, flog the rest, then get some lentil stew. He decided, in his infinite wisdom of life on the Soviet side of the border, that he could call it a day. Might even give them more time to plan a raid on a couple of farmhouses he knew about a few miles out of town.

He turned back to the soldier. "Tell you what. You stay out and scout for more deadwood. For tomorrow's run. Mark it near the road. We're going to head back with the sledge."

The soldier blinked away a gust of ice crystals. "What do I get, *arschlocht*, for doing that?"

Belzer grinned. "I give you something." He reached into his coat pocket and pulled out a pair of hole-shot woollen gloves and proffered them to the soldier. "What? You were expecting an interzone pass or something? Jesus, you really are an idiot."

The soldier pressed his nails into his palms and the pain enlivened his frozen hands. He reached for the gloves just the same. Belzer flashed him a grin again. "There's a lad. And you only have to give me five cigarettes tomorrow instead of ten. Fair enough?"

"It's not going to last forever, Belzer. Maybe not even another week."

His tormentor gave a dramatic shake of his head. "I just have to say one word to that Russian lieutenant who hangs out at the market—*Werewolf*. They'll have their boots on your neck before you can even piss your pants."

The soldier looked down as he pulled on the gloves. The others snickered and turned away. "Off you pop now," Belzer cracked. "We'll see you in the square for supper in a couple of hours, eh? If there's any left." Two of the men grabbed the ropes on the sledge while the spotty kid helped turn it from the back, steadying the wobbling load of firewood. The soldier blinked a few times to clear the crystals on his lashes and then walked into the woods, his feet sinking into the snow. He didn't look back.

The soldier wandered, half-hearted in his search. The forest rose up in front of him, birch giving way to dark pine. For a little while he thought about lying under one and just going to sleep, forever. Back in August, the Americans had opened the gates to his camp and let him go. Him and everybody else. Too many mouths to feed, they said. And if you weren't a POW anymore the US Army didn't have to feed you. So he had trudged back home to the Harz, to Wernigerode, flea-ridden and destitute. His parents had gone so he did what he had to, fell in with whom he had to. And bastards like Belzer knew how to survive, even how to thrive, in a dead-eyed world of despair.

The sun was just a small orange blob winking at him low through the trees. He realized he didn't have the pocket torch they shared. And part of him didn't really care. Facing west, the bald Brocken in front of him high above and distant, he kept walking. He hadn't gone far when he saw light through a dense stand of trees. A cottage. Likely some forester's hovel he thought as his feet start moving him towards it. It was a dilapidated mess, shingles falling off, but someone was there. The soldier knocked. And waited.

The woman who answered, middle-aged, honey-brown hair streaked with grey, did not look alarmed or even surprised to see him standing there, a derelict with ill intentions. She gave him a tilt of her head and ushered him inside without words. The warmth hit him immediately: a fire crackled gustily in a stone hearth. As he stepped inside, clumps of wet snow dropping off his boots, he quickly saw the cottage had but two rooms.

"Food?" she asked. The soldier wasn't sure whether she was offering it or expecting it. He took it as an invitation though and nodded. She motioned for him to sit on a trestle bench and then took a bowl down from a cupboard and went to a stewpot that stood on a tripod near the fire. He watched her. Her hair was tied back with a red bandana, pulling her gaunt face tight and giving her a look of meanness. But he had to admit she wasn't bad looking as he watched her bend over the pot in her blue twill trousers, bunched and tucked into her black rubber boots. While he waited he took in his surroundings, the smell of the stew exciting him even more than the woman. Sparse. A big wooden armchair, a table and two benches, a couple of oil lamps, black lacquer sideboard, some rug throws, and an old green sofa that looked like it had collapsed on itself. A long, birch-twig broom stood propped in a corner. Some old photos on the wall and a cheap bakelite Deco clock that didn't seem to be working. Motes of dust floated through the air, gently drifting towards the sputtering hearth. She called to him as she stirred slowly, then ladled the steaming stew.

"You in one of those work parties then?"

"Yes."

She turned, gripping the bowl in both hands. "A bit late for it, no?"

The soldier forced a smile. "I'm scouting for firewood. Dead trees that have already fallen."

She nodded and offered him the bowl. "Let me getyou a spoon." His eyes followed as she moved over to the sideboard, hips swaying ever so slightly, and she came back with a spoon for him. "All alone today? No comrades?"

She had sharp features, and pretty eyes. Sort of green mixed with blue. As he reached up for the spoon his eyes flitted to where her blouse fell open. "They left for town before me."

"Some friends."

The soldier returned her an awkward smile and hefted the bowl in his throbbing hands, all pins-and-needles now that the blood was circulating again. "Thank you." His teeth clacked on the spoon as he gulped a mouthful of the stew, molars sinking into a lump of meat that was fatty, chewy and satisfying. It had been an age since he had tasted pork.

"I haven't been into town for a while," she said. "Not since the Russians came."

He shovelled in another spoonful and wondered about how she survived out in the woods. Maybe she got things from a nearby farmer. But there weren't any up here. "Just as well," he replied after a pause, "it's no place for a woman these days. Everyone's an animal." The fire had eased his aches now that he was thawing out. He dipped the spoon and had another bite, this time getting a potato chunk. "You on your own now?"

She studied him a moment. "Is that a proposal? Or are you just sniffing around...for you and your comrades."

"Just curious. It's your business." He scraped the last few gobbets of meat onto his spoon and then into his mouth. "That was good. Very good. I'm grateful to you."

"Some *schnapps*?"

His eyes widened a little. Now that was a rare treat. "If you're offering...Have you lived here for the whole war?"

She lifted a terracotta jug from the sideboard and swept up a couple of shot glasses in her other hand. "Oh, I've lived in this wood for a long time. Very long time." She threw him a smile that bore a glimmer of mischief and poured him a measure. "And I have a few cigarettes left. Go sit on the couch."

The soldier felt himself becoming uneasy, a slow unsteady slide. She was either trying to placate him into being nice so he wouldn't rape her or—and this came to him rather suddenly—she wasn't the least bit afraid of him. But he obeyed and moved over to the overstuffed sofa, a ruined soufflé, sinking down in it. His eyes followed the packet of cigarettes as she caught it up in her hand. "You haven't asked anything about me yet," he said.

She stood over him and extended the packet. Kurmarks. He hadn't seen those in a year.

"You were a soldier. Captured. Released. What else is there, *na?*

He managed another awkward smile as he lit up the glorious tobacco.

"I need some chores done around here. Some wood chopped. If you want some food in return."

He had nothing to lose. "Sure. Tell me what you need done."

"And I've lost something out back. Something sentimental. I know where it is but I need some help to retrieve it. A cigarette lighter."

The soldier shrugged. "Sure."

She looked at him with her strange eyes, those colours fighting one another, studying him in just half a moment. "Let's drink to the arrangement then." And she handed him his *schnapps*. "You might as well stay here for the night. You'll get lost in the dark." The last was delivered with a flatness that carried certainty, even threat.

It would be dark very soon. That was true enough. He'd probably freeze to death before he got halfway back to Wernigerode. "I'd be obliged, *Fraulein…?*

She didn't help him with her name. "You can stay there on the couch. If I hear my door open, I'll kill you. Understand?"

* * * *

He woke to the smell of coffee, acrid and pungent. *Coffee.* She was standing over him with a cup, smiling. He hadn't slept so well in months, maybe ever. He nodded his thanks and wrapped his fingers around the cup.

"I'll fry up some sausage and potatoes," she said, turning to move to the stove. "Then we can go out back to the bunker. I'll show you what I need done."

His belly full, he followed her out back through the trees, the sun casting a feeble warmth in the bitter air. About a hundred metres away was a squat concrete blockhouse. The soldier thought it some Wehrmacht storage hut or an ammo dump. The snow had blown up high against the side but he noticed a door that was chained and padlocked.

"So, you lost something inside?" he asked, craning his head up at the slabs of concrete.

She smiled again, sheepishly. "Yes, my lighter dropped down the hatch while I was standing up top." She reached down and brushed the snow from a coil of rope near the door. "Climb up and I'll show you."

The flat roof was free of snow: black bitumen that looked like ancient elephant hide, wrinkled and bubbled. There was a square steel hatch near the middle and he squatted down to peer into the darkness. She settled down next to him, shoulder to shoulder, smelling of ration soap. "I couldn't go down, you see, as there'd be no way to climb out. But with two of us, you can. Get the lighter and I will pull you up on the rope." And she handed him a little square battery torch, something from a bicycle. The soldier leaned back, away from the opening.

"I find the lighter and you pull me out?"

"That's right. I'll tie the rope around my waist and pull you up. But you will have to shimmy too." She wiped a lock of hair from her face. "I'm not *that* strong, you know. Older than I look."

The soldier chewed the inside of his cheek. "Alright. Give me the torch."

His boots echoed as he hit the concrete floor, about a two and a half metre drop down. He saw her face framed above him, a short length of the rope swaying. "Go on," she said, her voice suddenly urgent. "Start looking. It's brass. Should be there somewhere." The soldier looked around, his torch casting a yellow beam. All around him was broken glass, the smell of piss, empty metal lockers that looked like steel coffins all lying at drunken angles. But there was nothing there. He moved the beam to the floor around him and scanned it. He saw it almost instantly. Square and shiny on the concrete floor. It was ice cold as his fingers grasped it and he held it to his eyes, curious as to why she wanted it so badly. It was rather plain, no inscription, old but not that old.

"Throw it up here to me!" She sounded agitated. Almost scared.

"Lower the rope to me. I'll bring it up."

There was a long silence. "I wouldn't want you to drop it. Just toss it up here. Then I'll pull you up and we can go have a bowl of hot stew."

She smiled down at him again. And the soldier knew then something wasn't right. He flashed the lighter with the torch and it shone back at him, enticing him. If this is what she wants and he does toss it to her, then she wouldn't have much of a reason to get him out at all.

"I said throw it up here!" She was waspish now, her face contorted. The soldier swallowed and decided to push his luck.

"No. Tie off that rope on something. I'm coming up."

Her voice, calm, was laced with ice; the mask now cast aside. "Then we'll see if you change your tune in a few hours. Once your bones freeze and the torch is dead. And you're alone in the dark." She slammed the hatch shut, the daylight winking out with a clang.

He knew he was trapped and the madwoman his only way out. But she wanted the lighter. Badly. As long as he held it she would be back for him. Already the torch was failing, going dimmer. He would be in pitch darkness before long. He fumbled in his shirt pocket for a cigarette, found one and tucked it between his lips. She had to come back. She couldn't leave him here. He hefted the lighter. Maybe it's gold. Why else did she want it so badly? He raised it and flicked it to light his smoke. A long blue flame sparked to life, purplish-blue as if from a gas stove. It was like nothing he had seen before. His cigarette crackled and he snapped the lighter shut.

"Looks like you need a hand."

The soldier let out a shout, his heart jumping, and he frantically waved the torch in front of him. It was the voice of a child, no, different— squeaky, but adult. And then the torch spilled upon the source. The soldier gaped. It was a tiny man. Dressed in an SS major's uniform. He looked just like the midget he had seen in '37 in Berlin, in a film about some circus freaks. The midget's black boots shone glossy in the fading torchlight, the silver *Totenkopf* on his cap glinting. The soldier stammered.

"You, you were here all the time? How?"

The manikin smiled up at him. "I've always been here. Question is, do you want to leave?"

The soldier nodded dumbly, still shell-shocked.

"Then follow me."

The midget did not need the light and the soldier shuffled behind him. They walked to one end of the blockhouse, crunching broken glass underfoot. "Push open the door, my friend." The soldier shoved and the steel door shifted easily on its hinges, swinging wide and bathing them in the light of day. They stepped outside and the soldier blinked, unable to take his eyes from the little man.

The midget tugged at the brim of his cap. "She'll be furious. She will, you know—now that you have the light."

The soldier squinted. "What the hell are you?"

The midget smiled up at him. "You hold the blue light. I serve *you*."

"I don't understand." A sharp gust blew past them, swaying the bare branches.

The little man smiled again. "Yes you do. Everybody does. What do you want of me?"

The soldier's tongue wet his lips as he looked around the trees. "Where is she now?"

The midget nodded and gave a wave for the soldier to follow him. And they headed back in the direction of the cottage. There was a woodshed nearby and the little man gestured for the soldier to look down at a mound in the snow, then laid a finger aside his nose. He bent down and wiped the snow away, revealing what lay beneath. "She makes good stew, doesn't she? Well, this is her larder."

The soldier staggered back a few steps when he saw the body of a child, naked and frozen blue. Large chunks of flesh had been neatly sliced from its thighs and buttocks. Mercifully, the boy was face down. The soldier gagged and fell to his knees, stomach rolling, and an instant later the sausage breakfast spewed into the snowbank. Then he saw other little feet and hands protruding from the snow, stiff and grey as the ash saplings around them. He wiped his mouth with his coat sleeve. "Where is she?"

The midget pointed to the cottage and the soldier pulled a short spade sticking out of the snow nearby. He was about to ask the little man something more but he was gone. Vanished, tiny tracks ending where the soldier stood, trembling. His hands tightened about the spade handle and he began to trudge towards the cottage. When the soldier burst in, the woman froze for a moment, the word *scheisse* coming from her lips as she instantly realized how he had managed to get out. Then she shook her head as if cursing her own stupidity. "It won't end like you think it will."

The soldier was almost shivering with rage, knuckles white around the shaft of the iron spade. He saw that she looked older. Actually, *old*.

"He's a clever one, that little *kerl*. And he'll get the better of you, believe you me. Give me the lighter before you regret ever having seen it."

The soldier's heart pumped madly—he could feel it thumping away in his chest—his mind not quite sure what to do, stomach still churning with the last bits of the children he had eaten. "You bitch," the soldier said, shaking his head, still unbelieving. "You murdering…witch."

She sprang for the sideboard and wrapped her fingers around a black-steel Tokarev automatic, wheeling again to level it at him. The soldier swung the spade and it smashed into her arm with a ringing sound, sending the pistol flying and her sprawling to the floor. He stepped back and then raised the spade again up over his head.

The woman let out a croaking laugh and pushed herself up, cradling her hand. "You liked the food well enough, comrade. And you've done far worse in the war, haven't you? You soldiers always do. I have *seen* it." She spat on the floor and turned her blazing eyes up to him. "You don't think a wolf can sniff out another wolf? I've known your kind for a long, long time." She placed splayed fingers under her eyes and then slowly started to turn her hand towards him. Those eyes stripped him bare in an instant, looking into what was left of his soul.

And he didn't like it. He swung the spade down on her head with a dull crack. And he struck her again with both hands with all his strength. And then, a third time. He stifled a gasp and fell back onto the sagging couch, shaking. It was quiet and the cottage seemed to grow heavy around him. The woman lay near the table, a red pool widening around her. The soldier pulled out the lighter and flicked the wheel, the blue flame jumping to life again. In the armchair across from him, the little man sat with folded arms. "Lost your temper, didn't you?"

"Get me away from here. You can do that, can't you?"

The little man laughed, high-pitched, like a naughty child. "It doesn't work that way, my friend. *You'll* have to do the walking back to town. Try again."

The soldier fought his nausea. "My tattoo. Get rid of it."

The midget gave him a knowing wink. "Done." And in the blink of an eye he was gone.

* * * *

In Wernigerode, people shuffled from house to house, bundled against the chill, speaking in hushed tones. Furtiveness born of fear. There, in an alleyway off the market square, a man in a tattered greatcoat hunched, a blue glow emanating from his cupped hands as he lit his cigarette. At his knee, a miniature SS officer looked up and grinned.

The soldier's low voice did not mask his desperation. "An interzone pass. Get me one."

The little man reached into his breast pocket and pulled out a buff-coloured piece of paper and handed it up.

The soldier looked around, anxious. Out in the square, he could make out a small group of men on the corner. Belzer and his cronies huddled together, no doubt planning something while at the same time trying to look innocent. From his vantage in the alleyway the soldier could see how they shuffled about guiltily, the eyes of Russian soldiers drilling into them from across the square. He looked down at the strange thing standing at his knee, a thing out of a child's tale, a thing that shouldn't be there but somehow was. "I wish you were less…conspicuous," he hissed at him. "It's rather poor taste."

The little man shrugged. "Then task me again. And I shall be gone."

The soldier bent down and whispered, the words deliberate and slow.

* * * *

Belzer and his friends spotted the soldier as soon as he had entered the square and were on him before he took ten steps, enveloping him in their false camaraderie. "Did you build yourself an igloo out there last night?" Belzer asked. The spotty kid sputtered with laughter. Belzer poked the soldier in the chest. "If you found a house out there you better had tell us all about it. Or I'll just whistle up those Russkies standing on the corner."

The soldier looked at Belzer's eyes, cold and shiny, noticing how very wolf-like they actually were. He didn't answer.

"What? Nothing to say? Well, you can start by handing over some cigs. It's my pay-day."

The soldier's gaze moved across the square to the brown-clad soldiers that were now coming towards them, machine guns slung over their shoulders. One of Belzer's boys tapped him and they fell silent as the Russians approached.

An officer stepped forward and asked for their papers. His German accent was very good, well-practiced even.

"He's the one you're after," mumbled Belzer as he rummaged through his pockets while thrusting a chin towards the soldier. "SS man. Seen his tattoo." The Russian looked at the soldier, his dead grey eyes looking him up and down. He then motioned to his men who seized the soldier and stripped off his coat. The soldier was as passive as a shop dummy as the coat fell to the cobbles. They tore off his shirt, buttons popping, and revealed his pale, blue-veined flesh. Pure and unmarked. Belzer's jaw went slack.

The soldier's voice was calm as he faced the Russian lieutenant, a whisker-less boy who had seen more in five years than most grandfathers had their whole lives. "He's the one you're looking for."

Belzer cursed as he was stripped of his coat but he fell silent, bare chested and shivering, once the black ink was revealed on the inside of his bicep. The officer lifted the arm roughly, brows beetling.

The soldier gave Belzer a small, self-satisfied smile.

"Take him," ordered the lieutenant, and Belzer was hauled away, shocked, eyes as big as saucers and stuttering cries of innocence tumbling from his lips. As soon as the Russians and their prisoner were on the other side of the street, Belzer's comrades fought over his shirt and coat like snarling strays. The soldier retrieved his own clothing and walked away. West, and out of town. He did not look back.

* * * *

The soldier began whistling—badly—once he glimpsed the American checkpoint on the road a hundred metres ahead. He'd been walking for hours, feet numb. His mouth was dry. He stopped and pulled out the lighter and fumbled for his last cigarette and managed to light it with a shaking hand. The midget was once again at his side and the soldier noticed he had now awarded himself an Iron Cross, first-class with oak leaf cluster. "I need some money…and a packet of Kurmarks." The midget nodded, smiled, then tugged at the soldier's coat pocket. The soldier reached inside and felt the wad of notes and the smokes. He looked down again at the little man. "This interzone pass…it is genuine? It will get me through?"

"Would I lie to you? You hold the blue light."

That cherubic face from the midget in the movie—from the screen of that *kino* in Berlin a lifetime ago—that same face was staring up at him, beaming confidence. The soldier swallowed the lump in his throat, took a drag, and forged ahead towards the black and white barrier. His hand in his pocket clutched the pass and the lighter while he eyed the gum-chewing GIs that were standing there, huddled in the cold. There was no one else on the road and they stopped talking once they spotted him. The soldier could hear his blood roaring in his ears but he still heard one of the Americans demand his papers in bad German, not well-practiced.

The interzone pass and the lighter came out in his clenched fist, together. His shaking hand tried to unfold it but the GI snatched it away and the brass lighter tumbled into the dirty slush at his feet. Before he could bend to reach it, the GI had beaten him to it, holding it firmly in one hand while he studied the pass in the other. The American gave him a long hard look, as if he was deciding whether to give him a kicking. But then he handed the paper back to him with just two fingers, as if it were tainted. "OK, fuck off! Mak schnell!"

The soldier was paralyzed, his eyes on the lighter that the GI was now examining. The corporal next to him added his own encouragement. "You heard him, buddy. Fuck…off. You can go through."

For one endless moment the soldier locked eyes with the man holding the blue light and the words sat on his tongue, desperate to come out. His mouth opened and then he saw the Yank move his hand to his holster. The soldier blinked a few times and before he actually realized it, his feet had propelled him into the American zone. He did not look back.

The GI entered the sentry box and stamped his feet, grinning at his prize. He pulled out a Lucky Strike, put it in his mouth, and flicked the lighter. The blue flame surprised him but not half as much as the voice at his side, a voice that sounded like something out of the Wizard of Oz.

"Hey pal," it squeaked, "Got a light?"

BLOOD PACT
by Sharon Cullars

Surrey, England, 1888

"The vicar is due any moment," Kleinfeld says, running a hand across a sweaty brow where strands of gray lay limply. His squat face is a robust red, most likely due to the discomforting heat.

We've been waiting in the church for what seems an eternity and I am becoming quite impatient. I, too, am sweating beneath my shirt and vest but I believe in the power of mind over matter, so force myself to ignore the heat, telling myself I am not uncomfortably warm, that I am perfectly comfortable. Oftentimes the mind bending does not work, but on this occasion I fancy a cool breeze fluttering in from an unopened stained glass window. It feels pleasant and my peeve recedes a bit.

Less than a couple of minutes later, the vicar, Reverend Johnathan Davies, walks through the double doors of the church, his rheumatic steps slow and seemingly painful. He is due to retire by the end of the year and has set about finalizing his tenure. An offer has already gone out to a Mr. Harold Stanton who presently resides in Leicester. A young minister of twenty-seven or so with an equally youngish wife and two young, healthy boys, he accepted the position within a fortnight. Presently, the niceties of the deal are being taken care of. As an addendum, the rectory will be freshened up to provide a more hospitable environment than that enjoyed by a seventy-year-old man set in his ways, refusing to acknowledge that time is ever passing, as are the dictates of a changing society.

"Good day, gentleman," Reverend Davies says as he reaches the foot of the altar, where Kleinfeld and I stand. "I hope I haven't kept you waiting long."

"Dickson and I only arrived within the half hour," Kleinfeld says, his peeve evident in the sputtering cadence of his voice. "Whether or not that is considered long is a matter of subjective opinion."

Leave it to Kleinfeld to make a production of every minor irritant. His is a choleric temperament, one which ran off Myrtle, his wife of nearly twenty years…or so it was whispered. Rumor has it that after years of suffering criticism of her cooking, she'd taken a ceramic tureen of chipped beef and unceremoniously dumped it over his head. Thereafter, she'd packed her things and left.

"Well, let's get on with it," I offer, feeling the fingers of ice freezing the beads of sweat on the nape of my neck and beneath my clothing. I have bent my mind 180 degrees in the opposite direction and am now suffering the consequential frostbite.

The minister gives a genial nod, unperturbed by Kleinfeld's show of spleen.

"Of course, gentlemen, I guess I do not have to remind you that this meeting and its purpose is to be divulged to no one," Reverend Davies warns unnecessarily, his shoulder partially bent, his sweating pate gleaming with moisture.

I answer with a nod as does Kleinfeld shortly after.

"Well enough, then. Worthington," the reverend addresses me directly. "You may proceed."

I am definitely chilled at this point but I push the creeping iciness from my mind, concentrating all of my mental strength on the task of setting my temperature back to normal. Heat sears my core, but then recedes until I achieve an equanimity that allows me to proceed unencumbered by physical distress.

I gather my thoughts, pulling the threads to the center of my brain, pushing myself past the limitation of the body of Michael Worthington standing at the altar of St. Thomas Church of the Angels. Soon I am traveling the miles to East End, London.

What hits me immediately is the melange of unpleasant odors. Stifling cigarette smoke hangs like a fog in the warm evening, intermingled with the noxious and overwhelming smells of unwashed bodies gathered in the close uncobbled street, the pungency a miasma that speaks of a hopeless poverty.

"This is a disgrace," Kleinfeld says with disgust, his voice somewhat muffled. He stands to my left, a kerchief held to his nostrils in an attempt to diminish the rank smells. Reverend Davies stands to my right, a step or two behind me, no handkerchief visible. As a minister who at times ventures into the slums of London on assignment to minister to the less fortunate, he has no doubt become accustomed to a plethora of smells. As for me, I have a strong constitution. Smells, even of the offensive kind, bother me little.

"Yes, the state of the disadvantaged is always a disgrace," I answer, hiding the mirth in my voice.

"You know that is not my meaning. Why do these people not at least try to live with some dignity?"

I deign not to give an answer to such a clueless question. It is hard to maintain a veneer of dignity when one is living a hardscrabble life. But then Kleinfeld has never personally known poverty. In the quiet verdancy of Surrey, one easily forgets that not all are born to comfortable stations, that not everyone is privileged to traipse along roads lined with quaint cottages of quiet complacency.

Dusk is drawing nigh and we have much to do before the strength of my teleportation power begins to wane.

We start our trek down a dirty street of tenements situated just north of the Thames. Walking together, the three of us draw suspicious stares from a group of men gathered in front of a public house, tankards gripped in grimy hands. Their clothes are dirty and threadbare, their hard faces unshaven. Their resentment in seeing us is palpable, even several feet away.

From their midst darts a young blonde girl of tender years, mayhap ten or such. She runs up to me without censure from the group of men and looks up, her face smeared with dirt. Her hair is tangled and filthy.

"Sir, can you spare a farthing or a penny?" she asks unabashedly. This then is her past time, begging for coinage from her betters. That is, if she does not spend an enormous amount of her days toiling in some workhouse manning machines twice her size.

"Bah, be away with you child!" Kleinfeld says before I have a chance to speak. "We have no money for the likes of you."

"The likes of me then?! And what be the likes of you, three fancy men dressed like the organ grinders funny monkeys?"

"Pretty cheeky for a street waif, aren't you?" Kleinfeld retorts.

In answer, the girl spits a wad of sputum that lands unceremoniously on Kleinfeld's pant leg.

"Why you bitch!" he says, instinctively lifting a hand as though he would slap her. At that moment, we catch sight of the tavern men hastening from their seats and Kleinfeld thinks better of his action. After all, we are outnumbered and not only by the men walking toward us, but by the common denizens walking about. He drops his hand, but it is already too late.

A dark-haired, mustachioed man leads the pack and gets right in Kleinfeld's squat face, which is a sight redder than it had been minutes before, fear and anger adding their own imprint.

"Hold on there, you dark cully, don't you even think about 'ittin' my daughter! Who the fuck you think you are? All you *fine gentlemen* comin' 'ere in the dark of the evenin' seekin' to dab it up with the laced muttons, you disgusting…"

"Sir, you misrepresent us," Davies interjects. "We are not here to partake in any carnal practice. We are simply here to be of service."

The man laughs bitterly. "A man of the cloth. Now why ain't I surprised? Wouldn't be the first time one of you high and holies has taken a detour to the East End of town to have your cock pinched, no matter your blusterin' otherwise."

"Sir, forgive my companion's impetuousness," I offer, attempting to allay the men's anger for we are quickly running out of time. "He did not mean to strike out at the child. It is just that we are late to an appointment, so if you would allow us to be on our way…"

"Appointment? Fancy way to say you're late meetin' up with your 'ores," another of the tavern men spews which engenders a healthy round of laughter among his cohorts. A few passersby have stopped to join in the gaiety. Obviously, they do not want to miss the opportunity to belittle those above their stations. Although I sympathize with their resentment against the hand that God has dealt them, the ridicule is simply a fruitless endeavor.

"If that is what you choose to believe, then far be it for me to disabuse you of your erroneous assumption," I say without rancor. The sky is darkening, time for children to be in bed but the little miss stands next to her father, her face a amalgam of curiosity and meanness. She is a child with a woman's sensibilities. So young, so lost.

"Huh?" the second man asks, his face confused. Basic comprehension must be beyond his abilities.

At this time, both Davies and Kleinfeld cannot hide their impatience and these good folks are not quite done with us. The crowd has grown exponentially.

The minister throws me a worried glance. The tavern men look ready for some severe rough housing which neither Kleinfeld or Davies would survive.

When I was but a child of eight, a rattler rose from a thatch of grass growing near my grandfather's farm. It drew back its head with a hiss, its fangs bared.

When it would have struck, a fire flared up around it and burned through its metallic body, which blackened to a pile of soot.

As my grandfather was standing several feet away, I could not be sure whether it was he or I who had performed the feat. I was still unfamiliar with my *gifts*, and my grandfather had had several millenniums to hone his powers.

At least a millennium of time stood between me and the child I was and I had sharpened my skills considerably since then. The flames were instantaneous; barely a scream as the crowd was consumed. No alarm raised to those within the tavern or tenements. The street was eerily silent.

The blackened ash rose on a sudden current of wind and the three of us retrieved and held kerchiefs to our mouths and noses, as we were blanketed with the remains of scores of men, women and at least one child who would never grow into a woman. In a way, a kind blessing for her. Better death than a lifetime in a hovel, begging on the streets for change.

We are running against time as we part ways, each of us with a duty to perform. I turn down an alley in which vermin of the four-legged kind scurry among the detritus. As I continue my way through the Whitechapel district, I see a disheveled woman standing sentry at an opened back door. She is unkempt, her hair unwashed and limp, her mouth drawn and pinched. An older version of the waif who is no more. A dab of red rouge on her drawn cheeks advertises her misbegotten wares.

"'ello guvner, would you be seekin' some company tonight, then?" she queries, her eyes lighting up at the possibility of a few coins to rub together.

I do not answer, but turn to see that no one has followed me, then turn back to see that no one is at the end of the alley.

The meeting is fortuitous and makes up for the minutes lost from the confrontation with the tavern men.

"Wha' will it be then?" she queries further. Impatience has taken some of the hope from her eyes.

* * * *

From the beginning of time, the gods required their sacrifices, an appeasement to satisfy their horrid lusts. In exchange for man's obeisance, these dark gods rewarded the ones who duly offered up blood, skin, and organs. No longer would these men be hindered by their flesh or mortality. In a sense, they became demi-gods with powers of the earth, the air, the water and of course, fire. But blood must be shed every seventy years (an arbitray sum of time, my grandfather complained once; why not fifty or one hundred years? he'd only harped that one time. Then he'd died by the blade of a reaper, his mortality rescinded. No one questioned the gods.). Just a half past midnight would be too late. They had to keep to schedule.

* * * *

Before she can react, I deftly retrieve the knife from my right pocket. She has no time to scream before I slit her throat. Her body collapses in the doorway.

I drag her corpse away from the door, lay her in the middle of the alley path. And then I set about my duty.

I quickly pull the scalpel from my left pocket and incise a precise opening into her clothing, her flesh, along her belly. The smell of bowels immediately overwhelms me, but again I am used to even the most offensive odors.

I remove her womb and one of her kidneys, a quarter size of the fleshy part of her abdomen. *Thus the organs, the flesh.*

I retrieve a vial, again from my left pocket and siphon the blood pouring liberally from her wounds. *Thus the blood.*

I place my offerings in a satchel that I pull from yet another pocket.

I do not wait. My duty is done. Now to meet at the appointed site.

I am the sole one with the gift of transportation and fire. Just one moment past the time, Davies and Kleinfeld will not be able to merge souls with their bodies lying in the church in Surrey.

The area is one large labyrinth of alleys and passageways, but the street we have agreed upon to reconvene is on the edge of the district, away from numerous prying eyes. I arrive within five minutes amid again more tenements. The distant peal of Big Ben travels the silence of the night from Westminster, down the Thames. It is striking the twelfth hour. Most of the denizens of this particular area, save but a stray harlot or two, have retired to their hovels, sleeping off their drunk in decrepit rooms, or are still feeding their ale lust in nearby taverns. It is fortuitous that no one notices me.

Within a minute Reverend Davies arrives, his own satchel held tightly in his hand.

"Where is Kleinfeld?" he asks. I am at a loss to answer for Kleinfeld is nowhere to be seen. We must return to St. Thomas at this very moment lest we risk our mortality. The gods must be fed and are an impatient, unforgiving lot.

"He must not have found a sacrifice," I surmise. Davies nods his concurrence.

"Too bad. He will be missed…by some, at least," the Reverend says. I notice the blood stains on his collar.

He grabs hold of my arm as there must be contact for him to travel back with me. Just as we begin our flight, I hear Kleinfeld's urgent appeal, see his corporeal soul hurrying down the street, his satchel dangerously dangling in his grip. But it is too late. From this night, he will be corporeal no longer.

Both Davies and I awaken in the church, prone on the floor near the altar. The interior is dark now but for the slight stream of moonlight filtering through the stained glass window.

It is still quite stifling in the enclosed church.

Kleinfeld's body lies soulless. In a few seconds, his wandering soul will dissipate from the streets of Whitechapel and become nothing but an ephemeral wisp of what he once was.

I rise first, then lend help to the rheumatic Reverend. He rises with an *oomph*, then both of us are standing over Kleinfeld.

We ignore him for the moment.

Wordlessly, I raise the pyre that burns upon the altar and yet does not singe the blue velvet covering that lays upon it. Beneath the cloth, unseen at the moment but observed by me on numerous occasions is the scripture from Acts 17:28 that is etched into the otherwise smooth wood of the altar: *For In Him We Live and Move and Have Our Being.*

He, the One of Light, is not the one to whom I appeal as both Davies and I empty the contents of our satchels, allow the flames to lap greedily at the wombs, the kidneys, followed by the blood poured from our vials.

As I say the words I learned so long ago, I remember:

And in the first caverns, the abodes of the hybrid between man and his prehistoric ancestor, fires burn, greedily receiving the woman's flesh, her womb, her organ. And the men surrounding the pyre receive a renewed infusion directly into their forms, their life's blood energized, their muscles strengthened. In some, even the outer surface is rejuvenated, and life begins again in a body newly invigorated.

Had I a mirror, I would no longer see the reflection of a man past his fortieth year, but rather that of a male still in his bonny youth. I have been both ages more times than I have kept count of. I am allowed only so many years before I must make recompense.

The Right Reverend Johnathan Davies is no longer a rheumy elder. He now stands tall and erect, the map of wrinkles vanished from his face. In their place is the smooth visage of a man just past his thirties, maybe slightly younger.

He is allowed to age further than I, but then again he is much older than I am by several milleniums and therefore ages much faster. My grandfather, had he lived, would have relived his thirties, forties, and would have been glad of it. We all have our different gifts, our different ages, our divergent paths.

Davies raises a hand and snuffs out the fire. He has received a renewed energy of his powers, which had dwindled down to a bare sliver. He has the gift of calling the air to strengthen and destroy. He was the one to clear the ashes of the unfortunate London denizens I had incinerated.

I look down at poor Kleinfeld. Had he made it back with us, his renewed gift would have been to call the waters and to shake the earth to its core. Mighty powers indeed that are now dormant in his dead body.

A much younger Davies looks down at Kleinfeld, then looks at me.

"What are we to say became of Kleinfeld?" he asks.

I shrug.

"*We* say nothing, as we will no longer be here to provide witness. Sacrifice sometimes require change. We cannot stay here. For all the parishioners and the town denizens will know, Kleinfeld was felled by a heart ailment. The physician will not be able to say yea or nay. After all, he was a man of a contentious temperament which can be stressful on the heart of a man nearing fifty. We will have to leave him here."

"Poor Kleinfeld," says Davies with a voice that is stronger, deeper.

My own voice is the lighter timbre of a young man whose voice has yet to mature into the depth of a much older man. The man I once was only an hour ago.

When the new minister arrives, he will find the rectory vacant, abandoned by the Right Reverend Davies, who will have unexpectedly left his post earlier than proposed due to a familial emergency.

For those who would seek Lawrence Worthington after this night, they would find that I, too, have left suddenly, purportedly seeking a cooler clime for my health. All of which would be explained in a letter that would be found on my dining room table by Mrs. Calvin, my housekeeper. As compensation for the abrupt termination of her services, I would leave her several hundred pounds, a sum that should last her until she is similarly engaged by another household.

In my life as Lawrence Worthington (I have already chosen a new name), I lived a solitary life without either wife or children (although my former incarnations have proven fruitful, at last count just over fifty or so). Only a select few of my descendants know of our familial pact; my oldest has to be several hundred years now, not that he would look it. The last time I ran into him, he went by the name of Martin Thompson, and was a respected barrister.

Tonight he would have taken on a new life, as well, and would have found reason to abandon his former one. He had several children this time around, if I recall correctly.

In cities throughout the world, in this past hour, pyres would have burned in solitary homes, empty churches, silent graveyards, and even caverns, anyplace far away from mere mortal eyes. Ceremonies would have been solitary or with one or two in attendance, but never with more than five. That many disappearances would call undue attention to practices that had been performed since time immemorial. And with each pyre, the gods will have feasted hungrily on the offerings, the wealth of which they would not taste for another seventy years.

"Well, then, so glad to have known you, dear boy," Davies says somewhat sarcastically. His wit is piercing, no longer with the dryness of an elderly minister. His rejuvenation has given him a handsomeness that was not evident in his older persona.

"You, too, Davies. Maybe our paths will cross again," I say.

He nods. "Yes, maybe so. Until then…"

With that, we both leave through the church doors, turning only once to give a slight nod to Kleinfeld. Then we take separate paths to our present homes to spend the last few hours or so packing so that we will be long gone by sunrise.

The next morning, I am on the eight-twenty train heading to Cardiff.

The ticket bears the name of Cadfael Rees. Mr. Rees is twenty-two and is seeking his fortune, maybe as an apprentice to a mason or such. Whoever takes him on will find he is a quick study. He'd been a mason a few hundred years before.

I settle into my aisle seat which adjoins that of a matronly woman traveling alone. Her gabardine dress speaks of someone with money to spend. Maybe I would strike up a conversation later. But for now I just want to sit back and read the early edition of *The London Times*.

The headline blazoned on the front is simply entitled *Murder in Whitechapel* the article of which describes the crime scene I have left behind. It is strange to read about one's handiwork as described by another who eagerly makes assumptions about a john who had gone amok.

Strangely, there is no reference to the other deaths that occurred that very night. Maybe Davies and Kleinfeld stashed the bodies. In time, the decomposing bodies would be found. The rules of the rituals would not allow us to use our powers to dispose of the bodies or I would have eagerly incinerated my victim. And Davies would have cast his unfortunate prey miles into the river with one strong gust. Kleinfeld would have moved concrete, rock and earth with his power to sequester his corpse.

As it were, I do not speak but a few words of pleasantry to my seatmate the whole ride to Cardiff. I am overwhelmed, not with guilt, but with wariness, lest I through some innocent action or word, give myself away.

The other two bodies are never found.

But strangely enough, in the next few months, someone else takes up where I left off. Maybe they became inspired by the graphic details of the carnage I left behind. As many details as the reporter got wrong, he did correctly surmise that someone with medical knowledge had used a scalpel. I had interned in an American hospital decades ago, the life lived before I moved back to England and settled in Surrey as Johnathan Worthington, a successful vintner.

Each headline in the Cardiff papers become more blatant than the last.

And now there are letters being written to the police and to the reporters.

By this time, I have found a position with a clothier, my efforts to find masonry work having proven fruitless.

In one paper, the killer is dubbed The Leather Apron. And yet, in another issue, they say that he has chosen his own appellation, Jack the Ripper.

Whomever the Ripper is, he is not one of us. He is most likely a mere mortal who has simply taken our...or rather, my...schematic and made it his own.

I am both flattered and offended, but do not spend too much time dwelling on it. That is in my past.

I have a future to look forward to.

I cut a seam with scissors and only for a second remember the many pounds of flesh I have cut into. I say a silent prayer in memory of the unfortunate sacrifices, then quickly work to finish the bespoke trousers that have been ordered by the lord of an estate. After all, there is a duty to perform and a schedule to keep. There is a price to pay when one doesn't keep to schedule.

May Kleinfeld rest in peace.

✗

SOMETHING I HAVE TO TELL YOU

by John B. Rosenman

"Martha," her husband said, "There's something I have to tell you."

They were walking through the park and at first she didn't attach any importance to what Fred had said. He was after all predictable, a man of no surprises. In a moment he'd say something quite ordinary.

Her husband was silent, though, and she felt a faint curiosity. What was it?

Fred stopped walking, making her stop, too. He stared at her.

"What is it, Fred?" she finally asked. "What do you have to tell me?" The words sounded strange, as if she should be saying them to someone else.

Fred cleared his throat. "Perhaps," he said, "we should sit over here."

To her growing surprise, he took her arm and led her to a nearby park bench.

They sat down. Fred cleared his throat again, sounding like a clogged drain. She watched him glance nervously around.

"What *is* it, Fred?" she asked. She waited impatiently.

"Martha, I've meant to tell you for a long time, even before we were married. But I hesitated."

"What?"

He wet his lips. "I…I don't really belong here," he said.

"Don't belong here?"

"No." His stolid face twitched, and he gazed at the trees and grass. "To tell the truth, I belong elsewhere. On another world."

"Another world?" She stared at him. "What are you talking about?"

"I should be flying in the sky, Martha, sailing on great golden wings."

She shook her head. "Fred, it must be your new medicine. You remember I was concerned about it." She started to pull him up, but Fred actually resisted.

"It's not my medicine, Martha. I felt this way before we even met." He reached out and gripped her arm in return, pulled *her* down.

"When was the first time you had this feeling?" she asked.

He gazed up at the clouded sky. "Somehow I think I felt this way even as I was born. That I'd slipped into the wrong realm, which was so sad and little. Wordsworth called it 'trailing clouds of glory' when he was born. Well, that's the way it's been for me. And gradually, over the years, I've remembered more and more."

"You mean you've *imagined* it."

"No, I actually remember. In my other life, on that other world, I flew in clouds of glory high above a divine land incomparably better than here. The air was filled with the fragrance of heavenly flowers." His gaze traveled about the park and rose again to the sky. "How far I have fallen."

She stared at him. She loved Fred, but he'd always been dull and predictable, a man she could depend on. Then one day they went for a walk and he told a mad story. He actually believed he had flown through the sky on golden wings in a previous life. It was an insane delusion which she found strangely disturbing.

She took his hand and pressed it to her lips. "So this is a golden wing, Fred?"

He looked down at his hand. "It's part of it, Martha. My wings were so long, beautiful, and majestic as I glided through the sky. Then one day…"

She swallowed, almost able to see it. "You slipped through."

He nodded. "Yes, I don't know how it happened. Only…"

"Only what, Fred?"

He trembled. "I just remembered something. One of our enemies picked up my trail and pursued me. A vicious, slashing Red Wing."

Something stirred inside her, a distant echo. "Red Wings. Is that what you called them?"

Another nod. "Yes, and I knew it would kill me, rip me to pieces. So I fled and used every trick I knew, rising and falling, darting and swooping. But the enemy was skilled and relentless. It drew closer and closer, until I knew I was about to die. Then somehow, I slipped through and woke up as a human baby here."

Her eyes were wet. "How can you believe such a thing?"

"It's not a matter of believing, Martha. I *know*."

"I see." And suddenly she knew too and could not deny it. "What happened to the Red Wing, Fred?"

He shrugged. "I don't know."

She sighed and kissed his cheek. "Maybe she slipped through too, Fred. Woke up as a child here and grew up. Then met you and fell in love."

He stared at her. Deep in his eyes she saw a glimmer of understanding. "What are you saying, Martha?"

She glanced about to be sure they were alone, then raised her hand. Slowly it grew and expanded, becoming a giant red wing.

"Fred," she said gently, "there's something I have to tell you."   ✗

THE CURIOUS SIMULACRUM OF DR. F

by Michael Canfield

"I felt grateful for your letter, sir," I said. "And to know that your 'blasphemous' profession still engages you."

"Quite," he answered, smiling in appreciated at my little joke—for time and experience had inoculated him against accusations made by that mob of incurious and superstitious souls opposing his work. Their barbs: blasphemer, sorcerer, atheist, (*et al., ad nauseam*) had long since failed to draw blood. "Another sherry, my boy?"

"Will I need it?"

"In all likelihood."

Dr. F— entertained in his study. On similar evenings, some years before, when I had first been taken on as his pupil, I had thought his rooms astonishingly small for a man of his standing. Though I now know that stature among men of learning does not correlate with stature in the mundane world. Once, however, I had assumed, like so many young men, that my passions and interests were also the world's.

Alas.

My host refilled my glass and placed the canister back on its tray, all without looking at me. It was his manner when deep in thought, as if too much contact with the presence of another would distract him from his important thoughts—thoughts only he could think. I took no offense at it as I was well used to the behavior.

"However, you mustn't say it's 'my' profession. It's our profession, our profession, Henry. Ours. How have your studies progressed? Never mind, never mind, don't answer. I know the answer, I know the answer well indeed, for I have followed your career with great enthusiasm since you first ventured out from beneath my wing. Great enthusiasm," said he, speaking in that rapid cadence of intellectual excitement that was his hallmark. I knew, from this alone, that he had had a great breakthrough of some kind. It only remained to hear what.

"I haven't learned half so much in two years at Oxford as I learned in your laboratory, Dr. F— "

"You need say, no more, Henry. No man can stay in his father's house forever. Nor his teacher's either."

He smiled bravely. Quite unexpectedly, he put his hand on the arm of my arm and squeezed. "We are colleagues now. I call you Henry, you must use my Christian name as, well. If you will not call me Victor then I must call you Dr. Jek—."

"Very well. I submit."

"Good, good. That's settled," he said and, nearly under his breath, followed with, "I am so pleased."

He suddenly stationed himself at the mantle and stretched his arm across it mahogany surface. Above, hung the antique dueling pistol that had been his grandfather's. The doctor had carried it with him, from country to country, during his exile. It was the sole legacy of his once-illustrious family—save for the possession of his hereditary genius itself.

He dug his thumbnail idly into the wood of the mantelpiece; patiently impatient, as it were, until I drained my glass and set it down on a side table.

Smiling, now that the conventions of hospitality stood satisfied at last, the doctor clapped his hands together loudly (his signature gesture of enthusiasm) and said, "Now Henry, if you're quite refreshed, do me the kindness of taking up that lamp there. I shall take this one—"

He reached for the gas lamp at the end of the mantle, pushing back his sleeve (for he wore no coat) as he did so. He turned to his desk and swept up an impressively-sized key ring that held an even more impressive number of keys.

"Now, were off!" he said with uncontained enthusiasm. "This way, Henry! This way!"

I grinned inwardly as I followed my host's lead, for it delighted me to see how giddy the fruits of his genius had made him. I could scarcely wait to see the results myself!

We wound our way along the hallway and out the rear of the flat, into the alley.

Holding our lamps high, we trod carefully upon the uneven stones, crossing to the storing house across the way. One end of the alley abutted the Thames. A light patina of snow had fallen while we had talked and was not yet blackened by the soot. Cold air enveloped my cheeks and my nose so fully and with such haste that the restorative comforts of brandy and my host's modest fire immediately fled—as if I'd not been inside after my journey at all.

The doctor, in his shirtsleeves, took no notice. Handing me his lamp, he worked a prodigious number of the keys into their corresponding locks—deadbolts, of which a great many had been set into the double doors since my last visit.

The warehouse was narrow (no more than the span two healthy-sized men side-by-side, arms outstretched) rather deep, and possessed a high ceiling. The doctor paid the merchant to which this storing house belonged a tidy sum—nearly as much as the cost of his flat itself—for essentially an oblong hexahedron.

Though, perhaps it is more accurate to say the merchant charged a small sum in rent and a somewhat larger amount for his discretion.

The doctor pulled one of the large doors open and, after taking back one of the lamps, motioned me inside.

The ceiling contained a skylight—of no use this moonless evening.

Research of the caliber undertaken by the doctor required a prodigious amount of light and we moved about in the dark, lighting the myriad lamps and candles set out atop the various tables alongside the doctor's array of equipment and instruments.

As soon as we had sufficiently battled back the gloom, the Doctor pulled shut the door, barring it now from the inside.

He took the added step of securing the bar with a padlock on the *inside*.

I found this strange and attempted a joke, telling my friend that if, for any reason, he succumbed to fumes from one or more of the many compounds stored in the jars on the crowded shelves and surfaces, that I hoped I would myself be able to remain conscious for sufficient time to take the key ring off his person, find the right key, and free us.

I was not serious and I merely meant on invoke the amusing memory of a minor accident that had occurred a previous year.

"What? What?" replied the doctor. He made a show of separating the key from the others on the ring and thrusting it outward to me. "Take it, if you must."

I demurred, somewhat embarrassed that my attempt at humor had failed.

"Simply a precaution," said he, with an inflection somewhere between perplexity and disinterest. With frustration, he tried to get the key back on the ring but suddenly gave up, dropping both the loose key and the ring into a chair—onto the top of his coat, as it happened, which he had evidently carelessly tossed there who-knows-how-many hours before.

The laboratory was much changed since I had last visited it, though this did not surprise me as the doctor's fields of interested were always varied and constantly evolving.

One could cast an eye over any surface, into any corner, any nook, any cranny, and find stacks of notebooks, sheaves of sketches; jars holding specimens of organs or small, exotic creatures; pressings of plants; potions and powders in vials stacked haphazardly upon bulging shelves; marvelous new devices to measure and explore the invisible forces of nature—gravity, magnetism, electricity, to name three—resting on the floor or on worktables alongside experiments in taxidermy; Petri dishes of cells and fungus.

The doctor's work was the work of life itself. Nothing stood outside his scope.

"Enough preliminaries," said he. "You want to see my research. That's why you've come. Is it not?"

"It is, sir."

"*Victor*," he reminded me, rather earnestly. "I am *Victor*. And you are Henry."

"Of course," I said. "Victor."

He nodded with satisfaction. Moving through the myriad tables, he nodded to indicate a heavy curtain of blood-red velvet drawn across the whole of the rear of the laboratory. It may have come from a dilapidated theatre somewhere, as it appears much too long and wide for its current purpose.

This same, he now went to. Grabbing its heavy folds, he dragged it along its track.

Revealing the iron bars of a cell.

And in the cell, a figure.

In contrast to the rest of the warehouse, the cell was nearly naked—nearly as naked as that small wretch sitting within it, in a solitary chair, with his head bowed, some distance away from a dented and rusty bucket that I suppose served as a chamber pot.

"What in the world—" I started in my surprise. I did not finish because, at that moment, the poor soul looked up to regard us with burning, yellow eyes.

Though the face was partially obscured with untended locks of greasy, graying hair falling across it, and the sallow cheeks blackened and filthy (as was the rest of his skin), and the whole, pitiable, presence being a shock to behold, one simple fact trumped all the rest:

"He—looks like *you*, Victor. "

"He *is* me," said the doctor.

I took a step toward the bars. The man—if he was a man—shifted his weight, kept his eyes fixed on me, but made no other move.

Nor did the poor soul attempted to speak.

Like an imbecile, I looked back and forth between the wretch and the doctor.

"Is he—?" I faltered.

"Is he what, Victor? Real? Oh, yes. Human? That is what we must determine. Is the specimen human?"

"The specimen?" I repeated appalled. "Victor, whatever else, I must tell you that the condition of this, this specimen, as you call him, is appalling. To be kept naked, in a freezing enclosure, sitting in his own filth. What could you be thinking?"

The doctor looked down. That measured, distinct, gesture of disappointment that I had come to know so well as his student after many occasions upon which I'd failed to grasp some concept that he felt I should have.

His shirt sleeve still rolled up, he turned over his arm, presenting it to me. Then he dragged his fingernails across the white underside of his forearm, heavily, reddening the flesh with streaks.

He displayed his hand, still bent into a claw, for my regard.

"What's there, Henry? Under my fingernails? What's there?"

"Dead skin cells, one imagines."

"Nearly correct! Skin cells. Yes, skin cells. But not dead. Not truly. For I have discovered a history, a blueprint, if you will, that lies within each cell of the body of which it is but a part. It's there, Henry, it's there. In each one of us. In every flake of skin, every drop of blood, every strand of hair. What I fool I was, poking around in graveyards! All the while I had all the material I needed," he slapped his hands against his trunk heartily. "Here! Within me. Myself."

"By what method did you—"

He swiped a hand derisively. "Oh, it's all in those notebooks back there. You're welcome to look them over, but have you not grasped the essential thing yet? We are immortal."

I hesitated, absorbing all he had just revealed—which, because I knew the man's genius, I did not doubt was true—and tried to form my next question thoughtfully.

The doctor became impatient. "Well?"

"I'm overwhelmed," I told him.

"I've told you nothing yet," said the doctor. "There is more, so much more. Producing the body—that was simple enough. I'd done it with animals and so forth. A side discovery from my previous research into reanimation proved the basis for accelerating the growth process. All perfectly banal, really. No, no, that was merely chapter one, verse one, of a *new Genesis*, for the resulting simulacrum was as a newborn babe. A blank slate. I went deeper.

"By a process I next developed, I then went on to subjugate the greatest marvel nature has ever produced—the human mind. I call this process the 'brain scan' and, having applied it to myself, I then introduced the resulting scan to my subject: making him fully me." The doctor suddenly seized both my forearms, shaking me vigorously as he finished. "He is as much myself as *I* am myself. The same thoughts, memories. Do you understand?"

I looked steadily into his watery eyes. "Doctor—" I said slowly. "Victor. Might I exam the—*ah*—subject?"

"Of course, of course. You didn't come here to listen to me prattle on. Of course, you will want to examine my work for yourself. Nothing would please me more, Henry. Nothing in this world."

"Might I have the key then?"

"Key?"

"The key to the cell. Is it on the ring with the others?"

"No," said the doctor, backing away. "No, I cannot allow that, not at this stage of the research. Examine him all you wish from here, through the bars, speak to him, ask him what you will, and, as I said earlier, my written records are entirely at you disposal. You can even take them with you back to the university if you wish."

"Yes, of course, and thank you," I said.

My friend now appeared to me to be suddenly next to exhaustion, as if the flood of his reverie had taken from him the last bit of energy remaining after what, I knew now, must have been many months of intense overwork. I resolved to send him to bed as soon as possible and which I would have done instantly—were it not for the more pressing matter of the wretch in the cell.

I continued. "I think we should perhaps take your papers back to the study and look them over together, but first I think I will, at least, speak to the…"

The doctor nodded, gesturing.

I turned back to the cell, approaching the bars.

"Stop!" said the doctor. "I insist you keep an arm's length away."

I pushed the folds of my coat aside and straightened my vest. "Very well," I replied.

"Hello," I said to the wretch. "My name is—"

"He knows your name," said the doctor, swiping the air with his hand.

"Oh, quite," I said. I began again. "Hello, how are you feeling?"

The poor fellow grunted.

"Are you eating?" And then I asked the doctor, "What is his diet composed of?"

"Just such as ours. As anyone's," he replied, shaking down the sleeve of his shirt and turning away. He went to a table and started gathering loose papers into a leather case. He did not look up.

I turned my attention back to the soul in the cell. His eyes remained fixed on me, and though I felt him to be human, the expression reminded me only of one other I had ever in my life witnessed, and that creature, though decidedly *non*-human, had also occupied a cage.

I speak of a gorilla I had once the misfortune to witness being transported to the London zoo.

The same wild intelligence. The same inarticulate—and profound—despair.

The doctor ran string around another folder and then gave it a satisfied slap. "He won't answer you," said he.

I turned my head. "Oh? And why is that?"

"I removed the brain pattern. It has served its purpose. That stage of the experiment is at an end."

"You gave the creature consciousness—and then took it away?"

"As much as I could. Some remnants remain—like vestigial organs." He smiled slightly, with one corner of his mouth. "The world is not ready for *two* souls such as a mine, Henry."

"No, indeed."

The doctor looked down his nose. "Now, now. I know what you're thinking, Henry. I know how your mind works: you reproach me for giving fire to Prometheus, only to snatch it away again! Such a petulant and fickle god!"

He thrust his arm out, as grandly and as steady as a fencer presenting his rapier. "That specimen, that *body* is nothing more than a system of cells, no more alive than an earthworm—half an earthworm, let us say."

"You may say it, sir, but I will not—"

"V-v-victor...."

I turned. The wretch had spoken

He stood, and was at the bars now, clutching iron in both his filth-covered hands. His cracked voice came again, air pressed through atrophied vocal cords. "V-victor. My name is Victor!"

I turned to the doctor. My own voice boiled with rage. "I will see to him, sir. I will! Open the cage!"

The doctor ground his jaw. He wiped his hands on his shirt, and then cross the laboratory, back to the chair where he had left the ring of keys earlier.

He took it in his hands and held it tightly as if wanting to twist and bend the metal ring in his grasp—all his rage at me compressed into his hands.

"Well, then," he said. "I suppose it's settled. Do as you like."

He flung the ring high.

It soared across the room falling well short of my feet and sliding under a table.

I looked at him with reproach. He merely leaned back on one heel and folded his arms—hugging himself, in effect, with satisfaction.

I stooped and reached under the table, groping around like a blind man until I touched the cold metal of the ring

Bringing it up, I shook it at him with impolite satisfaction.

He merely raised his eyebrow.

I went to the cell, smiling and speaking calmly to the wretch.

"I just want to come in and have a look," I said, "See if you're all right. See what I can do for you? Do you agree?"

He grunted, and made a slight head movement that I interpreted as an assent. He then, of his own accord, moved back to the rear of the cell, all the way to the wall, clasped his hands together before himself and stood with his head lowered.

These were the movements of a trained and pacified creature.

I look again the doctor, though I could only just bear to see him now, he had treated his doppelgänger so abominably. "Which key is it?" I hissed.

The doctor turned to some worktable and made is if to busy himself with bottles and beakers set there.

"The large one," he said.

The ring held twenty keys, at least—several of which made equally good candidates for the term "large one." However, I had had my fill of the doctor for the moment, so turned away from him and tried the most likely-looking key in the lock.

The tumblers turned with as satisfying wrench, and I pulled the cell door open. It creaked.

I turned to glance at the doctor with satisfaction.

He was already upon me.

I did not see the syringe the doctor held in his white grip until he had already raised it.

He sank the needle into my neck.

I fought him, pushed him away. The needle broke off, but it was too late, he had already squeezed the plunger.

The effects were nearly instantaneous.

I staggered, waving my hand to find something to hold onto—and failing.

The doctor stepped over me, closed the cell door and turned the key, locking it again.

The wretch, still at the back wall, wailed.

I looked up at the doctor's wavering form. I reached out, but he seemed miles away.

His voice echoed toward me through a cloud. "A pity you wouldn't listen to reason, Henry. You always were a damned fool."

The polluted cloud of unconsciousness overtook me.

#

I awakened—how much time had passed, I knew not—to find myself lying a gurney, trapped there, by heavy canvas straps.

I had been stripped and swaddled in bandages from my neck down to my feet. I moved my head around and blinked to clear my vision, which was horribly blurred.

I made out enough to see that I was still in the doctor's lab. It was day, and a warm, unseasonable sun shone through the skylight.

I focus on the shimmering image the at the back of the lab.

Still within it—though a blur to me—the doctor's wretch huddled in the far corner, face to the wall,—a crouch of emaciated flesh, breathing in fits, and sobbing softly.

"Ah, among the living now, Henry. Yes?"

I turned my head to see the doctor coming toward me, wiping his hands on a towel.

He tossed it aside. Coming next to the gurney, he leaned forward.

"How are you feeling?"

"Let me up," I rasped.

"In due time. You mustn't exert yourself."

"Water."

"You must be very thirsty," he said mildly. "How is your vision?"

"Some doubling," I said.

"All right. Nothing to worry you, a minor side effect. It will clear in a moment."

"What have you done to me?"

"Rest, now. Talk later."

"No! Damn you, I'm not one of your experiments. I want you to release me. Where are my clothes?"

"Your clothes are here, Henry. See?" He moved to a nearby work table and put his hand a stack of something which could well have been folded clothing.

"All laundered and waiting for you." He nodded at the floor. "Boots polished too."

"Let. Me. Free."

The doctor sighed, slumping his shoulders theatrically.

"Very well," he said. He moved to the straps. "The restraints are merely a precaution," he said, with the petulance of a child ordered to put his toys back in its chest. "For your benefit, really."

When I was free, I tried to rise, and the world spun. The doctor put his arm around me, perhaps to help steady me, but I shook him off.

"All right, all right," he said, retreating. "I'll get you that water."

He poured a glass from a pitcher. I managed to sit up, and then pulled at the bandages which tightly swaddled me.

"I'll cut those away," he said, handing me the glass of water. "Steady with this, now."

My hands shook, but I managed to take the glass and hold onto it. Raising it to my blistered lips, I drank down its contents as if I had never tasted liquid before.

The doctor found a pair of scissors and slid his hand under a layer of bandage wrapping my shoulder.

"This will take some time," he said, "more water?"

"I'm fine."

"Good." He cut. "Vision?" Another cut of the scissors.

"Nearly recovered."

"Verrrry good…."

He turned, finding a bucket and retrieving it to drop the strips of cut bandage into.

Centered at the small of his back, I saw the hilt of his grandfather's dueling pistol poking out of his trousers. It was cocked.

"Another precaution?" I asked.

He looked at me.

"What, this?" He removed the pistol and held it up, his arm crooked, looking at it as if the feign he known it was there. "Yes. Well…all things considered…. I had no idea what temper I'd find you in. However, I do feel now that you're unlikely to hurt me…. Therefore, I apologize."

He put the pistol down on the table, out of reach, next to my folded clothing. He did not uncock the hammer.

With a slight smile, he returned to cutting the bandages.

A cloud and passed above the skylight, casting a shadow, briefly. The rays of the sun shone again.

"Bright today," I said.

"Is it?" He looked away from his work and up and the skylight. "So it is."

"Warm too."

"Oh, yes…." He worked away. Cutting, cutting.

"What day is it?"

The doctor lifted his head, averting his eyes to think. "The twentieth? No, the twenty-second. The twenty-second of July. Or the twenty-third."

"That's months." Months since the dead of winter. Months since I had come to visit.

"*Tempus fugit*, dear Henry. So much done; yet, so much *more* to do."

Cut, cut, cut.

The bandages began to fall away into a great pile, overfilling the bucket between our feet.

"What have you done with me? What have you done with me in all that time?"

"The second phase," said the doctor.

"Is that why you lured here?" Not to see and share his work at all. "To be your Guinea pig?"

"Henry! Such talk—coming from a man science. *Guinea pig.* My goodness. Such umbrage you take. The entire world should be our laboratory, all its miraculous forms our—as you say—*Guinea pigs.* We are explorers, Henry. Explorers. And colleagues! Don't forget that. We're colleagues, after all. In any case, *I* did not lure—"

"What 'explorations' have I been helping you with, lo these many months? Colleague."

The doctor looked me in the eyes. He put down the scissors and, taking hold of the gurney in both hands, swung it—and me—around. The steel wheels—un-oiled—whistled.

That noise made the wretch huddling in the corner of the cell lift its head.

And he was not Victor's doppelgänger.

I screamed. I did not *know* I had screamed at first because the creature—*my* doppelgänger—was screaming too, and flailed its arms above its head as if vexed by invisible, winged demons.

"Henry! Henry! Calm yourself. Calm yourself. You see that you are upsetting the specimen. Calm yourself. We are men, need I remind you? Be calm."

I wanted to shake. Shake myself right out of my body, for whatever my shock upon first seeing the doctor's double the now long-ago evening, the shock of seeing my *own* was tenfold—no, a hundred fold.

The doctor continued his foul exhortations for calm. "Breath, Henry, breath. Deep. In. That's right. Out."

Whatever my thoughts for him, I understood his instruction to breath was sound. Exuberant emotion would do nothing to ease my shock. I forced air into my lungs and abdomen, again and again.

And I recovered myself.

"One must repeat one's experiments," said the doctor. "One must duplicate one's results. That is essential to the scientific method." He spoke as if to himself—as if repeating what he would have learned long ago—regurgitating from a copybook.

My doppelgänger had, like me, become becalmed, and returned now to its previous hidden crouch. I so pitied the poor wretch, yet I could barely stomach the thought of him.

Mustering my will, I turned to the doctor, looking at him through the diffusion caused by the welling in my eyes. I was nearly free of the bandages.

"And the other?" I asked. "Yours?"

For the cell still only had one occupant.

He gestured to a long trough among all the other debris of the lab. "Acid," he said. "Hydrochloric—together with a few other compounds of my own devising. A long process, and there were fumes to be dealt with, but I found that, with the skylight open, they mostly rose up. And it leaves no trace."

"No," I said. "I suppose it wouldn't."

"Mere organic matter, you know," he said absently. "Just an old shell cast off. Like a snake's first skin. Metaphorically."

"Or the exoskeleton of a pupa."

The doctor looked at me, brightening.

"Metaphorically," I said.

"Yes. Rather apt, Henry. A marvelous student. It was ever thus. May it be so again."

"Might I trouble you for my clothing, doctor? I have not quite the strength to stand yet; however, I should very much like to be dressed."

He went to the table.

Instead of picking up my clothes, he picked up the pistol. He turned it over with both hands, admiring the patina covering its muzzle. Then he looked back up at me, shaking his head and smiling. "Such foolishness." He release the hammer carefully and set it back down.

He brought me my clothes.

He helped to dress me, and then, my hand on his shoulder, I stood at last. I supposed I felt no better, nor no worse, than if I had emerged victoriously from a long battle against influenza or some other invisible invader.

When he was sure I could remain upright without falling, the doctor released my arm and clapped his hands together.

"Now! Next order of business. I had intended to begin the process of disposing of the remaining specimen in the cell this morning. I had not anticipated your awakening so soon. A pleasant surprise, but a surprise nonetheless. Would you care to assist me?"

"I have a question for you, doctor."

"Anything. Anything." He held his hand upward, cupped.

"Earlier—before my rather embarrassing outburst—we spoke of why you had invited me here—"

"To share in my work, of course."

I smiled indulgently. "No, doctor, you misunderstand me. For you have already answered that question. What you told me was, '*I* didn't invite you.'"

"Did I?"

"*You* didn't invite me. And between the time the letter of invitation was sent and my arrival, Dr. F—the *true* Dr. F—, at least the one I knew, was no more. And you, the simulacrum, had replaced him, wiping his brain to hide your crime."

He dropped his arms. "My boy, this is most embarrassing."

"If I am wrong, tell me I am wrong."

He did not speak at once. I watched his jaw grinding. He closed his hand into a fist and raised it, staring past me. Staring at the cage.

"He kept me there for months. I possess his intellect, his passions, his memories. We should have worked side by side, but he kept me penned up like an animal. Not at man. Not his equal!"

I listened.

"I formulated a plan and bided my time. One day, when he brought me my gruel—oh, the details are unimportant, Henry. We grappled, I emerged the winner, but it could have gone the other way.

"In any case, as you guessed, I wiped his brain and put him in the cage. But only so that he could not one day do the same to me, Henry! He was too brilliant. Too brilliant, it would have been only a matter of time before he devised a way to reverse our roles again.

"And then I left him there, empty-headed. I beat him. I let him freeze in the winter and I let him bake in summer, sitting in his own filth. I watched him devolve into nothing more than the mere mass of cells that he only ever saw me as. And then, at last, having done all I could, I extinguished the final spark with one ball of lead from his grandfather's gun. Think of that, Henry. All that complexity—of evolution, of the eons—undone in a moment by a few grams of metal and a reaction of powder. A simple... reproducible...predictable...function of chemistry and physics. As is everything!

"After that, I transported the lifeless body from the cell to the acid bath, where I erased even his carcass from the world."

He shook his head, as if banishing melancholy.

"Along the way, you presented yourself, Henry—unexpectedly, as I had no way of telling what letters my original had sent while I had languished as his prisoner. I thought first just to let you go, but I feared what might happen if you guessed the truth. So I took the extraordinary measure of the hypodermic needle—for which I do, apologize sincerely. From there, I could not resist duplicating the process of my predecessor. The process that lead to my own making. Curiosity, you see."

"And now that I *have* guessed the truth?"

The doctor—for I supposed I must still call him that—shrugged. "Do we not often find, Henry, when the things we most fear come to pass, we had nothing so much to be afraid of, after all?"

I said nothing.

"Now, Henry, ask me the question you *truly* want to ask."

I looked at the thing in the cell. Cowering, groping. Hideous.

"I have no further questions," I said, straightening.

The doctor arched an eyebrow.

"How you disappoint me, Henry. Have you so small a measure of curiosity in your soul?"

Have I even a soul?

I quickly banished the thought. Instead, I tugged and adjusted the sleeves of my coat. *Yes, it is your coat*, I reminded myself. *Your coat. Yours alone.*

"Very well," said the doctor. "If you won't answer, you won't answer. Let that lie. However, there is one thing left to do." He picked up the pistol and pulled back the hammer back again.

I froze.

Then he transferred the pistol to his other hand and held it, by the muzzle, out to me.

"I was going to do it, but seeing now as *you're* sufficiently upright…"

"It's got nothing to do with me," I said, looking away. I found my gloves in my pocket and began pulling them on.

"Hasn't it?"

I raised my voice in exasperation. "It's your experiment; it's your problem. Do as you will."

He frowned. "Very well, as you continue to be so difficult, I present you with a choice. I will do it, but you must tell me to. If you say dispose of it, I shall dispose of it. If you say nothing, then I will do nothing. And it lives. On and on, as long as nature allows. What is your answer?"

In its corner, the monster was peering out, peeking at us over the arm it held across its face, with its cowardly, yellowed eyes.

"Kill it," I said.

The doctor nodded solemnly, he turned the pistol again, taking it by the hilt. "Go across to my rooms," he said, his voice soft. "Cook will prepare something for you if she's in. New one, can't recall her name—doesn't matter. If she's already gone, pour yourself a sherry and wait for me and we'll make other dinner arrangements later. Oh, the times we shall have Henry."

"I am not staying."

The doctor took a step back. He let the hand holding the pistol drop to his side.

"I have my own life to live," I said. "My own work to do."

"Henry…."

"You know I must make my own way. You, of all people, know that I must. No man can stay in his father's house, forever." Or, if he is to be his own man, even very long.

He appeared to shrink. He was never a large man, but he looked even smaller, now. He glanced at the ground, shook his head and appeared to be readying himself to make a new argument. Then, all at once, he slumped.

"I'm disappointed, Henry, I will not lie to you about that. I'm disappointed, but I find I cannot stop you. Even if I could, I wouldn't. No, I couldn't, not after…. Well…" he trailed off, "…in any case. It *is* your life to lead. It must be so."

"Farewell, Doctor."

He took my hand and shook it, bravely. "Farewell, my boy. I—"

I turned, and before he could say more, left the laboratory, going out into the alley, where I squinting at the sun.

Absurdly dressed in my unseasonably heavy weeds, I nevertheless clasped my coat by the lapels, pulling it tighter around myself.

After traversing the alley, I pressed on toward the embankment. It was midday and life teemed everywhere around me: wheels of carts and carriages ground against cobblestones, hooves and the hobnail boots of women clacked, traders shouted, boatmen whistled.

I was some distance away by the time the muffled sound of the shot came from within Dr. F—'s laboratory—obscured and made insignificant by the rich noises of London—and I did not turn around.

d

A CURE FOR RESTLESS BONES

by Angela Enos

1: DESCENDING

They called us The River's Daughters, named after the deep wet road that bore our ships to the frontier. It didn't matter that we were actually the daughters of bakers and lords, laborers and scoundrels. We left those lives behind when we chose to leave the Waking World. Our reasons were not questioned by those who offered us motley few this choice. Neither were our future intentions.

I don't know who asked me to make the choice. It sounded like my own voice made a stranger by the screams of the woman I had been. I had an image of some holy thread of a thing that runs through the universe like unraveled yarn between the seconds of being a living breathing panting screaming thing and sloughing it all off that I made my decision. It didn't matter who asked. I answered. I chose.

I never asked the other Daughters who had given them their choice or how it sounded to them. My story, our stories, they were private things, kept inside and tangled up with truths that stung too much to cross our lips during the voyage. It only mattered that we made our choice and now shared the outcome of that decision.

My choice had been clear to me. I knew the change would not be easy. I understood what lay ahead, at least in theory if not yet in practice. I could feel the apron strings tying me to the table, the wooden spoon clenched between my teeth, the hurt of it all and the futility and the injustice. There I went, the all of me, the whole of me. I was disappearing with each gasp of air. In a certain frame of mind, the physical body becomes a destination just like a city on a map. A place either hospitable or not, capable of sustaining of life or a wasteland. My wracked flesh was not a home I cared to return to. There was nothing left for me in it.

The voice that might have been my own whispered in my eardrum.

If you go, none of this will have ever happened.

And I thought, *good.*

I bore no scars of who I'd been before, newborn and unmarked by my life before. My body may not remember who I'd been, but my mind was as untouched as my newly virgin flesh. The memories remained. I was who I had always been and it would be some time before I decided if this was a blessing or punishment.

The women, my fellow daughters, were a curving parade of infinite variety as they queued for the ships. Their faces were every woman I'd ever seen, ever spoken to, ever loved. We boarded the swaying gangways of the ships in our shrouds.

And then we weren't daughters at all anymore, but brides. Brides of the frontier. Brides of the ferrymen.

Sailing down the sulfurous river was to drift through our own abbreviated purgatory. Some wailed. Others prayed. One knitted tiny caps and mittens with smuggled yarn and furious speed because she thought her ferryman might take kindly to a wife with such motherly instincts.

I sat on a crowded plank bench next to a girl named Martine who conspiratorially showed me a glimpse of the pomegranates she had bundled in the corner of her shroud for the journey.

My eyes went wide. "How did you bring anything?"

She winked, pressed one of the fruits into my hand. "I bargained, silly. That's all you have to do."

Something in her voice told me that this wasn't the first time Martine's old soul had sailed on this ship.

The skin of the fruit was tough and I had no knife, but held the weight of it in my hand and considered the seedy innards of the thing.

I had not tried to bargain. I carried no treasures wrapped in kerchiefs that smelled of home. If there is something worth bringing, I had reasoned, there is something worth staying for.

Time would prove me wrong.

2: NEW TERRITORY

The river, they said was one of many, all named in a language my tongue couldn't get the knack of. The bodies of stinking water formed a latticework of rivers, intricate as lace, all adding up to separate the living from the dead. A "boundary land" was the proper name for this spartan settlement on the banks of the river, just a ferry ride from the afterlife. A place for the ferrymen to make their homes, earn their keep, and stave off death for as long as they were useful. But no one ever called it the Boundary Land after we set foot on the spongey shore.

Those who lived there called it New Styx.

They crowded around the docks as we disembarked, these ferrymen we'd traded ourselves to. The ladies on the boat were quick to guess at what sort of men would be waiting for us, what exactly they *were*. No one was certain, but rumors wormed their way into all our ears.

Some kind of creature, neither man nor devil, a girl named Kitty had whispered to me from her hammock above mine on the journey. Something neither living nor dead, who had long ago bargained for eternal purgatory rather than facing death themselves, kept alive to pole the dead across the river in perpetuity. A species with no womenfolk. *Unnatural*, Kitty hissed. She seemed to savor the idea.

Unnatural was dying three days ago and not being dead yet, I thought. I didn't say this to Kitty, because I thought I might need a friend in the new territory where death was an honest living and pomegranates never grew.

From the deck of the ship, the ferrymen looked enough like ordinary men that it was perhaps a disappointment to Kitty, but a reassurance to myself. There could be demon enough under any man's face for me to trust too quickly.

The bosun called names and matched brides to their new men. It was a coronation, a cotillion, we debutantes of New Styx listening with sharp ears and anticipation coiled tightly in our shrouded sea legs as we took turns swaying down the rope-bannistered gangway.

As our feet touched land, a shipmate stood waiting to hand us the tokens of our new afterlife. Each woman received the same handkerchief with two coins folded neatly in the envelope of it. Enough to buy passage across the river into true death, should we choose.

So there was still another choice, I thought as I waited my turn to disembark.

Some of the ferrymen lingered and looked at us travel-worn women like cuts of meat they wanted to devour. Others paid hardly any mind at all. Most just gawked. I wondered what they thought we should look like, if they had only seen dead women before. If they liked that better.

For our part, we gawked back. They were not quite men as we knew them, but kin enough. It was long past raising cane over. We'd known where we were going.

The river settlement was a city of men. There was a coarseness to the place, a muddy-streeted carelessness that gave the impression of having been constructed with great haste and temporary intentions. Eventually, surely, they had expected someone to come along and build it properly, craft each hovel and dock with greater care and skill?

But no one had come along except for us. One in a long line of bride ships, delivered sporadically, chosen haphazardly. We were cast onto the shore like dice.

I saw Kitty sent into the arms of a grizzled behemoth wearing the telltale oilskin coat of a ferryman. Not all the men here poled ferries, I discovered, despite the collective name they'd come to be known as. Some fished, others farmed, the restless ones roamed the shores of the waterways and traded with the other settlements as far as their weary legs could carry them.

Martine's man farmed goats. He looked a bit like one too, but she claimed not the mind the stubby horns.

My ferryman? He was what he was, no more and no less. The reason for my being in this shanty town on the edge of death, but not my reason for being anything else. He was kinder than some, quieter than others. He tried to tell me his name when we at the docks that first day, but I never could never quite master the unlikely syllables. People didn't speak their names down here much as it was, where such things needed greater protection than where I'd come from.

The first time I stepped across the threshold of the drafty cottage that the hell breezes drifted through almost sweetly, I was surprised by the gingham curtains hanging in the corner that served as a kitchen. For me, I supposed. He must have traded for them from one of the other settlements downriver. In the days and months that followed, I would watch from between those curtains as he and his brethren spent their waking hours pushing the crude bulk of the ferries back and forth across the river loaded with the fresh dead.

When he came home at night, it was with a fat purse of coins in the pocket of his oilskin coat. On the third night after I arrived, there was a corked bottle with a goldfish in his other pocket. I put it in a bowl on the windowsill between the gingham curtains and the shanty began to feel a bit more like a home.

My ferrymen and I gave each other little enough reason to complain, so we mostly didn't. Reliance breeds a sort of affection, I discovered and it could not be denied that my ferryman and I relied on one another. I was a stranger in his land and he was a lonely soul, it wasn't a difficult match to make. Before long, my hand didn't even flinch when it brushed the base of his tail and I never did ask about the scars where the wings had been.

In turn, he never asked how I'd ended up on the bride ship. I was grateful for this, rarely speaking of it even with Kitty and Martine, who remained my closest companions in this new world of ours until the dry wind scattered us.

3: BRIDEFOLK

The ragged river settlement was thick with men. Everywhere you looked, a pair of deep red eyes met your own. Some challenged you with their looks, most just registered your otherness. The shrouds that we had arrived in quickly proved impractical in the muddy streets and the women had set to cutting them down, stitching them into day dresses and petticoats until we were all marked by our grey homespun creations, a school of pigeons fluttering about the shores of hell.

Martine thought we were doing God's work, but Kitty claimed to know better. Soiled Doves, she called us. Soot-winged sylphs of New Styx. They were both wrong.

Kitty died in her first childbed and Martine's ferryman took her and their goats deeper into the dark frontier after the first dry season in search of new promises. I never saw her again, but I watched when Kitty's ferryman poled her across the river with coins on her eyes.

I missed them both more than I would have thought possible, but loss was traded daily across the river and the ferrymen seemed to have no concept of the feeling. I wept behind my gingham curtains and began to walk the shores as far as I dared by myself. A half-day's walk could take me all the way to the Bone Fields and back before supper.

The loneliness pulled at my chest like a stone. Not many of the surviving brides spoke the language of where I came from and most were occupied with their newly birthed broods of leathery winged boy children. The other brides had begun to bear children sooner than seemed naturally possible, though nature held little sway in New Styx.

A dark haired woman called Abigail had been the first bride from my ship to birth a ferryboy. She had risen early the next morning and tendered her handkerchief of coins to a neighbor and been poled across the river before the sun was up in the smokey red sky. No one ever spoke of it, but I'd seen her through my gingham curtains while I waited for the kettle to boil.

Kettles boiled quickly here.

If my ferryman disliked my walking to the Bone Fields, he never told me so. In the gnarled cartography of the afterlife, the Bone Fields were the long stretch of desolation that lay between the river settlements like New Styx and the far off Deadlands. The Deadlands were where the unrestful lingered, those who had paid their ferrymen and then got shy on the other side. Unfinished business or just remnants of warm-blooded fear, it was hard to say. They weren't whole anymore and sometimes they floated messages coiled in bottles like little serpents that washed up on our shore caked in river mud. I was told that if you read them, they would drive you mad. The Deadlands held no temptation for me, but I found great comfort in the sandy decay of the Bone Fields.

And I wasn't alone on my walks, either. I carried my secret with me. My river child. A ferry creature, still breathing inside me through gills like my goldfish in its bowl in the kitchen sill. My second heartbeat kept me company.

We walked, my creature and I, along the spines of the ruined train tracks that threaded the fields, appearing and disappearing under the dunes. The land here felt more like a dry riverbed than the wet muck of New Styx, and perhaps it once had been one of the veins of waterways that lead to the beating heart of hell. Now it lay dry and dormant, the very ground crackled and broken with tendrils of smoke escaping the sand.

This was not a land that took kindly to industry. This was not a place that cared to change its ways and ill-fortune met those who forged ahead. The remains of a steam engine was half-buried in sand and ash a good several miles from where the tracks ended. How it got there was lost to memory, but the hulking shell of it was now occupied by the Old Wives. I met them there, unwittingly, my river creature swimming in my belly and a petrified pomegranate in my hand.

The Old Wives were what became of us brides, after we'd outworn out welcomes and worn out our ferrymen. I met them by accident, I used to think, but now I realize I was mistaken in that belief.

I met the Old Wives because I was about to become one.

At first, I was affronted. They smelled, these women of age and experience. The sand and bones and petrified wood that surrounded them seemed to have blasted all the color out of them, bleaching their hair to steel and pearl, clouding eyes, and carving faces like the sides of mountain bluffs. The only familiar thing about them were the tattered coats that they wore. The oilskin coats of their dead men had become their widow's weeds as they traveled to the Bone Fields, ruling over the great vast nothing of it because no one else wanted to claim the wretched place.

You could tell how many teeth they had left because their mouths were always open, laughing.

The Old Wives laughed at everything. They laughed at me the first time I stumbled upon them, but I kept visiting anyway. Most of their talk was river-shit, but I learned things from them about my adopted land that no one else had ever spoken of. The young wives back in New Styx only talked of homesickness or bragged of their offspring these days. The Old Wives talked about everything, quickly and loudly, cawing like birds circling their prey and gnawing salamander meat that they plucked from cunning snares.

They cooed over my growing belly and told me about charms and half-truth mother's wisdom from all the places they had once come from, before they came here. They warned me of the Deadlands and taught me how to shuck a cicada. The one called Patient Myrna, with her grey hair plastered to her scalp with something dark brown-red that might have been river mud and might have been blood, spent one afternoon explaining the geography of hell to me as if she were giving me directions to the nearest dress shop.

"Best know how to get where you're going if you get there." She told me, always laughing. "And learn how to pole a ferry, the undertow is stronger than you think it'll be."

Myrna cracked her bulbous knuckles. Her hands looked strong enough to steer a ferry straight back to where we'd all come from.

I asked about her ferryman once, because Patient Myrna knew how to talk more and laugh less than some of the others whose parched minds darted too fast for conversation to take root.

She laughed too, but then she dredged into her memories and told me what she could remember of who she had been.

A woman, like all of us. This was how all of the bridefolk's stories began. Though Myrna thought she'd been short on time, or out of time, when she ended up in New Styx. It had been a long time ago, she wasn't sure anymore.

In her ferryman, she'd been luckier than some, less than others. A good enough husband, but none too gentle.

Patient Myrna shrugged her dusty shoulders and grinned, "But I hadn't been promised a gentleman. Those were what I chose to leave behind, weren't they? Bore five sons, two still breathing. Came to the Bone Fields when my man crossed the river and never came back."

The last time I visited Patient Myrna, I took her my goldfish as a gift. In return, she touched my belly and told me not to be frightened of it when it was born.

"It's always a shock, but you'll love 'em as your own once they de-wing it. Less fuss and sweet when they want to be, just like their fathers."

When I left, I couldn't remember the last time I'd seen a woman so old.

4: THE FERRYMAN

My ferryman died before my child was born. It was a quick thing, unexpected. Death usually is, even when we ought to know better.

They laid him out, his silent brethren, and knocked on my door bearing his oilskin coat and eyes that may have held pity or mercy or sympathy somewhere in the ruddy depths, but I neither looked for it there nor felt they owed me any of those feelings. I wanted nothing from them, but I took the coat because it had been his and because I knew what to do with it next.

Patient Myrna had taught me.

From my watch post at the kitchen window, I saw my ferryman laid out on a boat that wasn't his own, which was moored empty and waiting at its usual post. His eyes were blank like coins, with the silvery glaze of the dead glinting in his familiar face.

The coat was hanging on its hook by the door. My ferryman was ferrying no man, but waiting to be taken across the river as a passenger this time. I never would know how it happened, what had taken him away, but I knew it had left me with an oilskin coat and something not-yet-born in me. These were things that I knew I had, on a frontier I wasn't sure I'd wanted.

This is now decisions are made. Quickly. Without time to weigh and consider. In the breath between life and death, between the shores of the frontier and the afterlife.

I put the coat on, stiff with dried mud and sweat and the scent of my ferryman. It dwarfed me, but I rolled up the sleeves like I'd seen the Old Wives do and belted the waist over the bulk of my stomach and walked to the dock to earn my ferryman's fare back home.

It wouldn't do to use the coins that I kept folded in the kerchief that I'd been handed as my feet first hit the shore, all those months ago. Those were mine, marked for my own passage when I saw fit to take it, and a currency that could not be traded for another's crossing. Those, I kept. They could only belong to me.

The ferry pole was awkward and heavy when I took it up with sure hands, towering over me as I found my footing on the boat. Once the curious physics of floating atop the river balanced themselves in my body, the thing hardly felt like a hardship at all. I poled two lost souls across the river that morning, earning a coin from each and paying my own man's passage into hell with them. I laid the coins over his eyes myself, already sunk in their sockets. The other men rowed him across, ceremonial and solemn, while I watched from the shore while the ferry child tossed and turned inside me.

We were both restless with mourning. I poled seven more souls that night, just to keep moving. There was a comfort in it, adrift in the river and guiding my vessel surely to the most dreaded destination of most mortals. The souls fascinated me, ragtag creatures that they were. They made me forget my own woes and gave me silver for it.

Sometimes the lost souls I ferried were happy for a woman's sympathetic ear and wept and confessed to me. Others tried to grab one last handful of flesh before the afterlife rendered their hands, mouths, and cocks immaterial. I ferried them all and forgot them as soon as they stepped off my barge. Their coins clinked in the pouch around my neck and were the only sound I cared for. The ferrywoman did not care.

I grew large and rich that month, filling the cups and bowls in my kitchen cupboards with coins. Soon the washbasin and cookpots were full too. That was when I started throwing them into the river itself. My business partner, the Styx, whose waters I rowed daily and whose brine-thick air clung tight to my hair.

The slithering creatures who lived in the river must have been flummoxed by the hard metal coins. They liked soft things best, eyelids and tongues and flesh as tender as sweet words.

The Old Wives had warned me of the river, that there was good reason to never drift too long in between shores. That a soul could get lost in the middle of that water, neither here nor there, boundary land nor afterlife. I had learned that the division between one thing and another was infinite and inexpressible. I tried to pay heed and make my journeys from one shore to the other with a quickness that satisfied my desire to be in no place at all, constantly moving between points.

In the end, it wasn't me that the river got. It was my ferrychild. I'd grown careless in the surety that I could protect it as long as it resided within my own flesh, part of me that I could wrap the oilskin coat around and shield from the hot winds and bitter flames that licked the hillside shore. I had not anticipated what would happen when it was born, when it lived and breathed independently.

My ferrychild, my river creature, was born on an empty barge in the middle of the Styx. It caught me unawares, as I have since learned is its nature, but this was the first time we'd met. Halfway between shores, dragging the ferry through the bubbling waters with my pole, the ferrychild came.

There is no stopping such things. I surrendered and wondered with the last coherent thought of my mind what would become of a soul born between these shores, adrift in the waters the Old Wives had warned me about.

It wasn't a child, to begin with. Not a proper babe like I must have once been or even a chubby winged thing like the other brides had birthed. It wasn't either, or it was both, but it changed shape so quickly that I couldn't rightly tell what it was. In one blink it was a child, but just as soon it was a hedgehog or a snake, contorting it's shape and color and sex like a be-witched thing.

Like an enchanted thing. A changeling. My ferrychild.

I decided that it was perfect in that way only mothers can and when it had calmed itself enough to drink the air on its own and settle into a single shape long enough to touch, I picked it up as gingerly as I dared and swaddled it in the pocket of my coat. I could feel the second heartbeat that had thumped in my own body for so long beat from outside of myself and it felt like my heart was ripped in two and bursting with pride all at once.

It was a changeling child sure as Patient Myrna had warned the river could make, shifting from the prettiest infant I'd ever seen to shapes un-natural and bizarre. When it molded itself into a lizard and rode on my shoulder, it warmed my skin like summer. I called it Pocket, for that was where it kept itself most of the time when I ferried souls across its native waters. It was enough of a name until it decided on one for itself. Time would take care of those sorts of details. I never could tell if Pocket was man or beast and decided it didn't matter because I had made it and I loved it fierce enough to die.

The ferrymen of New Styx would never be my brethren as they had for my poor dead man. I knew this as sure as I knew the Old Wives would be waiting for me in the Bone Fields, ready to dust myself with white sand and laugh into the abyss.

But it wasn't time for such things. Not yet. There was work left to be done and I'd never shirked from the tasks dealt to me by fate. I took my changeling child upriver to the edge of the Boundary Lands, where the settlements were few and far between and for a reason. I ferried us there, with our cups and bowls and baskets of silver, and there we lived in a peaceful sort of way, most of the time. Fewer souls found their way this far upriver to be ferried across, but I took what business that came to me. Those who were especially lost were, as odds would have it, particularly good at finding me. The souls with bone-deep weariness and who had worn a lost look in their eyes long before death had brought them to my ferry. They were in-between souls, those who danced on the outskirts of their world and ended up in this one that I now called mine. The ones who had knocked on a door they couldn't see, but had trusted was there. I was on the other side of that door to guide them.

I always ferried them across if they asked me. I took the coins of those who had them and ferried those who didn't freely. I learned that a touch or a look could bring wistful smiles to the faces of the dead, that it didn't harm me any if their tears rolled off my oilskin coat or if I held the stray hand longer than was necessary as I helped them off the ferry onto the shore. A moment of comfort was a small thing for me to give them to carry into the afterlife. The sublime and the harrowing lived side by side on the Styx just as they did in all worlds.

Not often, I would see a spark of something familiar in their eyes as they boarded my ferry. Something that spoke of untold possibilities that could break worlds open like eggs. To those souls, I would lean close and stroke their hair like a mother, whispering to them so quietly that only my changeling could overhear.

If you go, none of this will have ever happened.

✗

HOMECOMING CORPSE
by Andrew Bourelle

Word travels fast in high school, especially when something big happens. So when Jenny Clarke was killed in a car crash, even I heard about it right away. Christopher Jenkins—he and I were always competing in gym class to see who got picked last—called me to spread the gossip.

"The queen of the school is dead," he said. "Can you believe it?"

I hung up on him.

I didn't know what to say. I'd been in love with Jenny Clarke for a long time, but of course she—and the world—didn't know that.

I lay in bed most of the night, dazed in a horrifically strange trance. I wasn't asleep and I wasn't awake; I was in some world in between. When I rose in the morning to go to school, I had convinced myself the whole thing had been a dream. But then, at school, everyone was talking about how it happened.

Coming home from cheerleading practice, she skidded off the road after a surprise early autumn frost, sliding down the embankment at Black River Gorge and slamming sideways into a tree before the slope turned into a cliff that would have dumped her one hundred feet into the canyon below. It would have been lucky the tree stopped her, but her Camaro crumpled, and she was pinned inside, bleeding to death. A dump truck driver saw her headlights shining through the evening fog, glowing like a signal beacon of a lighthouse. But I guess she'd been dead for a while. When they found her, she was as stiff as a frozen chicken breast.

I learned all this before first period, listening in to all the chatter. But then a hush went over the school, and we looked up and saw her, Jenny Clarke, the most popular girl in school, walking down the hall. She was stiff-legged and looked pale—still wearing her cheerleading outfit—but she was alive.

The whole thing had been a hoax.

Or so we thought.

At first, her friends were very excited. They hugged her and told her about the ugly rumor that had been spread. She listened silently, with a strange, empty look in her eyes. People thought it was just trauma. "She's just shell-shocked," they said. But everyone's discomfort grew, and by lunchtime, the whole school knew that she was, in fact, dead.

Jenny was the only one who didn't realize it.

Her friends still invited her to sit with them at lunch. Flies were buzzing around her, and already maggots were starting to fester in her wounds. When someone pointed this out to Denise Franklin, who was sitting next to Jenny, she threw up right on her lunch tray, pizza chunks coming out of her mouth and chocolate milk bubbling out of her nose.

Still, Jenny Clarke had been the most popular girl in school, so everyone tried hard to welcome her back. But it was difficult to speak to her. She only grunted syllables that resembled words. She had the vocabulary of a baby trying to utter her first word, and her voice sounded like she'd been drinking smoothies filled with broken glass. People said that when they actually got close to her, they could see just how awful she looked. Her lips were crusty, her skin turning pale and bluish and her eyes—milky and shrunken—starting to sink into the sockets.

"It's sad," said Troy Hannigan. "Before, whenever she was even close, it was like there was this magic force surrounding her. Her beauty seemed to affect time and space and everything else—turn the world into slow motion just like in a romantic comedy. Now," he added, "she's just nasty, dude."

I had loved Jenny Clarke for two years. Ever since I moved to this new school, from the moment I first met her at the start of our sophomore years. We had been in English class together, and we had been grouped together to discuss Emily Dickinson's poem "I'm Nobody! Who are you?" We talked awkwardly. She said she didn't "get" the poem. I said, "Well, I'm new here, so I really am a Nobody." She laughed, and then she got serious and said, "You know, I have a lot of friends but I don't feel like anyone knows me. Sometimes I think maybe I'm a Nobody too."

And that's when I saw her smile, a sad, honest smile that told me she was putting her guard down for the first time in years.

That was it—I was in love.

But then class ended, and her mask was back up. We never talked again because I really was Nobody and she most certainly was Somebody.

Two years passed, and I waited every day for a moment when we might be alone again, where she might show a glimpse of her true self one more time.

She died before that ever happened.

Like I said, her friends tried to hang out with her at first, but within hours, she was a bigger Nobody than me.

In Biology class, Darren Raymond made a joke about how he was tired of dissecting frogs and thought they should cut open Jenny. Everyone laughed and then Corky Johnson asked the teacher if he had any extra formaldehyde for Jenny because she was starting to stink. Jenny just grunted like a Neanderthal and looked around, confused. She seemed to understand they were laughing at her but didn't get the joke.

From what I understand, the cheerleading coach, Miss Carlene, tried to include Jenny in practice, but her movements were glacially slow and she remembered almost nothing. She had to look at the other girls to know what to do, and she grunted loudly the whole time.

"Good grief," Miss Carlene said to her. "So you had an accident. That is no excuse for not knowing your routines!"

When a veteran cheerleader is cut, you might imagine a scene of great camaraderie, with the other girls hugging her and crying, saying their goodbyes. I heard none of that happened. Jenny's former friends just stood by awkwardly, waiting as Jenny lumbered away, her pom-poms hanging limply at her sides.

I saw or heard stories like these all week long. I had never seen such an ostracizing. It was worse than when Randy Dexter was caught masturbating in the restroom and was tossed out into the hall by two wrestlers. It was worse than when Amanda DeWitt got pregnant with Assistant Football Coach Mark Reynold's baby. It was worse, well, than being the new guy nobody talked to even though you'd been in school for two years.

Jenny's boyfriend, Dirk Mobley, sat next to me in American History so he could copy off my tests. Before class, I asked him if he was still going to take her to the Homecoming dance this weekend.

"Hell no," Dirk said. "I don't mind if a girl's passed out, but I want her to at least be warm."

Dirk was a big football player and an even bigger douchebag. Real life is just like the movie clichés—girls as beautiful as Jenny don't actually go for good guys. But Jenny wasn't living a real life anymore. And I felt my love was stronger than anything Dirk ever felt. Or any strange infatuation that people like Troy Hannigan ever had.

So, on Friday, I waited in the hall after school. As the rest of the guys and girls filed out to their cars or the school buses, I looked for Jenny. When the halls were empty, I thought I missed her. But then I heard a sound coming from the girl's locker room, groaning like a sick person calling for a nurse to come administer morphine.

I opened the door and was hit with the stench of road kill. I found Jenny inside, standing in front of the mirror, practicing her cheers. She was stiff-legged and could barely move her arms above her head: her pom-poms flailed in herky-jerky motions as her legs did nothing more than twitch.

She had once been muscular and curvy, and the uniform, which she had been wearing all week, used to hug her sexy body. Now it sagged against her skeleton, making her bony frame visible underneath the folds. Her face was hollow, her yellowish skin tight against her skull. Chunks of flesh were coming off, revealing purplish, rotting meat underneath. And her hair, once golden and full-bodied, now hung flat against her head, dull like a cheap wig. The hair was coming out in clumps, showing splotchy red patches on her scalp.

"Hi," I said, walking toward her.

She looked at me and underneath all the nothingness that death brought with it, I could see her sadness.

I stood before her, my heart pounding, and I said, "Jenny, would you like to go to the dance with me?"

She grunted, and I took that for a yes.

I took her to the mall and bought her the most expensive dress we could find. I had to bribe the Nordstrom employee to help her put it on because Jenny couldn't do it herself and I was too much of a gentleman to go into changing room with her. The dress was silver and sparkling, with a sash over one shoulder and a bow around her waist.

"I think you look beautiful," I said.

"I think I'm going to be sick," said the employee.

At the dance, people stared when we arrived. They whispered as we walked in. I heard someone say, "Who is that with Jenny Clarke?" I ignored everyone. I had waited a long time for this date.

I offered Jenny a drink, but the punch ran out the rotten holes in her neck and stained her dress. We tried to dance, but the music was fast and Jenny's rigor mortis was too severe for her to move quickly enough. Besides, wherever we went, people scurried away because of the smell. We cleared the dance floor, and then everyone stood on the sidelines, watching.

Her facial expression was hard to read, but I could tell she was humiliated. She had once been the prettiest girl in school. The girl every guy wanted to date; the girl every other girl wanted to be. Now, well, now she was just a corpse in a dress.

I decided that we should leave to save her further embarrassment. As we were walking toward the door, me holding her bony hand, everyone stopped dancing and turned their attentions toward the stage, which was decorated with cardboard-cutout stars and crepe-paper streamers. Mr. Martin, the principal, was preparing to announce the Homecoming King and Queen. I tried to keep walking—I didn't want her to be here when she didn't win—but Jenny stopped, pulling on my hand.

"This year's Homecoming Queen," Mr. Martin began, and then he paused several seconds, either for effect or because he didn't actually want to say the words, "…is Jenny Clarke!"

The room was silent as the spotlight circled the crowd and then found Jenny. I began clapping, a hollow, empty noise in the silence. Then someone else joined in. Then another. And then the whole school was applauding.

Jenny looked at me with her sunken, milky eyes, and I nodded at her to take the stage, my eyes welling with tears.

Even though they had been treating her so badly, her classmates had at least given her this touching tribute in memoriam—crowning her Homecoming Queen, the seat of royalty she had been destined for since beginning high school. I was proud of them. I thought for a moment that perhaps I would be crowned Homecoming King to accompany her. But then Mr. Martin looked at the card he was holding and smiled with genuine excitement.

"Dirk Mobley!" he yelled, and the audience roared with approval.

I realized how naïve I'd been: the voting for King and Queen had concluded before Jenny died.

The spotlight spiraled through the crowd, trying to find Dirk. When it did, he put up his hands in protest and said, "No way, man. I'm not going near that thing." Then the room was silent again, and everyone stared at Jenny, alone on stage with the principal. The plastic crown twinkled on top of her head.

Mr. Martin looked around, unsure what to do. He seemed relieved when I mounted the stairs. I grabbed Jenny's hand and led her onto the dance floor. As if on cue, as if the whole thing had been planned, the DJ started playing Frank Sinatra's "The Way You Look Tonight."

This time, the song was slow enough that Jenny could move to it. I put one hand on her waist. With the other, I held her bony fingers. I couldn't smell her anymore, and I moved close to her, our bodies touching. We swayed back and forth under the swirling polka-dot lighting of a disco ball. The rest of the school stood around us, watching.

Her face was nothing like it used to be—skin so perfect, lips so full, teeth white—and yet I could still see the same girl I had been in love with for years. Only now she looked at me the way I had always wanted her to. Finally, I was the only one for her, just as she'd always been the only one for me.

I leaned in to kiss her.

Then her eyeball came out, sliding down her cheek like an egg yolk followed by a comet's trail of green mucus.

I reached up to catch it and stuff it back in its socket. It wouldn't go in. It was too gooey. Too rotten. Her eye ended up in mush all over my fingers.

"Oops," I said, trying to give her a reassuring grin.

She stared at me with her remaining cyclopean eye and then turned away, staggering for the door as fast as her stiff legs would go. The music stopped, and I realized the rest of the students were laughing. As I followed her through the door, the DJ played that song clip that's always used at sporting events: *"Na na na na, hey hey hey, good-bye!"*

I caught up to Jenny in the parking lot. I tried to hug her, but she shoved me away with surprising strength. If she had tear ducts, she would be crying. If she could talk, she would be cursing. But now she wasn't even moaning, as if she'd given up trying to express herself.

Finally, I put my hand on her shoulder and said, "I know what to do."

The night was foggy, and we drove in silence. I wanted to tell her how much she meant to me, but every time I opened my mouth, I felt like I would cry. If that happened, I didn't think I could go through with it.

I parked on the shoulder, right where her skid marks went off the road, and left the engine running and the headlights on. We clambered down the embankment in the moonlight, which came through the fog in a glow. I saw the scars on the tree she slammed into. But we kept going downhill until we were at the cliff's edge.

The drop was supposed to be about one hundred feet, but in the darkness, I couldn't see the water, just a vast, gaping abyss as deep as eternity. Cold air rose up from below.

Maybe it was the moonlight, or maybe it was my brain playing tricks on me, but Jenny's face seemed eager. Her expression never changed, yet somehow I had gotten good at reading it. I could see her pain in school, her embarrassment at the dance, and now I could see the relief she felt knowing what was to come.

I reached out and wrapped my arms around her, hugging her. She put her arms around me, just bones wrapped in skin. I lifted her up like a groom preparing to carry his bride over the threshold. She weighed nothing, but I felt like I was lifting my whole world.

She craned her neck toward me, and we kissed. A long kiss. I closed my eyes, so I could remember it forever. In that kiss, I tasted death. I was sure that's what it was: a flavor I wouldn't taste again until I was an old man.

I dropped her into the canyon.

I didn't hear her hit the water. It was as if the darkness opened its arms and took her home.

✗

A CHORUS OF SHADOWS
by Sarena Ulibarri

No one had told us that a recruiter from the Face of God would be visiting the temple that day, but somehow we all knew. Some of the more sensitive pupils claimed they had felt the vibrations when the monk stepped out of the Face of God and onto the mountain that surrounded it. I probably made that claim myself, ambitious as I was back then, though I certainly was not adept enough to feel such a thing. Our own energies that day were hectic, waves of anxiety and hope radiating off each pupil like raindrop ripples crashing into each other in a pond.

I walked to the courtyard with Boksen, as I often did, to listen to the morning voice vibrations.

"My water's muddy," he confided miserably. "I won't be picked. Again."

I assured him he still had a chance, though I suspected he was right. Each pupil practiced basic voice vibrations in a soundproof room so we could learn them without affecting the vibrations of the world at large. If the plants and insects in our room withered, or if the fountain ran anything other than clean and fresh, it meant some part of our vibrations was wrong. The visiting monk would inspect the rooms and decide who might be ready to ascend to the Face of God. A single voice could affect a room, but a chorus of voices could affect a world, and they ascended only those with near-perfect aptitude.

Boksen and I knelt in the courtyard and did breathing exercises in the cool morning air while we waited. The rest of the pupils and teachers filled in around us. A few wisps of cloud hung around the Face of God as it overlooked the Holy City with cavernous stone eyes, the Mouth a gaping dark oval. We all sat in silence as the morning voice vibrations flowed out of the Mouth. I closed my eyes, listening to the intricacies of the tones, feeling the ripples of our anxiety quiet and the silent vibrations of the world itself rise to match the monks' harmony.

Once the vibrations ceased, I raised my head. The visiting monk stood at the edge of the courtyard, hands clasped over his belt, head bowed. A light breeze tossed strands of his pure black hair. The sunlight that just now peaked over the mountains made his green robes practically shimmer. The monk lifted his gaze.

"Which pupils have studied at the temple for more than four season cycles?" he asked.

I stood, as did Boksen and half a dozen others. The monk gestured, and we followed, once again raindrops in a pond.

We lined up in front of our soundproof rooms, waiting for the monk to inspect. I looked down the row and smiled encouragingly at Boksen. He shook his head.

When it was my turn, the monk said to me, "I will inspect in silence, and when I nod, you will sing the voice vibration for blooming flowers, twice. Understand?"

I bowed in agreement. He pushed open the door to my room. The fountain burbled pleasantly, and colorful moths nearly the size of hummingbirds flitted between the leaves. I seated myself on the small round cushion in the center. Light slanted through the skylight in a different angle than it did during my usual afternoon sessions.

I watched the monk's face as he inspected my plants and filled a little glass vial with my water. His expression remained impenetrable. After an agonizing moment, he nodded. I turned my gaze to the plants, took a deep breath, and began.

The first time, nothing happened, but the second time, I concentrated on the enunciation of each sound, and halfway through, one of the plants burst, rather suddenly, into yellow blossoms. I finished the vibration and sat in silence while the monk inspected the blooms.

"Try it backwards now."

I concentrated for a moment, reversing the sounds in my mind. We did not practice the vibrations backwards very often. After I felt confident, I sang, and the blooms retreated into buds. The monk opened the door and gestured for me to follow him out. I searched for some sign of approval in his face, but his features stayed neutral.

He lurked around the temple for the rest of the day as we went about our normal routine of gardening, star chart study, and instrument vibrations—the various bells and bowls whose vibrations could only have positive effect, no matter how poorly we played. I supposed he was evaluating these skills as well, but I cared nothing for them. I wanted to be a cantor, seated in the Mouth of God, in tune with the world's vital vibrations. Someday I hoped to be Head Cantor, leading and adjusting as the world required. The visiting monk ate with us and slept on a pallet with the teachers.

"Why are you so worried?" I asked Boksen that night, leaning down to his bunk from mine.

He didn't answer at first. "It will be my third pass," he said finally.

He'd been at the temple longer than I thought, then. The monks visited rarely, and ascended pupils even less often. To be passed over three times meant either a monk must recommend you to the teacher's training, or you must return to the Holy City, or wherever you had come from, to make your own way as a merchant or farmer. Religion was not something that concerned most people on a day-to-day basis, even in the Holy City. It was the job of the monks to keep the world vibrations properly tuned. The skills we learned at the temple translated poorly to secular life.

At the end of the next morning's voice vibrations, the monk stood at the edge of the courtyard again, which meant that at least one of us had been chosen. We waited for his pronouncement.

He lifted his head. "Doane." I jolted upright at the sound of my name. "And Boksen." Boksen scrambled gracelessly to his feet. "Gather your necessities and follow me to the Face of God." Boksen and I looked at each other, his face oscillating between elation and confusion. We stepped around the other pupils, who gave little congratulatory tugs on our robes as we passed by.

The monk waited outside the temple. He bowed to us. "I am Ryt," he said.

I bowed. "Doane."

Boksen offered the same, but as he straightened, he said, "Ryt, I'm honored, but…my water…"

I elbowed him in the arm. Ryt smiled, the first expression of emotion he had offered.

"You will not be a cantor," he said to Boksen. "But the Eyes of God have need of those who know stars and measurements."

Boksen's worry faded into a beaming smile as my own face hardened. "And I?" I asked.

Ryt turned to me. "The Head Cantor will make the final decision," he said, and I asked no more.

We began our climb. Three hours of gradually gaining altitude, weaving in and out of the peaks. At times I swore we were moving farther away from the Face of God, but Ryt seemed confident in his path. Eventually, we emerged onto a thin cliff, the Face of God just across from us, so close that I could see the monks moving around inside the stone cavities of the Eyes. Evening voice vibrations were still a few hours away, so no cantors gathered yet in the Mouth. The wind whistled through a plummeting canyon before us.

Ryt trilled, and another trill answered. Ryt responded with a third trill, and a rope flew out of seemingly nowhere. He caught it and handed it to me.

I clutched the rope and peered down into the canyon. A bird soared far below.

"This is your final inspection," Ryt said from behind me. "If the world does not want you to be one of its caretakers, then it will pull you down into it."

I tugged at the rope to test its steadiness. I was not physically strong; few of us at the temple were, though we did daily stretches to stay limber. The hike had already tired me. A number of pupils surely fell into the canyon and never became monks.

The rope led into a half-circle jut of stone that had been carved to resemble an ear—a feature of the Face of God that could not be seen from the Holy City. I had worked my whole life to get here. I had to see what other secrets waited inside the mountain. I gripped the rope, and swung.

I thumped hard against the rock on the other side of the canyon. Bits of stone flaked off as I struggled to find a foothold, arms burning with effort. The ear was only half my body length away. Hand over hand, I climbed toward it, until I could release one from the rope and grab the smooth ledge. I tumbled in, and the monk who had thrown the rope helped me to my feet before throwing the rope back across to Boksen. I leaned against the wall and closed my eyes. Boksen had been the first pupil to be kind to me when I arrived at the temple, and had been a good friend ever since. If he fell, I didn't want to have that image among my memories of him. I opened my eyes when he tumbled to the floor beside me. Ryt followed with no struggle at all.

"Welcome to the Face of God," he told us.

* * * *

Ryt showed us the alcoves that would be our sleeping quarters, and the great candlelit cavern where we would dine. We climbed a winding stone staircase up to the Eyes of God. I had always looked up at the Face of God and wondered when I would be able to look out at the Holy City through those stone eyes. I imagined I would be able to see all the details of people's lives. Standing there finally, all I could see were rooftops and the farmlands that stretched west of the city.

The Left Eye was full of instruments to measure the health of the world through barometric pressure and temperature trends and other such scientific analysis. The Right Eye was full of telescopes, some pointed up at the sky, others pointed down toward the Holy City.

Ryt asked one of the monks to allow us to look through. There, as though we stood only a block or so away from it, was the temple where Boksen and I had studied, spires glinting in the mid-day light. I could even see people walking along the streets in front of it. This was much closer to what I had imagined.

Then Ryt led us back into the Mouth, and down a narrow ladder that descended through a long, dark tunnel. We emerged onto a brightly lit mesa a few acres wide. A small waterfall trickled down the cliff to our left and then diverted into irrigation between neat rows of vegetables and fruit trees. Past a row of corn, the land dropped sharply off, overlooking a valley.

"Behold," Ryt said. "The Stomach of God."

I laughed.

"Well, you didn't expect us to subsist on light and rain water, did you?" he said.

"The Stomach of God," I repeated, still laughing. "Are there other body parts as well? Will I get to see the gallbladder of God? The left big toe of God? The—" I almost said the scrotum of God, but I stopped myself, noting the lack of humor in Ryt's face. Boksen smiled, at least.

* * * *

During the evening voice vibrations, Ryt, Boksen, and I sat at the back of the Mouth and listened. The volume was overwhelming, the way the cave amplified the already hearty voices. I could feel the vibrations in my blood. Once they ceased, I hurried to wipe the tears from my face before anyone noticed.

The cantors began to disperse, and Ryt waved to the Head Cantor. He was a tall, thin man with straw-colored hair like I had only seen on pilgrims from the far south, and skin so pale it looked almost blue.

"Allow me to introduce our two newest members," Ryt said. "Both from the Holy City. This is Boksen." Boksen stepped forward and bowed. "He will be joining the Right Eye. And this is Doane." I stepped forward and bowed. "I recommend him for your open cantor seat."

I startled a bit at the pronoun, but didn't correct him. I had the body of a girl, but had cut my hair short and worn boy's clothes since I began adolescence. In any case, here it hardly mattered. Several of the other monks had feminine faces or curves concealed under their robes. My teachers at the temple had always said that the world was genderless, and so should be the monks who learned its vibrations.

The straw-haired man bowed back to us. "Welcome. I am Ktun." The name was foreign, and seemed to have an extra syllable that I struggled to replicate as I returned the greeting. "You will meet me in the practice rooms after eating," he said to me, and turned away. Then, looking over a shoulder, "Unless you're too tired from your journey."

I was exhausted, but I drew back my shoulders and declared I would be there.

* * * *

The Face of God had soundproof rooms deep in the mountain, lightless caves where my progression was measured not by the flourishing of plants, but by Ktun striking me across the back with his baton when I erred. My first whole season was spent back in those rooms, and it was the dead cold of second winter by the time I actually took my seat in the Mouth of God. I had come to resent Ktun for his harsh methods, but when he bowed to me after that first official session and told me my vibrations were excellent, I can't deny the thrill I felt. Though I had only just been accepted as a cantor, I was already imagining myself in Ktun's place as Head Cantor.

Now and then I would go up to the Right Eye to visit Boksen. One night I found him there alone, polishing the lenses. After a long silence, he glanced up at me.

"At the temple they always told us that the voice vibrations weren't made of words, just sounds that influence and sustain the vibrations of the world."

"Of course," I said, confused that he would bring up such a fundamental teaching.

"Is that still true? Or have they taught you a secret language to know what they mean now?"

I shook my head. "They don't *mean* anything. Or if they do, no, I haven't been taught any secret language. Why would you think that?"

Boksen held a lens over the candle and then placed it carefully in its case. He wiped his hands on his towel.

"Down in the Holy City," he said, "They always sounded like nothing but vibrations. But here, when I hear all of you down below, sometimes they sound like words to me. Like a language from far away, or a forgotten tongue. Sometimes I can't shake the feeling that you're calling to something."

"It's only because we're so much closer."

He smiled, but his eyes looked incredibly tired. "I know. I'm sure it is."

* * * *

On the first day of second spring, Ktun caught up to me as I left the dining cave.

"Are you satisfied with your position?" he asked.

"Mostly," I answered, and immediately regretted the honesty.

He raised a straw-colored eyebrow. "What else do you desire, Doane?"

I hesitated, but I had already started down the path. I straightened my robes and held my head high. "I want to be Head Cantor," I said. "Someday," I added, a bit late, and bowed.

Ktun nodded. "I'm gathering a select group of cantors to prepare a very old and complex voice vibration," he said. "You will be an important part of that group."

Taken aback, I bowed quickly. "Of course, Ktun."

At Ktun's bidding, seven of us met him in the practice cave. Torches burned along the walls, but nearly everyone's face remained in shadows. The vibration was complex, and left a strange sensation on my tongue.

"A shift is coming," Ktun repeated each time we practiced. "These are the most important vibrations the world will ever hear."

He denied us anything more specific than that. During the day, I would often sit in the Mouth alone and attune myself to the world's vibrations, trying to sense what Ktun knew was coming. What I sensed was only apprehension, and I struggled to tell whether the sensation belonged to me or to the world.

* * * *

"No, no, no," Ktun said while smacking each of us on the head. "It's *naft mglw*." It was a throaty, garbled phrase, and like his own name, the syllables seem to stretch out into extra sounds that were difficult for any of us to articulate. He smacked my head. "Do it again."

I couldn't repress a groan. "We've been over this so many times I know this vibration backwards and forwards."

"Don't be silly," Ktun said. "This is not a vibration we would ever sing backwards. One more time, and remember, *naft mglw*."

The vibration felt different this time around, not the clunky mess it had always been, but smooth and clean like the traditional morning vibrations. We were nearly trance-like with their perfection, and once it ended, we sat silently, listening to the reverberations echoing back to us against the walls. I opened my eyes, and thought I saw something moving in the shadows, but the image disappeared just as quickly as it had arisen.

"Tomorrow," Ktun said, "Tomorrow we change the world."

I slept hardly at all, the vibrations echoing through my head as they had echoed through the practice cavern. Ktun's words bothered me as well. The cantors were meant to maintain the world's vibrations, not change them.

After our usual evening vibrations the next day, the cantors rose and headed to the dining hall, but the seven of us stayed in our seats. Ktun led the ancient vibration, and the sound rolled out of the Mouth of God even more smoothly than our last practice session. Once we finished, Ktun's face froze in ecstatic serenity. Suddenly, he frowned. His face scrunched as though he were about to yell at us again.

Then, a gust of wind burst against our faces, coming from everywhere and nowhere all at once. Vibration guides and seat cushions went flying. Stones shook loose from the ceiling. The air swept out of the Mouth and roared down into the Holy City.

* * * *

After the windstorm passed, Ktun ordered us to go to the dining cave and then to bed, but I could neither eat nor sleep. How could everyone just keep going on as though nothing had happened? Boksen was not in his alcove, so I checked to see if he was in the Right Eye. As I climbed the stairs I worried that perhaps the winds had knocked monks out of the Eyes, that perhaps Boksen had fallen. The thought made me queasy.

But I found him there, sweeping up glass from one of the broken telescopes. Night encroached on the sky, and dots of lamps and hearth fires appeared in the City.

"Did you see anything?" I whispered.

His hand shook as he dumped the glass shards into a bin.

"Tula, will you go find me another bin?" Boksen said.

Tula seemed to register that the floor was clean and the bin only half-full, but went anyway. Boksen sat down and tugged his green robes around his knees.

"I don't know what I saw," he said. He paused so long that I poked him in the arm to continue. "Just before—" He shook his head, lowered his voice. "Just before the windstorm…have you ever seen how a shadow can split when there's more than one light source, like there's two of whatever you're looking at?"

"Boksen, what are you talking about?"

"Just before the wind, it was like that."

"What was?"

"The whole City. Just for a second. Like it split apart, both sides faded and misshapen. Like it was just…reflections of its own shadow."

He was even more shaken than I was.

"Did you see anything else, anything more…concrete?"

Tula came back in with a bin and set it beside the door. Boksen didn't even acknowledge it.

"A lot of roofs and windows in the Holy City were damaged," Boksen said. "Some of the smaller houses, nearly flattened."

"Can I look?" I asked.

Tula answered for him. "Everything is off its targets."

"Then it won't matter if I use one to look around a bit."

Tula gave a "do-what-you-will" gesture. The light was fading, but enough remained for me to see. The Holy City was a mess. People picked through the rubble of their homes. Tree branches had been stripped bare. Shattered glass sparkled the streets.

I swung past a smear of blue and went back to see what I had missed since it was such an unusual color in the Holy City.

I tried to focus the telescope, turning the image fuzzy, then clear again.

Seven figures stood on top of the flat roof of one of the Holy City's tallest buildings. I thought at first that they all wore costumes, but that notion faded once I focused. They were that rare blue color from head to toe, and they looked more like upright lizards than people.

"Boksen," I said, "You should see this."

But before he could join me at the telescope, one of the creatures turned and seemed to looked straight through the lens at me. It startled me enough that I stepped back, bumping the telescope. When I found it again, the rooftop was vacant.

* * * *

The next morning we gathered in the Mouth for our morning vibrations, but Ktun was gone. Ryt occupied the Head Cantor's seat, and when we asked where Ktun had gone, told us only, "He has gone down to the Holy City."

"Should we go down there as well?" I asked. "People must be in need of help."

Ryt scoffed. "Vibrations are in need of alignment, now more than ever. We can do more good up here than we can by hauling trash and mucking out pigpens."

I wanted to ask what mucking pigpens had to do with a windstorm, but refrained. His answer sounded pat. I peered out of the Mouth, but could see nothing other than sky.

Ryt led us through our morning vibrations, and the frazzled energy began to calm. We did two extra sets of the clean air vibration and one for the soothing of human pain, which I had studied but never sung before. I had recently become more adept at feeling the world's silent vibrations, so much that I could at times detect the echoes of a great war long ago and far to the north. Those were all buried now beneath the echoes of the recent windstorm. We could have kept singing all day and not soothed all the suffering I felt from the Holy City.

* * * *

The next morning, Ktun had returned. After our usual set of vibrations, Ktun passed out new vibration guides and announced that the whole group would be singing the secret vibration. My throat grew cold at the thought.

"Ktun," I said, standing to get his attention. "I don't think it's a good idea to do that one again."

Everyone turned at once to look at me. I swallowed a lump of anxiety but stood strong.

"Oh?" Ktun said, the syllable a challenge. "And tell me why exactly a cantor not even one cycle out of the temple thinks he knows what vibrations the world needs?"

"I think," I said, then hesitated. Ktun folded his hands and fixed his gaze on me. Did he think I was merely trying to usurp his position? He knew I dearly wanted to be Head Cantor. "I think the vibration caused the windstorm." I wanted to tell him about the shadow-shifting that Boksen had seen, and the reptilian men on the rooftop, but those things seemed silly in the face of Ktun's withering stare. It occurred to me that the windstorm may have been the very shift he had spoken of, and our vibration kept it from being worse. But I had already spoken my initial fear. "If the vibration didn't cause the wind, then tell us what it is for."

"It affects the vibrational alignment of underground rivers and the purity of the water in those rivers. So, center yourselves, we begin on eight."

Someone beside me tugged at my robe, and I took the hint and sat back down. Ktun tapped the count with his baton.

I did not sing. I listened, and the vibration sounded as perfect as last time. I twisted my robe between my hands, wondering if I would be kicked out. At the temple they told tales of monks expelled from the Face of God for less.

In the silence after the vibration, a rumbling began deep inside the mountain, shimmying its way up to the surface. Wind beat against our faces, tore at our robes. The sky split, like a book snapped open, and then suddenly closed with a bright blue flash. The others cowered or ran. I stood and pushed my way to the edge of the Mouth, bracing myself against the wind. I held onto the stones at the edge.

Then Ktun was beside me, yelling at the sky. His chant had similar sounds to our secret vibration, but he spoke them flat and fast like language. Past the Holy City, the farmlands were on fire. The vibrations of the world felt in total disarray.

"You did this!" I yelled at him.

He glared at me. "A great new era has just begun," he shouted through the noise of the wind. "You can be part of it, or you can be destroyed by it." He turned away, hands to the sky, yelling his incantation again. The sky split a second time, and out of the blue flash emerged an ethereal creature. It seemed somehow both solid and transparent, both near and far away. It did not fly through the air so much as swim, turning with flicks of a great spiked tail, paddling with clawed reptilian feet. I threw myself backwards at the sight of it.

The creature fixed eyes on Ktun and swam straight for him. Wind stung my eyes so I could barely keep them open. Its mouth opened and a dozen arms like multi-hinged lobster claws shot out and lifted Ktun off his feet, pulling him into the sky.

"Integrate me!" he shouted, and the monster appeared to inspect him.

Then, the tentacles retreated and Ktun fell straight down into the Holy City with a surprised scream.

I crawled backwards. One of Ktun's vibration guides tumbled toward me. I caught the book just before it fell, staring at the upside down tones.

"I have an idea," I yelled. A few of the cantors still in the Mouth turned to me. "We sing it backwards."

Something screamed outside, an animal roar laced with child-like shrieks. One by one, the cantors returned to their seats. I took my place at the Head Cantor podium. The baton was nowhere to be seen. Wind threatened to knock me over. This was not how I had pictured my debut as Head Cantor.

We began low, awkward, starting and stopping a few times until we got the hang of the new, modified vibration. It had a completely different tone when sung backwards, far more pleasant.

The creature screamed. "Again!" I yelled.

They sang it again, and the cave flashed with pulsing blue lights. I dared to look behind me.

I could see much more through the Mouth from the Head Cantor's podium than I could from my usual seat. The creature was being sucked back into the sky, through the same split where it had emerged. The vibration ended and the split sealed up with a pop. The wind ceased, silence strange and hollow in my ears. I walked to the edge of the Mouth and looked out.

The farmlands were still on fire, the Holy City was still in rubble, but the creature was gone. The cantors mumbled uncertainly amongst themselves.

"Come see!" I beckoned, but they saw only destruction.

Noisy footsteps clambered down the ladder. Boksen's wide face appeared.

"It's gone!" he announced, and then told the others what the Right Eye had seen.

* * * *

We scoured the Face of God for all the vibration guides containing the damaging vibration, and sent some of our stronger monks rappelling down the canyon to search for any that had been caught in crags or branches. Once they were all gathered, we added more smoke to the sky. In Ktun's quarters, I found a book so faded it was barely legible, alongside Ktun's fresher transcription. It was in a language no one else at the Face admitted to knowing, and the illustrations were of odd blue reptilian people. This book we kept, locked in a vault deep in the mountain, along with the story of the skyquake. What had caused Ktun to stray so far from his role as caretaker, to think he could trample so many in his pursuit for power? We all had theories, but he'd left few clues. Ryt sent Tula and one of the others on a quest to the south, to see if they could find any more clues in Ktun's homeland.

I left too, before sunrise the next morning. Ryt had assured me that I would be granted passage back into the Face of God whenever I decided to return. I'd had a moment in the Head Cantor's seat. Someday, perhaps I would go back and continue working toward a permanent position there. For now, I could not sit up above the world while those below suffered and toiled. If my voice had helped to cause this damage, perhaps my hands could help repair it. Raindrops pelted me on my hike down; the hems of my green robe turned brown from the mud.

From the Holy City, I looked up toward the Face of God. The whole mountain was swallowed in thick fog. The morning vibrations rang out from somewhere behind the clouds. I closed my eyes and felt the vibrations of the world shift to align with the voices. The world was hurt, yes, but it would heal.

✗

GRAVEYARD WINE
by Joshua L. Hood

A point so fine that it would hardly need honed glowed salamander orange and coal forge hot against the slave's skin. Smoldering flesh vaporized like grains of incense. The slave watched the far wall, waiting with blank subjugation.

"No, no, no!" the smith bellowed. "Not the bowels, fool. Use an arm or a leg. Keep it alive!"

The apprentice pulled the glowing iron back.

The slave looked down at the wound with something that would have been curiosity in a better person. The small pock mark left by the curved blade was already beginning to clot. He watched it hurt and vaguely regretted something he didn't care to remember.

"But in my old master's shop we used the belly," the smaller man said.

"Your old master was a bigger fool than you are. Use the limbs first so you get five blades without killing it. Six if you have another one ready, though the skull will flatten the edge, so only if you want to spend more time grinding later."

"But you can just use the body again, can't you?"

"Did your camel dung of a master do that? Do you wonder why his blades broke and his head even now decorates the general's balustrade?"

"Some smiths use just a pile of hides," the little man persisted. "They're doing fine."

"Fine isn't good enough. You're in the palace forge now, you make the best." The big man stooped lower and spoke conspiratorially. "Look, boy, it's the life, not the meat that tempers a strong blade. Don't douse your iron in death. Douse it in life, let it pull vitality into its edge."

"In that case, can't we get more than five blades?"

"No, slaves die too quickly, and if they don't then there's no vitality left in them to give. Just one per limb is the most. Then the gut. Forget what I said about the head. Slaves don't have life in their heads at the best of times."

The slave ignored the smiths and watched his belly wound dry in the heat of the kiln. It wasn't deep or wide. When the scab fell off it'd look like nothing more than a pock mark from the wasting disease or an angry flea bite. It would blend right in, a drop of ink on a canvas detailing a short, hard life.

"In time I'll forget all about it," the slave figured.

"Like this," the smith said, and thrust the glowing blade through the slave's left arm.

The slave's world screamed and went black.

* * * *

Long ago in some Stygian crypt, someone cruel beyond imagining discovered the alchemical properties of flesh upon hot iron. That person is lost to time, but the remedy for weak blades has survived through the black centuries and is rote in every anvil and forge.

Some claim it's the human suffering. Some, like the smith, claim it's the life force. Most just do it and don't ask questions of the darker arts – but everyone knows that the best sword is one quenched in the body of a living beast after being newly beaten.

Once up on a time they used the flesh of worthy foes – generals of renown or princes of great power and wisdom – but as the price of capture in battle grew, these great men knew well enough to die before they ever made it to the forge, so they grew few and hard to acquire. The demands of market and production came to settle for the lives of slaves.

* * * *

As the soft, hot iron entered into this slave's arm a hand span above the elbow, in the meatiest part of the bicep, barely as strong as a child's, it became an adamantine weapon of gods and kings. And then Fate intervened.

Taking the life of the arm into its edge, the tempered sword nicked the link of the binding chain that bound the slave and gouged it. If the smith noticed, he didn't care. He was making a point, after all, and iron chains are not weak things to be worried about. Usually. But the iron of this chain wasn't flesh tempered. It was old, rusty with years of sweat and blood and tears, and it had become brittle. On that fortuitous link, where the sword nicked, it was brittle enough for even a child to break – if his incentive were high enough.

* * * *

"That's enough for the day," the smith said, showing no relish for his job, nor remorse. "Learn what I teach you. Get out that dung your old master put in your head. And don't question me again, you show yourself to be a fool for it."

"Sorry, master," the apprenticed said. "What about the slave?"

"We'll be done with it tomorrow. Leave it be. I smell supper." The smith took a deep breath through his nose and smiled. "You'll quickly learn the benefits of staying in the good graces of the palace." They left the forge in the flickering darkness of the kiln's embers.

* * * *

The slave woke up to raging thirst. For the moment it burned worse than the curdled wound in his dead arm. He nearly swooned again, but blinked it away.

There was a quiet shuffling of other slaves, penned in a row of cages along the deep shadows of the back wall. They watched him and offered whispered condolences. The slave ignored them, searching until he found what he wanted. Then, to the silent irritation of the other prisoners, he heaved himself and the chain noisily to a tall bucket of dirty water used for quenching hot metal. It tasted like new swords and rusty chains. "Metallic," the slave thought peripherally, "even the water here is iron."

It was true. The bars, the windows, the door. This was a place of black steel—more secure than a prison if someone wanted it to be. But despite its cages it wasn't a prison, and so no one did.

Once watered the slave went back to the step on which he was chained, absently fulfilling the unasked requirement of waiting for the morning's work to begin. He thought about nothing and did nothing. The other slaves quickly grew bored of him and their snores began to lumber across the room in a reassuring way.

"Foolish thought." The words came unbidden from his own mind. In his head he glowered at the words like so many masters had glowered at him when he became noticeable or inconvenient in a moment of unprofessional blunder.

"Silence, slave," he told the words in a habitual sort of way.

But they wouldn't be silent. *"Foolish thought. 'In time I'll forget about it,'"* the words mocked. *"Just a flea bite of a wound."*

The slave tried to ignore the words and sleep, but the foul water and dead arm proved to be too uncomfortable to ignore, even for one who'd led a profoundly uncomfortable life.

"Like you'll have time to forget."

"I am a dead man. I was born dead. Leave me be," the slave thought, pressing his eyes harder closed. He was beginning to wonder if it weren't witchcraft speaking in his head, through his own voice.

"Who would waste witchcraft on you? Who would dare?" the voice admonished.

The slave wasn't accustom to being asked questions, or answering, so he thought nothing back to the voice.

"Survive," the voice said plainly, and then was silent. The slave knew the word. He'd heard it echoed in the dimmest recesses of his mind for his entire life. But he didn't understand what it meant. Not really.

But now, when that dimmest recess was most needed, although perhaps least wanted, it came to him louder than ever before. *Survive*, it demanded, and he was repulsed by it. If only it were witchcraft he could explain it away, but he knew that it wasn't. It was a disgusting part of himself that he long refused to believe existed. The part of himself he didn't deserve.

Thirst returned, inevitably. The slave was a man who could die of thirst if it was required, or even seemed required. He ignored it, knowing he'd live long enough for his purpose and not wanting to waste water.

"Drink," the voice said.

He kept ignoring.

"Remember," it said, and to his annoyance he found himself remembering the morning before, when another slave screamed out her last on this very step, when the apprentice had hauled out the tall bucket and refilled it from the well.

"Start fresh and cold," the smith had said. "Replace your water often, the colder the better."

"Well, since they're throwing it out anyway," the slave justified. He drank more, with a loud rasp of the chain across the stone floor. It was even more metallic at the bottom of the bucket, but the sludge was almost appetizing, like the charred remains of burnt food that the kitchen would sometimes send. He tried to imagine charred meat as the sludge solidified quickly in his belly. It was a short fantasy that ended as he vomited onto the floor.

With terror, the first real terror of the day, he looked at the vomit. Then his eyes darted around the shadows looking for something to clean it up with. It was mostly water, but it smelled of bile and the thought of the smith returning to a soiled forge was repulsive to him.

In the corner there was a bucket. It had a flat edge for brushing scale into. With that bucket and what remained of his old rags he could do the job that he was mechanically compelled to do—clean it up. He went towards the bucket, weakly with one arm dangling, but the chain stopped him a hand span away from being able to reach the handle.

He strained, grunted, stuck out a foot to try and hook the bucket, but couldn't reach. The chain was around his waist, and his legs were no better for reaching than his one good arm. A sense of professional failure came over him as he thought of giving up. The idea of the smith being angry didn't bother him, nor of the whipping he'd probably receive from the apprentice in return for having to clean it up. The thought of it being him who they all looked at with realization terrified him. To be noticed, acknowledged, considered as an event worth altering a moment of time for. It was an anathema to him. A dishonor.

So with the strength of a child and the motivation of his life's purpose, he sought to stretch out the chain, or himself, far enough to reach the bucket and clean up the sick that he'd left stagnating behind him. He strained harder, grunted louder, pulled with more fury than his skin and bones should be allowed to have.

"Yes. It feels. It feels good," the voice said.

"It needs done," the slave replied.

"Pull harder. Use the fear. Feel it."

"I am."

"That is life."

"It needs done."

"Survive."

The chain sprung like a over-wound clock. Particulate crumbles fell from the wounded link. A short but splendid rending sound punctuated a loud clatter as the link fell in two and the anchored end of the chain crumpled to the floor.

The snoring stopped. Hushed gasps sounded from the barred darkness.

The slave stumbled, then stopped, turned slowly, froze.

"Survive."

* * * *

The vomit was cleaned, the bucket returned, the rags burned. The broken chain went unacknowledged. The slave avoided its gaze like avoiding the hypnotic terror of a poisonous snake. As long as the job needed done, the floor cleaned, he had a purpose, and he set to it with fervor. But that purpose didn't last, and now the vomit was cleaned.

"Go! Git out!" whispers from the darkness said.

"Take me wich'ya!"

"Don't be a fool!"

"We'll all pay for this!"

"Go!"

He ignored the voices like he ignored the chain. Only one voice registered in his dulled mind, and it was getting louder each time it spoke.

"Survive."

He thought of continuing to clean. Forges are dirty things. He could work until morning and never need to stop and think. The place would be sparkling by the time the smith returned. He'd be impressed, but what did that matter? He may, though, be so impressed that he'd keep the slave around to do more cleaning, maybe even earning a spot here permanently to…survive.

The thought surprised the slave as it was the first time he'd ever thought of doing something for a reward of his own imagining.

"But who'd keep a slave with one arm?" he thought, uncomfortable at asking even a rhetorical question. "They could get any slave. I'd only slow things down, get in the way. They'd just kill me and move on. But the forge house would be clean."

"That's not enough."

"What is?"

"Survive."

"What are you waiting for?" a shadowed voice interrupted.

"Listen to them."

"Geddout!" it whispered again. "Go!"

"The door's locked," whispered another.

"T'isn't. Oy' didn' hear no latch."

"Try it, boy! Go!"

The slave tried it. He didn't know why. By now he was too confused to know his own thoughts, which frankly wasn't new. The door swung open with a screech.

"Take me with you!" a voice said, no longer whispering.

"He can nae. There be no keys fer the locks. Jes' git, lad. Go!"

The slave looked back at the shadows but didn't see any faces in the dark. Fresh air pushed past him into the hot room, and it was wonderful. How had he never noticed fresh air before?

"Run!" his own mind compelled him along with the whispers of the slaves, and he did so because it was a command and he had no other choice than to obey.

* * * *

The stink of coal and the grime of the stacks had placed the forge house a long distance from the main bulk of the palace. A kitchen between the two protected the gentry from its industrial stench by erecting a wall of fresh bread and roasted meat throughout the day. Because of this, visitors to the forge house past dark were rare and the slave's departure went unnoticed. He crossed the grounds, climbed over a short wall, and ran into the darkness. He followed the moon though he barely realized he was doing so. The stub of the chain left around his waist rattled with each step, but the thought of being noticed was far from his mind. He'd never escaped before and didn't know what to fear from it.

Instead, his mind was filled with uneasy freedom – sensuous, vast, terrifying freedom. It was new to him, intimate in a way that he'd never known. Solitude had never sat right with him, being left to his own contrivances, and now he ran towards a lifetime full of it. A short life, sure, but a free one. Only the promise of the moon to follow kept him from turning back, but while it glowed above him, two points of a crescent like an ox's yoke, he had chosen a master and he dutifully followed.

Paving stones became sand under his feet. Torchlight and walls gave way to smooth silver hillsides better visible in his periphery than when he looked straight at them. Paths of scorpions and snakes crossed his own and he idly wondered what it was that they were following.

He didn't stop moving until he had no choice, and when he did he was well lost and mostly dead. Cold desert stretched around him for miles. Cramps and splints wracked his body. Even the cauterized wound on his arm was trying to bleed, but his blood didn't have the water to spare, so it only inflamed, oozed and throbbed.

Breeze had already begun erasing his tracks backwards, and he was thirsty again. He would have given up and died then except that he stopped near a graveyard. In graveyards there was always something to eat, if you knew where to look.

"Survive."

He first saw the geometric forms of rock cairns from the left of his pulsing vision. They disappeared when he looked directly at them, but when he glanced away again he saw the columns of vizier's tomb defy the gentle curves of the dunes. Looking still at the moon, he traversed his way towards it until near enough to look fully onto the graves.

If he'd been a wiser man he'd have known never to approach a grave-yard sideways, nor ever under the horns of a setting moon, nor with your own blood out as tribute to the restless souls of the dead. But he didn't know stories and he didn't know magic.

Jackals and rats had made away with the previous day's offerings, bread, dried fruit, milk, but as far as the common man knew it was the dead who came up in the night to consume them. The common man would never eat funerary goods, but the slave, in this one instance in life, was no common man. He'd spent a short period of his life, never knowing how long, burying corpses in cemeteries like this one until he was sold to someone else for something else that he couldn't quite remember.

What had always struck him as perverse was the way that men buried other men with a fortune of food stuffed in their bellies where their innards used to have been. Then they fed them every night as though they still needed more to eat. As far as he knew, the dead had ever arisen from hunger in any case and it was a wasteful thing to do. But no one had ever asked him.

A fresh mound of dirt bulged over a recent burial. If he was lucky, the gutted belly of the corpse beneath would be stuffed with well preserved food. He began to dig with his good arm. The dirt was mostly sand and came away quickly. The first smell to greet him was more familiar than food, but far less appetizing. He had already vomited once that day and didn't see the purpose in doing it again, so he pushed the scent of rot from his mind and kept digging.

Rough funeral wrappings poked up from the loose dirt, dyed bright purple. The slave would have known purple under better light. He'd seen it from closer than most commoners, on the other side of iron bars, often welding whips, but in the moonlight it looked black. Black was worse, but he wasn't being picky. In this case, though, a plague victim's grave would have been better.

Rarely is a person unhappy to see gold, but when the slave pulled back the rind of grave cloth and saw the swollen belly of the corpse overflowing with it, he sighed and felt like weeping. Rarely is hunger or thirst ever sated by gold either. Tasteless, flavorless, unsatisfying gems twinkled in the moonlight between glimmering disks and chains of unblemished yellow. There was no food for this corpse who apparently would rather travel rich through the afterlife than well fed, eternally starving.

In frustration the slave struck the corpse with a limp palm. The scatter of gold was deafening and a jackal yipped nearby. Even if he wouldn't have been arrested for using it, he would never make it back to town to spend the fortune lying before him. He wailed and struck the gold again.

This time the treasure sprung up at him, as though it were striking back. His first thought was that the organs had been left in the corpse and the gold piled on top of it, but that was too foolish to consider. A man may live in the afterlife without food, but not without well prepared organs. The slave pushed the rest of the gold aside and his hand brushed against something springy and cold. He shoveled out more sand revealing more of the corpse, which turned out not to be a man, but a woman.

If he'd have known stories, or magic, he would have known what it looked like to bury a witch, but he hadn't come across such arcane knowledge when he was digging paupers' graves.

Thrusting his hand into the hollowed cavity of the corpse, he gripped the cold thing from under the ribs and pulled it out with a squelching, suctioning sound. The moonlight revealed it as a sheep's bladder full of liquid, stopped with a gem encrusted cork.

"A wine skin!" the part of his brain that insisted on survival said. *"Drink! Hurry, while you have the life to do so."* At that last part the slave felt suddenly weak, collapsing into the grave, feeling the last of his energy wane.

"Survive!"

"The blood of a witch does indeed become wine after death. It's common knowledge to the learned." A voice that wasn't the one in his head came from above the grave, near the humble cairn of rocks. "Drink it, slave, and live forever." It was a woman's voice.

With a shaky hand, the slave pried loose the jeweled cork and smelled the richest aroma of spiced wine that he'd ever smelled. It was intoxicating, even as fumes. The moon became brighter, almost like the sun, and the sand tumbling around him became soft like down. Like it almost wasn't there anymore.

"No!" instinct screamed.

"Yes," the woman's voice said.

"But wine anoints the body, doesn't get stored in it," he muttered.

"And what do you know of death."

"Much."

"No matter. Drink," she said. "I command it."

He fumbled the wine skin to his lips and drank deeply. Not a drop allowed itself to stray down his cheek, not a dribble touched the sand. He smiled around the spout. Energy, vitality, fervor flooded into his body – even as life flooded out.

When he found the strength to stand again he found himself in a white world, where the moon shone bright as day and the real things around him shimmered like ghosts. Before him stood a hungry woman, emaciated with drool running down her chin.

The slave said nothing.

"You'll do," the woman said and fell upon him biting and chewing away at his thin flesh. There was no pain, no death, and when she fell back, sated and fully rounded as though she'd never skipped a meal, the slave found that he was quickly becoming whole again. Only his dead arm was untouched, having passed to this plane hours ago and not bearing with it the life that could feed the dead.

The woman pointed to a pile of gold and jewels wrapped in purple cloth and instructed the slave to carry them. With his left arm he did so and the witch nodded. "Food, riches and a serving man. Fate saw to it that I have died well," she mused and turned towards the hills. The slave fell in behind her, mind curiously silent as the part of himself that demanded he survive, keep on living, fight for freedom, slowly ebbed to silence in a world where survival was a long lost dream.

And then the slave felt something he couldn't understand. It wasn't happiness, but close. His purpose had returned, and there was no pesky, selfish longing to challenge it. He smiled as he followed the witch into strange lands.

✗

MY LAST SIXTEEN HOURS
by Angela L. Lindseth

8:00 AM

It's never all the way dark in here. Like they's worried bout what we'll do without the light. Like it could be any worse than what we done out there.

Think every one of us murdered somebody. I only done the one, but I did her up right. Did her up so good they couldn't identify her body for weeks. Now they got all that new-fangled computer technology and such. Prolly coulda pulled me off the street by the look in my eye, for all I know. Been in here so long don't rightly know what year it is, let alone what they been inventing.

All I know is they caught me, and I confessed. I knew I done wrong. Can't tell ya why I even done it. Something inside me just made me do it. Like there was somebody else taking hold my hand, guiding that knife. I heard her screams, but they was like in a different room of my brain. Does that make sense? Prolly not.

Round here, down on the row, we call 'em hanging days. Course they quit hanging folks years back. Too cruel and unusual they says, but I reckon whatever brung us here in the first place, well, let's just say we deserve cruel and unusual. Maybe me more than any of them for what I done to that little girl. Don't know why they waited around this long to finish me off.

9:00 AM

I start my day out slow. They give me a brush and some paste. Every day I make sure I get my teeth pearly white. Want 'em to last, ya know. I go bout my routine: making my bed, doing my exercises, rinsing out my extra pair of underwear. I like me a clean pair every day. Just cause I'm in here don't mean I can't be clean.

They give me my breakfast bright and early, but I don't wolf it down like I used to. I cut it up in tiny pieces. Make myself wait. Then give myself a little reward throughout the day. Pretty sorry excuse for entertainment, I know, but any distraction is better than nothing.

I run my hand through my hair, or what's left of it, trying to tame the mess in the back. When you is young you got hair, you got your looks, you on top of the world, but life sneaks up and steals a strand here and there and adds wrinkles when you ain't looking. Pretty soon the person who stares back at ya from the mirror is a stranger. Things you done in your past just memories that twinkle at you like stars in the sky, too far away to mean much, but you still hold 'em dear.

Not that I got a mirror, Lordy no, they don't give out no sharp objects down here on the row. The shiny sheet of metal bolted to the cell wall does good enough for me, in fact the blurry face staring back is pretty much what I member bout my time. Days blurred to weeks blurred to months. You get the picture. I look back, and I don't member nothing since I been here. I swear it. Yesterday same as day afore and same as day afore that. Time lost all meaning years back.

I got too much time, or at least I did up till today. Used to count out the seconds, mark 'em down in my mind adding up the minutes, and piling 'em up to make hours. Never made it through a whole day, though. Me and math never did get along too well. Now I couldn't give even give ya a number as to how many years I been here. Don't want to know, Lord no. Those kinda facts might make a man crazy.

10:00 AM

My lawyer feller shows up just like always, all sad and feeling bad for me.

"I've put in a final call to the Governor for a Stay of Execution."

"Now why you go and do that for? Ain't I been in here long enough? Ain't you getting tired of fighting for me? I know I'm tired. Tired of counting out them bricks, tired of reading the same ole books, tired of that shit they call food. Why can't ya just forget about me like everyone else done?"

"Junior, I can't. There are reasons why you shouldn't be executed."

"You saying I ain't right in the head, but I know what I done. I'd like to think I'm ready to go. Like to think that there's some kinda higher power who'll show some mercy, but that don't seem likely. I don't deserve no mercy."

"Don't you want to live?"

"I ain't lived a day since I been on this row. You think I got problems with my head? Well, damn straight I do! This row got all sorts of brain problems. The ones of us that been able to escape into our minds are the lucky ones, let me tell you. We all been dead the moment they locked us up."

"I have to represent you, Junior. I have to do what's in your best interest."

"Best interest be damned. Now, don't get me wrong, I appreciate all you done, but it's time for you to get. Find yourself some other fool who got a chance, cause I done used up all my chances."

His heavy sighs just piss me off, like I'm a disappointment to him, like I'm his failure. Well boy, I done failed long afor this whipper-snapper ever got a law degree.

"I'm sorry, Junior. I did what I could."

"Don't you go blaming yourself, now. I got no complaints about you. I'm fine. Fine as rain."

"There's a few things you need to sign before you…before I go. This paper explains that your… You will be…your final resting place will be in the state cemetery outside the prison gates."

"Don't get all choke up, boy, I know I'm gonna die tonight. No need to sugar-coat it."

He clears his throat and takes a glance around the eight by ten room. "This form identifies who gets your possessions."

I cackle to high heaven. "Lordy Lord, there ain't nobody that wants a worn out copy of Old Yeller and my newspaper clippings. Burn all of it with me. Write that down on yer paper. Burn it all."

"All right then." He sticks out a hand, and I shake it. "I'll be in the witness room. I've contacted your family few weeks back, but I didn't hear from them. I'll be there for you though, Junior. Is there anything else I can do for you?"

"Think you done all you could, sir. Good luck with yer career and all."

11:00 AM

"Daddy, is that you? Can't hardly recognize you."

"It's been long time, boy. You was just a skinny thing last time we seen each other. What you go and do? Why they put you in here?"

"Kilt a little girl. Did more than that to her." I'd run over the picture show of the murder in my mind a thousand times. Hell, a million times. "She was my first, you know? Pretty sure I was her first, too, being as young as she was, and the way she fought me."

"Now why would you go and do something like that for? You go to hell for that."

"Learned it from you, daddy."

"I got no idea what you talking about."

"Everybody in town knew it was you, but ya got ole Leroy down at the bar to vouch for ya, but I seen ya. Seen ya haul that girl by the hair behind the bleachers. Emily Sue Cartright was her name. Yep, I member it good even if I was just a kid. She weren't much older than me at the time."

Daddy leaned back against the cell wall. "Ain't nobody prove nothing."

"Nope. I guess you was the smart one, not like me going and getting myself caught and all. Don't make it any less true though. And I seen the way you treated Momma. You was always making her cry, cry like the devil was in her. She always toll us she hit her head or fell or some such nonsense. Us kids, we didn't want to think you was knocking her around, but we weren't stupid. How come you so evil, daddy? How come you made me evil? It just ain't fair."

"Shut your trap, you rotten little liar. You never had a lick a sense. You ain't too old for me to teach you a lesson." He starts to unbuckle his belt.

"You kin keep yer belt on, daddy. Ain't nobody listen to a thing I got to say. Anyhow, it too late for Emily Sue. Too late for that little girl I did. Just want to know why I got that bit of ya in me. I know there's good too, but that bad speck took over. Me and her never stood a chance."

"Stop yer whining, boy. What I always say? You ain't worth the shit stain on my drawers. Don't surprise me none you ended up here."

NOON

The door to my cell opened and ole Gus came in carrying my lunch. This was a treat. Usually he just slid it through the slot at the door.

He ignored my daddy who took his chance to escape without so much as a goodbye. Good riddance, I guess. Don't know why he bothered to show his face now. Maybe just to rub in the fact that's he's free, and I ain't. That would be just like him.

"I brought you a cupcake. My Polly made some last night, and I thought you might like one." Gus held up a glorious dessert covered in a thick layer of chocolate frosting. "Hope you like white cake. I had her put chocolate on top just in case you don't."

"Why that's awful nice of you folks." I took it with both hands careful not to drop it on the filthy floor. "You tell Miss Polly thank you. She just wasting a sweet on me, ya know."

"You been a good man all the time I've known you, Junior. Never caused a fuss, not one time. Wished it could have turned out different for you."

"Getting what's coming to me, that's all. Just wish it hadn't taken so damn long."

"Well, enjoy. Have you figured out what you want for supper yet? Anything you want, you know."

"I been itching for some fried chicken and biscuits and gravy. You think you could russle some of that up?"

"Sure thing, Junior, sure thing."

1:00 PM

"Sissy! Man oh man, is it good to see you! Been a long while now hasn't it?"

"Sorry, I ain't been to see ya, baby brother, you know how it is."

"Well you're here now, that's what counts. Sit down for a spell. Don't have nothing to offer ya cept a drink of water."

"Don't worry bout it none. Just came to see ya off."

"Well I sure have missed ya. Seem like it been years since I had company. They ain't never let anyone come into my cell afore. How ya been? How the kids? Reckon they all growed up by now."

"Kids are good. Little Jack done broke his leg last summer, but he healed up all right."

"Sissy, you ain't changed a bit. After all these years, you don't look a day older. Taking care of yourself, I reckon."

"Living the good life. High on the hog and all."

I didn't know what else to say. We sat there looking at each other, but it wasn't uncomfortable like. Fact it was kinda nice. Kinda like when we used to share the tire swing when we was just kids. It was a great big tire and our skinny butts fit in there fine. Kinda snug, but kinda comfy, too.

"Member that big ole tire swing, Sissy?"

Her face brightened. "I do. We used to have us a fine time."

"You ever go back there? It still there? I betcha them young'uns of yours would like it just fine."

"Don't rightly know. You know momma sold off the place after daddy run off."

"That's right." I tap my skull. "Sometimes things get a bit mixed up in the ole noggin."

Daddy never was good for much more than drinking, cussing, and smacking us around went he got a belly full. Loved his whiskey a lot more than he ever loved us."

"Ya know, he came to see me today. Sat right when you sitting now."

Sissy's lip curled like she done smelt month old milk. "He was here? Right here? He got a lot a nerve showing up like nothing happened, like he never left us high and dry."

"Better him leaving than staying."

"Well, you got that right."

"Glad you're here. Gives me a chance to thank you for all you did fer me."

"I ain't done nothing."

"Ya say that, but ya know ya did. More an once you took the heat fer me, and Daddy let ya have it."

"Had to, Junior." Sissy's face turned red trying to hold back the tears.

"You was so scrawny. He woulda broke ya in two."

"And mommy never was right after daddy run off. Like he punched the life right outta her. I wished I'd knocked his lights out. I mean, what I got to lose?"

2:00 PM

Sissy left me quicker than sand through a sieve. Don't recall Ole Gus coming for her. Guess maybe I fell asleep. I do that.

Sleep is my best friend. Ain't always easy cause of the sobbing down along the row. Some of these sad-sacks still got hope. I done give up on hope long ways back. Hope ain't nothing but a gut ache. Nothing but a thousand knives in yer heart twisting and poking and reminding you that you ain't nothing nobody wants. Ain't nothing but a speck a shit on the shoe of society.

Sure, they lawyer you up, schedule appeals, put you on the docket, but none of it means a damn. Hope is what kills ya in here. Hope is what takes yer mind and plays tricks on ya.

Naw. None of that shit fer me. I done put my hope away. Hid it so deep under my skin I would have to cut it out with a blade.

Thinking, now that's something ya can't shut off. You'd think a person would run out of shit to think about, especially since nothing new ever happens in here.

I think a lot bout Billy Thompson. Me and him used to run together. He was a mean some-bitch, tell you what. Cats was his favorite target. Folks on our street knew it was Billy when their tom disappeared, but not many had the courage to confront him, Lord no. Billy had himself a reputation, that's for sure. Suppose I did too, since I run with him.

Anyway, he was real inventive when it came to cats. Lots of times kerosene played a part. Lordy those thing would scream! I member ole Billy rolling on the ground laughing and wiping tears. They would tear around the parking lot bumping into cars all the while screaming like the devil. Looking back, seems fortunate we never set nothing else on fire in the process. Or got caught as much racket we made.

Here's a fact for ya, I got a thrill outta what me and Billy done to them animals. I knows it was cruel, but I had a lot of cruel living inside me. He unlocked a part of me that the Lord knows didn't need to be unlocked.

But he didn't give me the idea to do that little girl. Daddy did. Or maybe it been hiding inside me since I was born just waiting for the opportunity. Little girls ain't suppose to be walking round all by themselves at night. Where was that girl's momma?

Sounds like I'm making excuses, and I guess I am. I used to blame her folks. If they had just been taking care of her better then I couldn't have done it. But I don't feel that way no more. It's my fault, that broken part of me that can't be fixed.

3:00 PM

My only possession I give a lick about is my newspaper clippings. Gus been kind enough to share his paper with me on the days he's here. I point out the articles I want and he cuts 'em out and lets me keep 'em. Sometimes he finds a good one and brings it in fer me. He a good man, that Gus.

They's all from the local Scottsdale Tribune which ain't too far from where I grew up. You think me being this close to home I woulda had a visitor or two. I mean, I did at first, but they tapered off quick enough. Till today, I can't remember the last person who come to see me.

I won't lie. I'm glad they quit coming. I don't want a reminder that there's an outside world. Them first years you think about what other folks might be doing, like going to the picture show or having a picnic, but no good come of it, Lord no. That's when the crying starts, and once it starts it real hard to close up the dam.

I'll let ya in on a little secret. I got me a son. Only met him once, and he don't know I be his daddy, but I know and all 'em clippings are about him.

His name is Jacob, and he turned out fine despite having some of me in him. Fact he sort of a big shot, sharp as a tack, captain of the football team and the basketball team. Well at least he was. I'm sure he out of high school, maybe even went to college. Imagine that? A son of mine going to college? I never finished high school myself. Had to get me a job, then that little girl come walking along.

His success just proves to me that I ain't all bad, that there's a part of me that's worth dog spit.

4:00 PM

"Momma, toll ya not to come." She never was one to listen. Hard-headed she is. Always was, prolly always will be.

"Hate having ya see me like this. You pretty as a picture. Daddy said you was a looker, and he was right."

Momma blushed. "Now I wasn't gonna let you leave this world without seeing ya one last time." Tears filled her eyes. "My baby boy and all. Stand back and let me look at ya." She clicked her tongue. "What they feeding you, boy? You look like the scarecrow down on Mr. Jetter's farm."

"Momma?" Tears I've been holding back for years finally break loose. "I'm afraid. I don't wanna die. He gonna send me to Hell for what I done. Sweet Jesus, I'm going to hell. Don't matter how sorry I am. I deserve to burn."

"Now honey, God's got a forgiving heart."

"I ain't asking for forgiveness."

My momma looked at me like I was from Mars. "Well, they's still time, boy, they's still time."

"I just can't. You believe in hell, momma?"

"I do, but baby, I think you been in hell the whole time you been here."

"You ain't wrong, but I'm sure they're levels of hell carved out special for some of us."

"Them be the levels for those who don't repent, Junior."

Momma brings out a Bible from her purse. Shoulda known. She never went far without one. Growing up, we never knew when the power of the Lord would strike her. I always wondered where the Lord was when daddy was giving her a beating. She pulls me in her arms, but I can't say I feel it much. She feels like a cloud around me. Then she's gone like she never been there. I rock myself back and forth making believe she still with me.

6:00 PM

Had the nicest dream. Well, any dream is nice. Anything that takes ya away from these walls. I dreamed about Brenda Jenkins from seventh grade. Boy howdy, did I have a crush on that gal. She had the nicest lips and smelled like fresh air and sunshine. I used to sit behind her in civics class and lean in to smell her hair if I thought I could get away with it. I would leave my hand at the front my desk just hoping her hair would touch it.

She was always nice to me even though our family was one of 'em that people warn ya bout, wrong side of the track and all.

One time on Valentine's Day I got a card. All the other kids got cards, but usually not me. I know it was her give it to me even if it wasn't signed. She was that kind of girl. I didn't have the nerve to ask her. I just liked thinking it was her.

I never was sweet on anyone else, not even Sherry. Sherry let me have her. That's why I did that. Billy told me a girl couldn't get pregnant the first time, and Sherry toll me it was her first time. I didn't care. Just wanted to get my pecker wet.

But Brenda weren't nothing like Sherry. Brenda was like butterflies. Sherry was one of them crows on the fence cawing at ya. Girl couldn't keep her trap shut even when I was going after it.

7:00 PM

"Hey Junior, you doing all right?"

Chuck was locked up in the cell across the way from me. He in here for murdering all four of his kids. Said God told him to do it. Anyway, me and Chuck spent hours talking quiet. They don't like us talking at all saying it's part of the punishment, but when Gus is on duty we can get away with it. Me and him been here the longest. Got pretty close over the years.

I sit down on the floor next to the door and peek out the food tray slot. "I'm doing all right, I spect. Doing the same as yesterday and day before. Glad we're finally getting to it, if you know what I mean."

He did. If anyone did, Chuck did. We talk about ways to take our own lives like we was decided what kinda ice cream to eat. We both agreed doing it quick-like is the best. I picked a gun. Figure can't be much pain if yer brains scattered to high heaven.

Didn't matter much. If I had figured out a way to end it, I woulda done it years ago. There was a time I felt *real* bad, like *real* bad. Bashed my head against the wall a time or two, but all that did was get me a trip to the psych ward and I tell you what, that made me appreciate my eight by ten.

Not to mention the treatments. Guess I got a preview of tonight's activities. I don't mind being dead, kinda looking forward to it, but the getting there got me worried some. They say you soil yourself, and I pride myself for having clean drawers, like I said afore. They say you can ask for a diaper. A diaper, believe that? Not sure what would be more embarrassing, wearing a diaper or shitting my pants.

Ain't that a weird worry, now? I worry bout that more than heaven or hell.

"Hey Chuck, I just had me an idea. I'd like to give you my newspaper clippings, I mean if you want 'em. You don't have to take 'em. He ain't yer kid, but you've known about him about as long as me."

"Chuck, you there?" I hear Chuck blowing his nose.

"Yeah, I'm here. I'd be honored, Junior. I'll keep track of Jacob for you, for as long as I can, if you know what I mean."

"I do. That's be fine, just fine. I like thinking that, you watching over him for me. You a good man, Chuck. I know ya is. You and me, we just got a bad shake on life."

"That we did, Junior, that we did."

8:00 PM

"Awful nice they let momma and Sissy come visit. Coulda done without seeing my pa though."

Reverend Frank lifts an eyebrow. "You had visitors today, Junior?"

"Well, yeah. I reckon cause it's my hanging day and all. Sure was nice to see 'em one last time. Funny how they looked the same as they did afor they sent me away. Momma pretty a picture. Wore her Sunday best, I can tell. She always wore a flower in her hair for special days. Daisies was her favorite. Sure miss the color. Ever think bout that Gus? There just ain't no color round here. Everything grey. Even the food." I laugh. Always been the funny sort, yep that's me, even in the thick of it.

"It's me, Junior, Reverend Frank."

I jerk my head up and give him a good stare. "Well sure, I know that."

"Is there anything you'd like to confess, my son?"

I slap my leg. "Well now, ain't that the ten million dollar question. I think I done confessed all there is to confess. Nobody wanted to hear it. You won't be saying no last rights fer me neither, you hear me Father? I don't think I'm much of a believer anymore, and I sure as hell ain't been no follower."

"The Lord is full of mercy, you can ask for his forgiveness, and it will be granted."

"See that's the thing, I can't ask fer no forgiveness. Don't get me wrong, I'm sorry for what I done. Sorry don't even cover it, but I ain't asking. Now if He sees fit to have mercy on me, well fine and dandy. He know I done my time, took my punishment and now I'm gonna die for it. I ain't one to beg, never have been, and I ain't starting now."

"That's not how it works, Junior. You must take Jesus into your heart. His glory will make you weep. I guarantee it."

"I guess bottom line is I don't think God gives a rat's ass about little ole me. I've had a lot a time to think, and I done my fair share of praying, but not one thing come of it. I loved the Lord as good as any southern man, but he done turned his back on me. Left me to rot in here. I come in here a young man, but I ain't young no more."

"God would never turn his back on you. He loves us."

I give a whistle. "That's a mighty strong statement. One I don't believe for one minute. I gave up on believing long time ago, tell the truth. And I ain't going to beg for his love just in case it is true. I done what I done, and if there be a hell, then that's where I'm headed."

Reverend Frank hung his head. Made me mad. One more person I went and disappointed. I knows I failed. Failed everybody I ever met, but he don't need to act like that. Ain't his place to judge, ain't that right?

"Let me ask you this, Reverend. Now I spent me some time out on the main floor before they put me on the row. Some of those men lot harder in the heart than me. Done a lot of damage out in the world they didn't get caught for, but that don't mean they don't brag about it. Fact is they do. They like sharing every detail.

"Now these same men got tattoos, ya see? Tattoos of the crucifix, tattoos of the Lady Mary, tattoos saying 'Jesus loves me.' And they all go to the chapel and pray like the devil was in 'em, figuring that would get them up to Heaven. Well now I *know* there ain't a speck of sorrow in their heart for what they done. I *know* that if they was to get out they would do it again. Tell me Reverend, them men going to heaven? Even if they got no remorse?"

"I can't say what is in the mind of God, but I know he has bountiful love, even for those who don't seem to deserve it. Maybe he loves them the most, because they need him the most. It's not my place to judge."

"Well, I'm a judging. Don't seem like fairness to me. Them fellers, they ain't good. Not a speck of good in 'em. That's why I say, let the chips fall where they may. If he's a loving God like you say, then he should find a way to open his heart to me without me going to him. I tried that, I tell you. He don't listen."

"He listens, my son." The reverend stands and makes the sign over me. "Would you pray with me?"

"Tell ya I'm done with that. You do what you gotta do and get. I hope death takes ya to Him, I really do. I'll give ya a wave from down there."

9:00 PM

Here we go. They move me to a little room outside the execution room. I see the chair as I shuffle by. I hear the wood they made it with came straight from the ole gallows, back when they had real hanging days. I wonder just how many ghosts live in that wood. How many poor souls let loose their bowels after praying and begging forgiveness?

Gus lathers up my head and takes a straight razor to what's left of my hair, then does the same down by my shin.

"What you doing that for?"

Gus won't look at me. "It's where they tape the wire. So they get a good connection." He pats my knee. "It's best to have a good connection."

It's nice to feel a human's touch, even if it was a man. Lordy the years were long.

There's a knock at the door, and Gus fetches a heaping plate of fried chicken and biscuits and gravy. My, oh my it smells good.

"Wish I was still on the row so I could share with the boys. Think you could give them some, Gus? Way too much for me here."

"You know I can't do that, Junior."

"Could you eat with me? Sure would like that."

Gus looks at the door prolly wishing he had a polite way to escape, but he pulls up a chair across from me. "Hate to see it go to waste."

Can't believe how much I ate. Figured with one foot at the gates of Hell, I might not have an appetite, but I wolfed that chicken down. Prolly ate six of them biscuits. Lord, that was some good food. I'm gonna make a mess of that chair when the time comes.

"Now if only we had a nice cigarette for dessert. It's the little things like that I missed most over the years. You smoke, Gus?"

"Used to. They say it's not good for your health. The wife made me quit."

I chuckle. "Wouldn't want to do anything that might jeopardize my health."

Gus gives me a weird look, and we break out laughing. Now that's a good feeling. Not much to laugh about, but we make the best of it.

10:00 PM

Dear Lord, why they just get down to it? Ain't never been so scared in my life. Oh Jesus, oh Jesus. I ain't praying, mind you. Not even at this late date. I'm fearful for the pain. Never been much for pain. Inflicted it was another matter.

I was always a pussy when it come to Daddy. I felt his pain a time or two. I would start to blubber, screaming out "I'm sorry, I'm sorry!" even though I ain't done nothing. Maybe that's why Sissy always had to step up. She used to take his whippings in silence cause she knew crying would just egg him on.

Kinda like 'em cats. The more they screamed the louder Billy would laugh. Fuel on the fire, so to speak.

I walk a mile around the little table still littered with chicken and biscuits. All the food I ate bunches up in my gut and afore I know it, it's coming up. Got most of it in the toilet. Bet that toilet seen more than its fair share of puke.

11:00 PM

They're coming for me. I hear the rattle of the keys as ole Gus opens the door. Everybody awake. I know they is. Ain't nobody sleep on a hanging day.

"Time to go, Junior."

"Yes sir, I'm ready." I say that, but I can't get my legs to work. There's a tightness in my throat like a constrictor got ahold a me and was squeezing. Gus grabs my elbow and helps me to my feet. He's a good fella, for a black man.

"You think you can make it from here?"

I stand up tall. Maybe for once in my life I can be brave. "I'll try."

It's only a dozen steps, but it seems like it takes a lifetime. Or maybe no time at all. They sit me in that chair with wire and straps hanging all over it. Gus steps back and finally looks me in the eye. I just barely make out a nod. He was saying his goodbye.

They strap down my arms, my legs, and run a couple round my middle.

I hear the electricity makes a man dance something fierce.

They wrap something around my leg that's connected to a thick wire snaking over to a big ole switch on the wall. They put this leather contraption on my chin and around my head. Look like the muzzle ole man Hinckey kept on his fighting dogs.

Lastly they take a sponge soaking in some water and put it on my head, fit me with this helmet-like thing that has more wires running out of it. They strap it down tight. Water runs down my face into my mouth. Tastes like a river of tears.

Sitting on the other side of the room is a half dozen folks. The only one I recognize is my lawyer. There's a man and woman I reckon is the little girl's folks. There ain't two tears between 'em all. Can't sees I blame 'em. I been gone too long for anyone to mourn me. None of my family is attending. I guess one visit in all these years was plenty.

I reckon it's a good thing. From what I hear bout the procedure, it ain't no picture show. Nothing you want to watch over and over again. The lucky ones die first try, but I hear some take a couple jolts to finish the job.

The clock on the wall gives me nine more minutes.

Jesus, why can't they just throw the switch?

MIDNIGHT

The phone sitting on the table don't ring. Like there was a chance in hell the governor gave a shit about a piss-ant like me. There's a clank, clank, clank from down on the row. The boys' way of saying goodbye. I'm a'shaking, I can't lie. I don't wanna die. Jesus take me. Oh Jesus. My heart keeps time with the tribute on the row.

One of the guards puts a black mask over my head. I'm glad it ain't Gus. Oh Jesus, oh Jesus, oh Jesus.

The first bolt rips through me. Holy mother of God.

"Ladies and gentlemen, this concludes the legal execution of Butch Walker, Jr. Time of death, 12:24am. Please exit the room."

WIDE WIDE SEA
by Jackson Kuhl

Martine's suicide is the third in five weeks. It surprises Dupont because they were approaching a city. The most dangerous time wasn't arrival—it was departure, when despair and loneliness settled on the crew like chains. The week before docking was a period of anticipation, of cautious excitement that this one might be different.

"There's another thing, captain," Georges tells him. He is first lieutenant. "The man who found him saw something."

"Yes?"

Georges hesitates. "It might be better if he told you himself."

Dupont relinquishes the bridge to a junior officer and the pair move aft, ducking under bulkheads and shimmying down ladders, the sailors pressing themselves flat against the walls as their commanders squeeze by.

The milling crowd jerks to attention. Martine hanged himself in all places from a pipe in a utility locker no bigger than a cupboard. This was the suicide's dilemma, Dupont supposed: with privacy nonexistent on the submersible, locating a spot where one could do it without interference was an insurmountable Matterhorn. And yet somehow twenty-six aboard *Telesto* had scaled the peak.

A sailor holds open the panel door, his face shaggy from avoidance of the ship's barber. Dupont has had all knives and straight razors confiscated. As a result appointments at the salon are difficult but Dupont has told his officers to ease the discipline over shaving. Anything, any small thing, to inject an ampule of morphine into morale.

"I don't need to," Dupont says, looking away from the locker. The black tongues, the sliced arteries and throats: déjà vu. He turns to Georges. "The man who found him?"

"Here, sir," says a sailor. He is short and pale, almost blue with either fear or lack of sunlight, and his voice shakes.

"What did you see?"

"My mother," says the sailor, "I saw my mother." And he proceeds to explain to Dupont, in an unsteady tone that grows stronger and higher through the telling, that as he proceeded along the passage on his way to retrieve two washers and a nut to fix a corroded container bolt, he was stopped in his tracks by the apparition of his dead parent before him. She regarded him squarely with an expression the sailor could not exactly define but which he takes great pains to describe, then turned away to walk forward and vanish through the locker door. When he opened the locker, the sailor made his discovery.

"Your mother," says Dupont, "she died tragically?"

The sailor nods. "Her life was very difficult, sir."

"Listen," says Dupont, his voice raised so the others hear him clearly. The instructional opportunity he has wanted is finally materialized. "What you saw is proof—proof of a kind of going on afterwards. This man, Martine, thought he could escape from the situation we are in. But we cannot, at least not that way. A life taken in despondence is not an escape. He is still here, trapped with us. Only a natural death leads away from this world. That is what your mother was trying to tell you," he says to the sailor, "To warn you."

The campfire tale ended, its moral delivered, Dupont spins and stalks forward again, trailed by Georges.

"Cut down Martine and eject the corpse," he says to Georges over his shoulder. "No ceremony. No more Christian burials for this."

"What about the sailor? He's not the first with a story like that. He seems so adamant."

"Oh, he *believes* he saw his mother," says Dupont, "Of that I'm satisfied. But it had nothing to do with Martine. Have the doctor examine him, make sure he gets bed rest."

With a skeptical glance Georges drops back to complete his assignment while Dupont returns to the bridge. As the crew scramble to fulfill their orders, Georges catches his reflection in the thick glass of a porthole. He pauses to adjust his hair, to tighten the knot of his cravat. Outside, something swims close to the ship, something with black exaggerated eyes and a mouth of thorns and his brother's body. It grimaces at Georges before veering off into the murk. Georges shakes his head. His brother is buried kilometers above him under a gravestone he will not read again.

Though he has never been here before, arriving at Progrès Deux is a homecoming—the settlement, like *Telesto* and Georges and everyone onboard, is French. Its flowerstem spires rising from the sea shelf identify it immediately, ripped like an old Mucha poster from a Parisian café. Only French architects, and maybe the Belgians, had considered matching the cities with their landscape. The Americans built theirs like railway stations, blocky and pragmatic, while the Brits constructed in nostalgia, aiming to reproduce their Londons and Manchesters under the waves. And of course the German cities were like fortresses—although Georges has to admit they have charm, softened by Neuschwanstein towers and windows. He supposes there are others out beyond the Atlantic, Russian and Chinese and Japanese and Australian towns, but he doesn't know them.

Returned to the bridge, Georges watches the arches and asymmetric facades emerge from the gloom and recalls that other captain, an invention of the writer who had, in his way, inspired them:

"I can imagine the foundations of nautical towns, clusters of submarine houses, which, like the Nautilus, would ascend every morning to breathe at the surface of the water—free towns, independent cities."

It had all happened so fast, although it took decades to design and implement once the peril was realized. The submersibles, the great *sousmarins* like *Eurynome* and *Metis* and *Telesto* filled the yards; the pilings were sunk; the cities that, like the vessels, would become arks for humanity, grew from their seabeds. The navy, once the singular domain of men, recruited and trained women, integrated cadets from the colonies in Africa and Asia. So had the other nations, to some degree, but Georges took pride in his having done so to the greatest extent. Theirs were republican virtues. *Ègalitè.*

With sweaty hands clenched in fists, Georges observes the approaching cityscape, the lights that burn behind Progrès's ports offering hope that today their odyssey will end. Silence lies in the troughs between curt statements by the helmsmen and instructions from Captain Dupont as *Telesto* glides forward and through the gate. Full stop, and then they rise into the docking bay, the water running down the ports. At least there is air outside, never a guarantee. Monroe D.A., an American city, had suffered a catastrophic rupture; *Telesto* had found its galleries and passages infested with sharks gorging on corpses.

In the airlock, Georges gives final instructions to Soyer, the expedition leader, then retreats. Soyer and her team don their tanks and masks and equip themselves with tools and bags; the mission is as much a provisioning trip as an exploratory one. The needles of exterior gauges measuring atmospheric pressure and air quality lay within tolerance zones. The interior door seals behind them, and Soyer turns the screw to the deck and goes out.

They stalk through lonely arcades and loggias, past deserted cafeterias and storefronts. Any other city would have been designed on a grid, with wide avenues and easy-to-determine addresses, but Progrès strove to emulate the old places, the lost places. The streets wind like vines, narrow but with high ceilings to suggest open skies and the concrete floors patterned after worn cobblestones. It is easy to become disoriented, and more than once search parties, thinking they have departed at a crossroads in opposite directions, reunite at some new *carrefour*.

They encounter no one, save for a single cadaver splayed across the threshold of a grocery. Soyer surmises from his ragged pajamas and the hand basket of dry spaghetti and chicory coffee that the wretch had ripped himself from his bed to gather staples, yet somehow expired in the effort.

"Check the residences," Soyer tells her team.

That's where they find them, in their flats: in their beds or next to them, or nearby, extinguished in mid-crawl toward lavatory or kitchen. In the hospital too, when they discover it, whole wards full of rotted flesh, doctors and nurses and orderlies dead at their stations.

A sailor pulls a file from beneath the elbow of a white-coated carcass, seated as if he had simply rested his head on his arms for a cat nap. She leafs through it, then rushes over to Soyer.

"Influenza, sir. An especially aggressive strain."

Thank God for the air masks. The virus, expectorated into the air by its victims, had circulated and spread through the city's ducts. The entire settlement, poisoned.

"Everyone," says Soyer, "grab whatever unspoiled food you can and any necessary equipment for the ship. We leave within the hour. *Move.*"

Ever since Queen's Drop, where the scrubbers had failed and the city slowly asphyxiated, *Telesto*'s people had worn air masks when exploring settlements. Human life, Soyer had learned — they all had learned — was not easy to sustain underwater. Quatorze had starved, their crops and livestock failed and their fishing machinery inexplicably undeployed. Some kind of civil unrest had struck down Unterköln, leaving nothing but bodies broken by factionalism. And what of *Aethra*, floating derelict and empty, her lifeboats deployed, but otherwise operational? The only clue to the mystery had been the strange tanks of experimental gas Soyer had found, which she had been instructed to transport onboard *Telesto* for analysis. The things they had taken for granted above, the air and the sun, even sanity itself, is questionable down here. They had been cast unwillingly like seditious angels into a lower world of eaters and eaten, where everything is absorbed into the next order of life. A small mistake, an imperceptible flaw, and the teeth just beyond the glass were upon you, and the assumptions and calculations once made in a room of warm sunlight melted into bubbles rushing out of your lungs.

A scrub team meets Soyer and the rest in the airlock and they are stripped, regardless of rank or distinction, and soaped and hosed. When Soyer emerges onto the bridge, hair wet, still buttoning her fresh uniform, it takes only a nod for Captain Dupont to issue the command to dive. The waterline rises over the ports and they back through the gateway.

Progrès Deux recedes in the silence of the bridge. These are the most dangerous times, when the disappointment is at its sharpest, when the hopelessness of ever leaving *Telesto* punches hardest. Dupont confers with

Georges and the navigator, agreeing upon a course for a new destination: New Oslo, far above the Circle. A voyage of little over a week. More than enough time to sharpen a loose screw into a blade to drag across the brachial artery or hang a noose in a utility locker.

Soyer glances at Georges, who nods. They have steeled themselves for this moment.

"Captain," says Soyer, "Might now be a good time to order the review of our food and water stores? The hallucinations—the visions and ghosts, whatever they are—are always worst after departure."

Dupont regards her. "You think it is ergot on the bread that is causing them?"

"I have no explanations, sir. Only hypotheses."

"It might be good to keep the crew busy," says Georges, chiming in. "To keep their thoughts from turning to darkness."

"If we find mold on the bread," says Dupont, "And we destroy it and the ghosts keep reappearing—what then?"

Soyer has no response to such a contingent scenario; what if they destroy the mold and the ghosts disappear?

"I do not believe ghosts are evil things," says Dupont. "Only they must be harnessed to work for the living. The sailor who found the hanged Martine—he now credits his dead mother for watching over him, perhaps even keeping him from self-harm. These suicides, they are an attempt to flee from our predicament. But the ghosts can stop them, if we allow it."

"So if there is mold on the bread," says Soyer, "You would have the crew eat it anyway?"

"What good is a ship if there are only corpses to man it." Dupont clasps his hands behind his back. "But I agree the process is a helpful distraction. Order a review of all stores and rations, and remove anything you think is harmful."

Soyer salutes and departs, and the captain turns the bridge over to Georges, whose doubt has made him quiet and introspective. Dupont retires to his cabin, locks the door behind him. He eases himself between the steel canisters crowding the already cramped room. Dupont turns the dial on one, feeling no resistance—empty. The testing of another is rewarded with a hiss. Carefully and with effort he muscles the tank into a jerry-rigged cradle consisting of an overturned chair balanced on the desktop, then opens the screw. The invisible gas streams directly into the cabin's return vent and throughout the ship.

Dupont observes his wristwatch. The last time, right before they uncovered Martine, he had opened the tank for a minute-and-a-half; this time he would let it go for two. Then he closes the valve and lays back on his bunk, dizzy. It is always most intense at the source. He watches as lights pierce the bulkheads which have become like paper and phantasms stream into the cabin. Strangers, an old schoolteacher, his wife who swallowed a bottle of pills rather than abandon the sky and earth and live the rest of her days entombed by steel and water. A hundred visitations creeping from the locked attics and basements of his mind and the gas holding a ring of keys in its hand. He could bear it, for them, for the diminishing populace of what increasingly appeared to be an extinction. Diversions and premonitions to keep them alive for another day, another work shift. To make them forget for even a moment the weight overhead.

THE SAFARI
by Michael S. Walker

The video game was called Buck's Safari. Or something like that. As long as Henry had been coming to the bar, the game had sat there in one corner of the dark room: a squat box, lurid computer graphics flashing on a flat, square screen. It was a shooter game and for a dollar (or whatever the price was (Henry was no too sure) a player could bring down, with the aid of one or two plastic rifles, a bounty of digital big game. Like Teddy Roosevelt going all crazy over the African veldt. Leaping gazelles and antelopes. Charging elephants with small red eyes and lethal curved tusks. Lions. Leopards. Tigers. Etc. Etc.

Kill or be Killed. Os and 1s…

Henry had never played the game (Buck's Safari) in the two (or was it three years now?) that he had been coming to the bar. Henry did not like video games. To tell truth, Henry did not like much of anything. Everything seemed to be a damn game: Work, Love, War, Peace, Politics, Education, Play… And Henry was SICK of games.

All Henry wanted to do was sit quietly at the bar and drink slowly, as the afternoon dissolved into dusk. One Long Island Ice Tea after another. And ogle the bartender's ample breasts as she brought him one more, warming round. What the hell else was there to do?

"You want another?" the bartender said, standing in front of Henry, her face as impassive as always. Her breasts as impressive as always.

"Does the Pope shit in the woods?" Henry mumbled, looking down into his (now) empty glass.

"What?" the bartender said, looking at Henry, her sleek forehead creasing, not getting this most innocuous of remarks.

"Yes, another…" Henry sighed, trying his best to smile.

The bartender went away to get Henry his fourth? fifth? Long Island Ice Tea. As she did, he just sat there, looking around at the dark bar, wondering why he came here to drink at all. What was the attraction? It was like this vast, gray warehouse sheltering almost everything Henry hated in the world. Just flotsam and jetsam of Corporate America. Beyond booze and breasts, what was there that kept him coming back? There were like four or five flat-screen TVs in the bar, screwed up high, affixed to various corners, and they were all tuned into sporting events. Games games and more games… Baseball here. Soccer over here. Football in all its grid-iron glory. It just made Henry feel completely alone. Completely desolate.

The bar that Henry was sitting at was a large horseshoe structure—burnished rosewood and ceramic tiles the color of sand. On the other side of that horseshoe, far away from Henry, two men sat, hunched over plastic mugs of draft beer. Like the video game, they seemed to be permanent fixtures in the bar. They were always there, every day, on the exact same stools—two middle-aged men about Henry's age. One of them had short, sandy hair and a pulpy, boyish face. The other was always dressed in a Cleveland Browns starter jacket and jeans, no matter the weather. And there they sat, every day, drinking drafts. Frequently they would become very animated, and get into an argument about something. Henry could never really catch these arguments, but he was pretty certain they pertained to football. Occasionally he would hear words or fragments as their voices rose in volume and pitch: "Rushing…Their defense SUCKS…Your quarterback cannot PASS…"

Sometimes Henry thought they were going to start throwing punches over such trifles, and the one with the pulpy, boyish face would get quite red. But they never did…

Games games and more games…

The bartender returned with a fresh Long Island and sat it down on the tiled bar. "*Good Better Best,*" Henry thought, as he stared into the cool brown depths of the drink. Like Ponce De Leon at the shores of a murky fountain of youth.

"Let us forget all games…" Henry mumbled, foisting the heavy glass to his (always) dry lips.

"What?" the bartender said, her forehead creasing again.

"Nothing…" Henry mumbled. "Nice game…"

"Well, we were behind in the first half, but yeah, I think we might pull it off…" she said, managing a slight smile.

Henry had no idea what she was talking about. There was a baseball game here. There was soccer over there. And there was football in all its gridiron glory. Maybe she was referring to all three of them? Maybe the planets were in alignment, and everyone was coming from behind and WINNING… All Henry knew was that he wanted to keep the conversation with the bartender going. God she was so lovely, with long black hair framing a gaunt, olive-tanned face. Large dark eyes. A dimpled chin. How old was she? Twenty-three? Twenty-four? Henry was old enough to be her father, easily. It was so incredibly sad. Could he not just cut through the games for once and tell her he thought she was lovely?

"Yeah…cool," Henry said, again looking down into his Long Island.

The bartender grimaced and walked away from Henry, towards a cash register on the other side of the massive bar. Close to her, sandy-haired guy and Cleveland Browns jacket guy were shaking their heads, waving their hands around frantically. Another argument…

About

Love War Peace Politics Education Play…

Sure. And football…

Henry looked around the bar. It was growing darker by the minute. Daylight Savings Time had just ended two days before. Most of the lightning in the bar was natural and came through a series of long windows that comprised one whole wall of the place. Beyond that was a pebbled patio where, in the summer, patrons often sat and drank and took their meals. It was 5:30 according to Henry's iPhone, but it was already as dark as midnight out there…

"Maybe I should go home…" Henry thought sadly, foisting his Long Island once again, clicking the hard ice against his front incisors.

And that idea saddened him too…the idea of trudging through six blocks of dark and cold to the tiny studio apartment he lived in and had rented for what? Nine, ten years now? He could see it in his mind's eye. The beige carpet in the narrow living room pocked with beer stains. A TV and a computer covered in dust. A thousand paperback books crammed into a flimsy blond case.

A study in losing…

NO NO NO

His eyes scoured the bar, looking, seeking some kind of escape beyond the poisoned forgetfulness of one more Long Island Ice Tea. They fastened, as they probably had a thousand times in the past, on the video game called Buck's Safari.

There, on the flat video screen, a cartoon goddess was strutting across the even flatter CGI veldt.

"Hmmm…" Henry said, into his heavy glass.

The cartoon goddess was dressed like a big game hunter, of course—a study in winning khaki and camouflage. She was wearing khaki cargo shorts that came down to her shapely knees. And a long-sleeved hunting shirt, its cotton fabric an autumnal Jackson Pollock splattering of greens and browns and orange. On her shapely head she wore a British Empire pith helmet—a single black strap slashed against its khaki brim.

"Hmmm…" Henry said once again, loudly.

Her face and her body reminded Henry of that one pin-up queen from the 50s and 60s. What was her name? Betty…Betty something. Henry couldn't remember but he had, he was certain, at one point in his life, been pretty obsessed with her, with black-and-white photos of her. Games games and more games. Solitary games that went nowhere and proved nothing. Yes, the CGI Goddess really looked like her. She had long, shiny black hair (very much like the bartender's hair) that fell straight down from her outlandish pith helmet and ended in a storm of curls around her padded shoulders. There was something feline, predatory about her face in profile: the sharp arch of one thin eyebrow perhaps? Or the aquiline nose? Or the long, blood-red lips? It was almost as if she herself was some kind of jungle cat (albeit with a gun) trudging across the lurid, out-of-focus background, in search of smaller cats to bring down.

And the gun? The gun she held, pressed close to one very shapely camouflaged breast? Henry knew that gun. It was a Remington deer rifle—an auto loading shotgun with a walnut stock. His father had gone hunting every fall with the exact same gun. As a matter of fact, it was the only thing Henry had inherited from the sorry old fucker, when he died from pancreatic cancer in 2001.

Why hadn't he noticed these details before, on the computer screen? The shapely girl? The Remington? The video game had always been there in the bar, but today seemed to be the very first time he had given it much thought. Before, it had just been a garish box on the periphery of his vision. Just another game in a dark warehouse full of games.

Now, he was noticing. His 4th/5th? Long Island Ice Tea sat on the bar, unattended, as he noticed.

He was stone-cold sober now, as he noticed.

And so, the shapely hunter moved across the screen, like Elmer Fudd in one of those old cartoons when he was stalking Bugs Bunny. But there was nothing comical about it at all. Henry's heart jolted with every fall of her black hunting boots.

Suddenly, a gazelle appeared, as if from nowhere, and began to leap across the two-dimensional screen, its forelegs seeming to grasp at the very air, as if it was bringing the atmosphere close to its taut caramel and white body. The cartoon goddess did not seem to even blink. She brought the Remington up and sighted it with one graceful, sweeping motion. She fired at the gazelle...

And the screen exploded, A supernova of red and green bubbles engulfed the computer, obscuring the CGI veldt. The bubbles fell like snow, slowly slowly down to the bottom rim of the monitor, leaving behind this legend in bold, black pixels:

"*100 POINTS! GOOD SHOT!*"

And then the goddess was there once again, as before, gun at the ready, ready to stalk the big game.

"Big game...big game...big game..." Henry's mind seemed to echo.

As if in a dream, the beautiful hunter girl turned to stare directly at Henry, where he sat, transfixed at the bar. She gave him a broad, mischievous smile.

And she winked at him…

"What the hell is going on here?" Henry whispered.

In quick succession, a lion, an antelope, and an elephant appeared on the screen of the video game, like living road blocks in front of the great Betty Page hunter. In every instance, she was nonplussed. She brought the rifle up, just as she had with the unfortunate gazelle, and fired with deadly accuracy.

"*200 POINTS! FANTASTIC SHOT!*" the computer exclaimed, as, once again, red and green bubbles evanesced on the glass screen. "*300 POINTS! YOU WIN! 400 POINTS! YOU ARE THE GREAT WHITE HUNTER!*" And, after every shot, the sexy girl turned her face toward Henry and gave him a wink and an inviting smile…

Henry shook his head violently. "This can't be happening," he mouthed. By fierce will of effort he managed to pull his gaze away from the game, from Buck's Safari. He felt strangely disoriented. Absolutely nothing had changed in the bar. The flat-screen TVs were still blasting out myriad games. Boyish guy and Cleveland Browns guy were still opposite him, gesticulating like mad. And the bartender was still at the cash register, methodically counting out bills from the till. But everything seemed, to Henry, completely unreal now. More vapid and two-dimensional than the action on the video-game console. He stared down into his Long Island Ice Tea, looking for solace in the muddy, swirling poison. But there was none at all now…

"You want another?"

The bartender was standing in front of him now, glaring, her hands on her hips.

Henry glanced at her for a brief second, and then back down into his glass. The bartender was so beautiful, so self-assured. And he…

Henry continued to stare into the Long Island, as if he was some fortune-teller who could discern the future in its gentle, Brownian motion. The FUTURE. And the future was shaping up to be a shabbier version of the present. Which, in itself, was just a shabbier version of the past. A thousand watering holes just like this one. A thousand-and-one Long Island Ice Teas. Crushing hangovers, sitting alone in a tiny studio apartment, wishing desperately that he was far far away from the squalor and the dust. That he was someone else…

Maybe Robinson Crusoe on some lovely tropical island, surrounded on all sides by peaceful blue waters…

Or maybe…

The Great White Hunter

Henry looked up at the bartender, and shook his head so furiously that he managed to startle her.

"Just the bill…please," he managed to say. He just wanted her to go away now. He wanted everyone to go away now…

As the bartender turned away from Henry, and toward the cash register to ring him up, Henry glanced back toward the safari game. Betty Page, African hunter, was still up on the screen, once again moving slowly, stealthily, from left to right, her trusty rifle ready for further sport…

She reached the center of that screen, and that very sport appeared…

It wasn't a gazelle this time.

Or an antelope.

Or a lion…

No. It was a man. He materialized in front of the girl as if he had suddenly been teleported there from some distant, more civilized planet. He looked around in bewilderment, his brown eyes almost as big as saucers. Like before, the girl did not hesitate. She brought the rifle up to her padded shoulder, aimed the glittering barrel directly at him, as his mouth became a perfect "O" engaged in a mute, cartoon scream.

The man was dressed in a brown-and-orange jacket. As he raised his arms in terror, Henry could just make out the letters "WNS" in large, blocky print across his chest.

The girl fired the rifle directly at the man's head. Instead of the explosion of red and green bubbles that had followed each of her previous kills, this time the screen was splattered with red, with blood, like it was the eye of a camera filming some Grand Guignol movie. The blood ran slow in rivulets down the screen, like rain down a picture window.

And through the haze of blood, Henry could see the girl still, one shiny black boot propped up on the slumped, headless body of her most recent kill. A new, pixelated legend appeared in the sky above her, as the blood cleared, and the background became green once again.

"HENRY LOVELL! YOU WIN! YOU ARE THE UNDISPUTED CHAMP! PICK UP ALL MARBLES RIGHT NOW!"

And the girl, under her ludicrous pith helmet, winked once again at Henry.

And licked her lush lips…

"Hmmm…" Henry said, staring at the safari game, as the last of the blood dissolved on the screen, Betty Page still there in tableau, one thick vinyl boot propped on one think inert body. A body in a Cleveland Browns starter jacket.

"There…" the bartender said, placing Henry's tab on the tiled bar, and walking away before he could say anything at all.

"There…" Henry said, not even glancing at the damage done. He just automatically reached into his pants, drew out his wallet, slapped his debit card on top of the bar receipt. The bartender came back immediately, like some insect drawn to the nectar of a pitcher plant.

As the bartender walked away once again with Henry's card, he went back to the video game. The girl was gone. The man's body was gone. All blood was gone. On the screen, a lurid jungle background competed with mug shots of gazelles and antelopes and lions.

Etc. Etc. Etc.

0s ans 1s.

Kill or be killed.

"There ya go…thank you…" the bartender said, bringing back Henry's debit card and a new receipt to sign. On the other side of the bar, Cleveland Browns guy and boyish-faced guy lurched at each other over their draft beers, their arms and hands moving wildly, as if they were having an argument in sign language.

"Hmmm…" Henry said, as the bartender walked away for the final time. On the flat-screen TVs in the bar—on a baseball diamond; on a soccer field; and particularly on a football gridiron—the planets were all aligning now. Everyone was coming from behind and winning. EVERYONE.

Henry rose to his feet. He was stone-cold sober now.

He knew exactly what he needed to do.

✗

THE WATER HORSE
by Bill W. James

August

Father went into the woods again today. He took the wagon and hitched it to our new white horse from the breeder in Ingolstadt. That's very far away. Now he is far away, and I am alone.

It is warm, but I am not to play outside; only look through the blurry window at the woods curving our farm. The low sun makes the sky amber and grows the trees' shadow long over the field and our house. It will already be dark around the river. Mother said I was never to play at the river or its branches, even when I wasn't alone. She isn't here.

Father will not be back until near dark. I will not get to play at the river today. He does this sometimes; goes wandering. I never know what he's looking for. The dying summer reminds me of his drawn out face, pale and broad. Always sullen and dragging too long. I have not yet been able to convince him to take me to the woods with him. Whatever he's looking for, I'm sure I can help. Or, at least play by the forbidden creek. He's more lax about it than mother ever was. He seems distracted, and will let me get away with it.

There's a spot where it shallows. The water runs downhill into a brook. Rocks crop up out of the ground and make the river run over their face. If you stand down stream, you can almost hear it talk. I tried to hear what it was saying once. Then, I heard it start to trot.

I see the white horse appear at the forest's mouth. It drags the wagon along, slowly but surely, with a slouched little man, my father's shrunken form, at the helm. I'm no longer alone.

September

Cool air has begun to filter into the breeze. Father stokes the fires more warmly at night. He seems so sad now, and has ever since winter. I don't know why mother wanted to leave, but father has left too. He is so distant. I hate being alone.

I begged him today to take me into the woods. He walked around the house, reading letters and picking things up. He spoke in half-sentences like he didn't want to hear me, like I was a thought he could put out of his head. I told him I could help him look. I grew increasingly more desperate as he grew more distant, like he was chasing an idea. At the mention of mother, he turned on me with surprising quickness, like a man woken from a nightmare. And in much the way of dream, he didn't seem to remember it. I wanted to play in the woods, as she and I used to do, and he thought that was a good idea. He hitched up the wagon with Máni, the white mare, and we rode down the long, dusty trail and into the woods.

Somewhere along the way, he told me to jump down and play in the clearing. He would never be more than a shout away. And stay away from river. The summer had been long and the flow from the mountains had evened out, but that it was still too fast for me. So here I remain.

I play in the rich, black dirt and hear the river babble from a short distance. I must not be too far from the rock fall, because through the trees, I can almost hear it speaking. As I play with my toy soldier, and his little wooden horse, I begin to hear something oddly familiar in the pattern of the distant gurgling – a song. Someone is singing. It's absently playful, and mockingly melancholy. It sounds like she is calling my wounded soldier to ride his horse to her. It sounds almost like my mother.

She is on the river, but my mother would never call me there. She always told me to stay away from it. She said that if I ventured too far, or too close, that if I heard the galloping—

And may father calls me. I drop my toys, quite unaware that I had been carrying them, or how I had begun to leave the clearing. He is at its edge with Máni, and we are to go home.

I collect up my toys and depart.

October

We have venture to town today. It is a good many hours drive from home, and road is bumpy, but if I am good, father will get me something. So I hold my complaints and jostle to town. Though the wagon creaks and clanks, I try to engage him in conversation. He seems to hear me very little. I am excited for the bustle and trade, to see all the people. He is not. I think they will tell Máni she is a pretty horse. I think they will give her carrots. He does not.

Eventually we leave the pine trees behind and find our way to Arboga. It is big and old. I can tell from the buildings. I am excited to see the other farmers selling their crops. Their children run and laugh, and wave. I wave back, and father tells me to go play. But not to stray far. He goes into a building off from the scattered market to talk with the other grownups.

For awhile, I frolic in the street with my friends, our neighbors from over the hill. Even though the cold begins to sting my ears, and they ware on me after some time, I don't want to bother father. I hope that his business will bring him closer, as it always did. He and mother wouldn't fight for a long time after the haul from market. They always fought over money. Even the last time. Maybe that's why she wanted to leave.

I do not stop playing until I hear two women, occasional friends of my parents, talking about father. He has not seen them as he stands halfway out of the building, talking to another man. He looks happier than I have seen him in a long while. One of them says he is a broken man. I do not know what that means, but I feel somehow it is my fault. I hope it is not over money, and no longer want to play. I wonder if mother were still here if we would be broken.

The cold hurts my ears, and I want to be alone.

November

The men in black came from Arboga today. They were constables, the three of them. Aunt Irena wired them. Mother never made it to Stockholm. Father didn't understand. He was confused; was she okay?

They had hoped he could tell them.

Apparently, she had planned a trip to see her sister—with me!—sometime late last year. They had corresponded via letter and wire until last February. Aunt Irena said she had stopped receiving replies around then. Father said he had thought mother had gone to Aunt Irena's then. Yes, he had the letters. No, he hadn't opened them. He couldn't bear to. He thought they had been from mother, explaining why she left. He didn't need an explanation. Yes, they could have them.

The men asked to take a look around. He told them they could, though it didn't seem like a question.

One stayed with father, and they continued to talk. He wondered why my mother would leave, and for so long. I would have listened in more, as the other two constables explored the house, but one found his way to my room. He wanted to ask me some questions. He stooped low and played with some toys, took off his hat to seem less threatening, and spoke down to me like adults do. He wanted to know if I had seen my mommy. I told him I had, and he wanted to know where.

I had dreamed about her. She was in a big frozen palace. A castle made of ice. She was wearing a dress made of leaves – they were long like snakes—and clasped in icicles. She rode a white horse around her throne room; it was beautiful, and the same color as the moon in winter, like the full moon when it has a halo. Even the carpets and banners were ice, woven frost from windowsills, dyed red and sticky. I rode a horse too. A big stallion. He was wet, and cold, and slippery, but big and strong, and wanted to take me to see my mother. His hooves were heavy and his stride long. I could remember the big, ice double doors opening. They had crystal ring handles and no one attended them. I woke up cold.

The constable smiled sadly. He wanted to know the last time I had seen my mommy that wasn't a dream. I told him, the night she left. He scratched his stubble and asked if she and my daddy had fought that night. I told him they had. He asked if I knew what about. I said money, I think. He got a side-long look on his face like an adult does when they think they know something you don't. His eyes were blue, and sharp, and smart like crystal. Smarter than his friends. His eyes reminded me of the horse that took me to see mother.

I asked him what being broken means. He didn't understand, so I told him about the women in the market. He told me that it meant to be sad; so sad that you couldn't get up. He struggled to explain it further when one of his friends, the one wandering around, called to him from the front door.

The constable rose and thanked me. He put on his hat and began to turn. I asked him if he thought my father was broken. He didn't know, but he hoped not. I asked if I was broken, and he faked a smile and told me no, before leaving to meet his friend.

The other constable, the one talking to my father joined them and spoke their farewells. With a tip of his hat, he said they would be leaving, but close by. They were going to take a walk in the woods this afternoon, and might be visiting again soon. My father thanked them, though I could tell he was angry. He spoke like stony gravel, and escorted them off the porch.

They took to their wagon and were gone.

Father looked worried, so I tugged at him. He smiled reassuringly and went back inside. He has remained worried ever since. Even now, he crouches by the fire. He stokes it, thinking inwardly, unresponsive to the world. I go to the dark window, and even though it's cold, I open it and listen for the river. In the quiet of winter, you can hear it from here. The babbling turns to singing, then flows into galloping, and I am not so alone.

December

The nights are dark and long, the days are cold and short. I hear the winds howl at night; they bring gales and snow. The ground is covered when I wake up, and the windows are sheets of ice. I can see my breath and the air bites. Sometimes, I hear the sound of something giant in the woods. I wake up afraid, because I think it is a massive beast. Father tells me this is chunks of ice breaking off the river and falling into the brook. I think the falling ice will make the monster angry. I tell him it is a creature, and he tells me he thinks I just like to be scared. He gets a chuckle out of this; it is the first I have seen in a long time.

I beg him to tell me scary stories as the long night falls. He does.

He tells me about the lindworm of lake Storsjön, that can circle a boat with its body, and crush the hull. Sometimes, it comes out of the water to stalk lonely marshes. I can see its big, flat jaws and gnarled fangs.

He tells me about trolls and witches that roam the land between midnight and morning, and how they search for innocents to use as food or sacrifices. Especially about a girl in a nearby town who escaped two witches on the road by fleeing to a church. Only once inside did she find that she interrupted a Christmas mass held by spirits of the hungry dead.

He tells me about mylings. They were all once children, left to die by their mothers. They wander the earth as twisted little people, perpetual infants, searching for a back to jump on. Once they've found a victim, the creatures leap upon them and demand to be taken to hallowed ground. But the mylings grow heavier as their victim approaches a church yard, and they may drown people in the grave soil as they seek to inter the screaming ghost. None know why this is. Perhaps the creature seeks vengeance more than rest. Perhaps they cannot be buried because they are unbaptized.

I asked him to tell me about the Bäckahästen, the Brook Horse. The story mother always told me.

His words ebb, and his eyes see far away. I ask him to tell me again, and he suggests I tell him.

I tell him it's why mother never wanted me to go near the river. She said that in the waters lived a brook horse, a creature which appeared as a beautiful white stallion or mare. You could hear its hooves in the breaking water over the rocks. It would emerge from running streams or still pools and offer rides young children or lonely young women. It would tell them of its wondrous home beneath the surface, like the world inside a mirror. The water horse would let you pet its mane, but you would become stuck, and no matter how hard you fought, you wouldn't be able to pull your hand away. Then, it would up and drag you down with it, into the depths, and never surface for air. You would drown there, and remain its guest forever.

Sometimes, when you're alone, you can hear it trotting through woods, or on the stepping stones around the water. Sometimes, if you listen close, it dances on the ice in winter. When the water flows fast, you know it's there, running with the stream.

Father does not say anything. He is gone. He sits with his knees at his chest and his hands on his knees. He stares off into the distance imagining mother.

The fire slowly dies.

January

The constables came again. The older one in the middle advised my father to engage a solicitor. They say they will be searching the woods again, though I don't know what they hope to find. They declined to come inside. Instead, I could see them, three black, cloaked figures outlined against the winter white of the snowy field. They simply tipped their hats and promised to return with a search party.

This has sent father into a state of complete ruin. He refuses to do much more than wander the house and talk to himself. He will not give me the key to the pantry. He cannot acknowledge me. I have to venture into the woods if I wish to eat. I catch rabbits in snares there. They are all as snowy white as the field.

When I'm alone, sometimes I can hear the stream babble. Today, I heard the song as the ice broke. She was singing to me. She wants me to come to her on a horse. To ride to her. Cracking and crashing of ice became hoof-beats, and I knew it was real. I could hear it galloping around the banks. As I approached the edge of the clearing where I had set my traps, I could almost hear it whiney. It trotted and jumped. It leapt over fallen logs and onto miniscule stepping stones. It avoided branches and danced on blocks of ice—blue ice with frosted edges, jagged like icicles.

I would have gone to it, but I heard the barn door break. Máni was screaming and running wild. I had to run all the way back to the house, dead rabbit in hand, to keep her from escaping and hurting herself in the process. The ruckus was so great it even brought the constables back. The snow had held them. They were half a mile away.

Father barely came outside except to yell at her. We cannot live like this.

Mother, save me.

February

Father has taken to wandering at night now. He is truly lost to me. He bumbles through the forest calling mother's name. I don't know how doesn't hear her singing. I worry that if he goes too close to the river the great horse will run him down. Trample him.

I am alone now. More so than I have ever been. Even more than the night mother threatened to leave for the last time.

He is out there, this instant, holding Máni by the reigns while he stumbles over fallen branches and breaks fragile stalactites of water. The cold will kill him.

The house is freezing. No fires kindle here. We have no dry wood. I cannot abide it and venture into the night.

I find my way down the trail, and over the howl of the wind, through the crunch of snow under my boots, I can hear her singing. She wants to see me.

She sounds happy. Not like the night they had fought over debts and she had sworn to go live with aunt Irena. I follow the sound of her voice like I followed her out to the water's edge that night. I remember how she stood there fuming with her back to me. I couldn't believe she was willing to leave me. I hate being alone.

The trees are dark and I can hear father in the distance. His voice is a cry now. Carried away by the wind.

I step through the clearing and into a gentle clam. It's standing there, facing me, not at all like mother that night. She had her back to me. The great horse raises its head from the frozen ground. It's not at all like I imagined it. It is a horse, but it's woven of sea weed, long and snakelike. It looks slick and wet despite the freezing temperature.

Máni is screaming somewhere.

The deep green horse lets out a snort of spectral mist and paws at the ground anxious for my arrival. It flexes a muscular, sinuous back.

All I can see is my mother's seething shoulders. She rants to herself about my father and his financial ineptitude. I cannot let her leave. I must keep her here. I hate being alone.

I reach up and touch the water horse's mane. The strips of sea weed eagerly greet me, tying like a knot I have slipped into. I cannot say how, except by some slip of my hand, as they have not seemed to move. He bows his head and accepts me as rider. I mount him with swiftness I didn't know I possessed, and we are off, in long, loping, powerful, but delicate strides. He breaks the icy ground beneath him and trods the snow. My legs are wrapped inside him. I can feel his ropes, cold and slimy. We approach the water's edge quickly, and he finds a space where the ice is broken. He wants to take me to see my mother.

I remember the sound as the log cracked her head. As she fell into the river. I couldn't let her leave. She would be with me forever in the brook.

As we descend, I remember her falling over the rocks' face and into the babbling stream.

When we hit the water, the cold steals my breath in one sharp exhale, and no more ever enters my body. I resist somewhat at first, but quickly lose the will to do so. We sink into the icy water, the wonderful land below; reflected on the solid surface, the other side of the mirror. We swim for a time in the muted, elongated continuum of water-noise, ever deeper until strips of black/hunter-green weeds rise from the bottom. There I see my mother, wrapped in them by the legs looking up at me. She floats with her arms out, still frozen, crystals of ice gathering on the features of her face like an icy masque. She forgives me. She just wants to see me. She wants me to come live with her after all. And the water horse has brought me to her.

To live here.

Forever.

THE LONG WAY HOME
by S.E. Casey

Charles Southworth didn't want to answer the knock at the door. It wasn't that he didn't want to be neighborly, he just didn't want to endure the cold. This would be his first winter here, and despite it being only October, he already had felt the icy sting of northern Canada.

He opened the door halfway. Raymond Wallace and his two sons stood on the porch seemingly impervious to the chill. One of the boys was dressed as a vampire, the other a pig. They both looked bored.

"Trick-or-Treat," they droned.

Charles's mind raced to account for the day. However, he was certain it was the day before Halloween.

"Well, I hope this is a trick. You're a little early I'm afraid. Halloween's tomorrow," he stumbled.

"Of course, Halloween's tomorrow!" Raymond guffawed, "That's why the kids are out today! You *are* coming trick-or-treating with us tomorrow, right?"

Charles had gotten the same invite numerous times over the last month from the other men of the town. He had dismissed the offer as a joke, or some neighborhood hazing. He had stopped trick-or-treating when he was fourteen. He hadn't attended a costume party since freshman year of college. Charles studied Raymond for sarcasm, but couldn't find any. His new neighbor seemed entirely sincere.

"Well, if everyone is going, then I guess so," he answered.

"That's the holiday spirit! Best night of the year, Buddy, I promise! Okay, so it's settled. Now, where's the candy for the boys?"

The boys mechanically raised their bags. A habitual procrastinator, Charles had planned to pick up something the next day. He didn't have a single piece of candy the house. He didn't like candy anymore: he had lost his sweet tooth over the years.

"I'm sorry, but I'm afraid I don't have anything. I thought Halloween was tomorrow."

Raymond sighed, "Yes, Halloween is tomorrow so today's the day before when the kids celebrate. Jeez, Charles, we told you this like fifty times."

His neighbor, owner of Wallace's Hardware and Tools, shook his head in disgust. The older of the boys lowered his bag and rolled his eyes. Charles tried to remember his name. It was either Timmy or Jimmy.

"It's okay Dad, let's just go," Timmy-Jimmy said pulling at his father's sleeve. However, Raymond didn't budge.

"Well, Charles, looks like there are more kids coming down the street for you to disappoint. Wouldn't be surprised if you get egged tonight."

"Sorry," Charles muttered.

"Well, maybe you can make it up next year. Anyway, we'll pick you up at four o'clock tomorrow! Can't wait, it'll be a blast!"

Raymond raised his arm for a high-five. The same as with anyone over forty, it was an embarrassing exchange. Charles slapped his hand too softly and left it there too long.

Timmy or Jimmy winced. His little brother pulled his pig mask over his eyes.

"C'mon, Dad," they droned.

"Yea, hold your horses kiddos, I'm coming... Be ready tomorrow, Charles! Can't wait to see your costume!" Raymond called over his shoulder as he was pulled away.

Charles still wasn't sure if he was serious. Braving the cold, he stepped out onto his porch to survey the street. Raymond was right: there were children in costumes going door to door with their dads. Maybe Halloween was reserved for the adults here. He might be going trick-or-treating after all.

* * * *

The pickup truck drove onto the lawn blaring its horn. They were early, but the night approached quickly. The town of Mersault was so far north the sun went down noticeably earlier each day. It was also colder than it had been the day before as if by consequence. Charles wore the heaviest coat that he owned, but as he stepped out of his front door he realized that it wasn't heavy enough. He anticipated moving here would require a new wardrobe, but he had put it off rationalizing that he would have another month of tolerable weather.

He had convinced himself that Raymond and the others were probably not going trick-or-treating, rather it some euphemism for going to a strip club or the like. However, the rowdy group of middle-aged men were all in costume. There were convicts, Mounties, hockey players, and even a forgotten character from Star Wars.

"Where's your costume Charles?" Raymond jumped from the bed of the idling truck to playfully punch him on the arm.

Charles rubbed his bicep. "I didn't know you were serious. Maybe next year, eh?"

The men in the truck hissed. Charles didn't quite have the local affectation down yet.

Charles winced at the prospect of riding in the truck's open bed. However, he could see the passenger seat was unoccupied.

"Hey, can I ride in here with you?" Charles asked the zombie driving.

"I guess, if you really want," Frank said.

Frank Salamano managed the only bank in town. He accessorized his elaborate zombie make-up with a ridiculous top hat that brushed the ceiling of the cab. It was strange to see him out of his business suit and not the least bit self-conscious about his adolescent costume.

Charles climbed inside delighted to find the cab well heated. He decided not to comment about the suffocating cold. He still felt like a guest here and worried that it would be taken as an insult. Charles had already made the mistake of complaining about the smell of Kousaboo Lake.

When he had moved to Mersault in the spring, the town's lake was frozen, a scenic sheet of skate scored ice. After the thaw, its water was disappointingly muddy and a breeding ground for all manner of insects. With no rivers to feed or drain it, the trapped water stagnated and whatever muck that lined its bottom reeked. It was as if some giant sea creature had gotten landlocked during the last prehistoric flood, its carcass still slowly putrefying. However, the lake was a big part of the town, and they took exception to his criticism. Maybe they had gotten used to its stench. Hopefully, in time, he would too.

"Wanna beer?" Frank offered.

Charles grabbed the longneck bottle in the cup holder already opened.

"Hey! What the hell are you doing? That's mine!" Frank scolded. "Jesus Christ, Charlie! Under the seat!"

"It's Charles," he quickly corrected. He hated being called Charlie, or even worse, Chuck. He wasn't a kid anymore.

Finding a half filled six-pack at his feet, he took one but didn't open it. He was too cold to drink it.

They traveled along the road that circled the lake. Charles could smell its rot even over the truck's leaky exhaust. He wondered what decaying matter made that odor. He hated it. It didn't help that the prevailing wind blew across the lake to where he lived. Maybe that was why the house had been so affordable. If he had known the direction of the winds, he would have sought a house on the other side. However, those upwind homes didn't seem to be for sale. In fact, everyone he worked with and had met were clustered with him on the southern shore. While he could see the houses across the lake, he hadn't met a single person who lived on that other side.

It was to that end of Kousaboo Lake where they were headed. Its elliptical shape made for a lengthy trip, the lake much wider than it was long. Charles imagined that when it iced over it would be a relatively short snowmobile ride across. But that would have to wait for another month, the water stubbornly resisting to freeze.

A horn blast startled Charles. They were passed by another pick-up despite the road being a single lane. Frank honked back hitting the gas trying to keep up. Charles gripped the dashboard as the road swung to the left and there would be no warning should another vehicle be coming the other way. The fog that had suddenly rolled in from the nearby lake further decreased the visibility. However, there was no one coming from around the bend, and the faster truck completed its pass jerking back into its lane.

Charles breathed a sigh of relief.

The men riding in the back of the other truck were also dressed-up for Halloween. They triumphantly hooted and hollered in celebration. The men in Frank's truck whooped back. Someone threw an empty beer can that missed everything sailing off the side of the road into the bushes.

"So where are we going?" Charles exhaled.

"Same place as every year. Marinere Street. You're gonna love it," Frank responded.

Frank burped and tossed his empty bottle out the window. The men sitting in the back cheered when it smashed on the pavement. Charles didn't envy his friends sitting in the freeze of the open truck bed. However, they seemed content, drinking and swapping dirty jokes.

"Make yourself useful and hand me another brew, eh?" Frank ordered.

Charles did so reluctantly. He decided a lecture about the risk of being pulled over for drinking and driving would have been futile. After all, dressed as a polar bear, the chief of police rode in the back.

With the arrival of the night, the fog spilling off the lake grew thick. It was a regular autumnal occurrence due to the sudden temperature plunge. Indeed, the last two mornings Charles had woken up to ice on the surface of Kousaboo Lake. It melted quickly once the sun came out, but it wouldn't be long before it set for good. While he wasn't ready for winter, he looked forward to the freezing that would trap the stench underneath.

Without warning, Frank slammed on the brakes. There were eight other trucks and one van carelessly parked in a pull-off. They had arrived at the neighborhood across the lake. Frank roughly skidded to a stop hemming in two other vehicles. The hollering gang leapt from the truck bed with their empty pillowcases in hand.

Charles gaped at the surreal scene. There were several dozen men in costumes crisscrossing the street with childish exuberance. He was reminded again of the town's propensity of men of a certain age. It was as if Mersault had had a mini baby boom some forty-five years ago. However, there was no time to contemplate this useless trivia as Raymond pulled him into the fray.

"C'mon, Charlie! It's Halloween!"

The houses on Marinere Street slumped in varying states of disregard and disrepair. They were of a similar style, and had probably had been built together many years ago. While the homes were somewhat neglected, the street was well lit. The same could be said of all the streets of Mersault. Charles supposed in these towns above the Arctic Circle where winter nights lasted more than twenty hours that reliable lighting was essential.

"Don't be such a drag Charlie. First house!"

Charles was pushed up the walkway of a peeling ranch, its shingles hanging loose off the roof. However, it appeared cozy inside, warm yellow lights aglow in the windows. The boisterous gang kept knocking until an elderly couple opened the door.

"Trick-or-treat!"

The old man and woman weren't threatened or alarmed, doling out candy as if nothing was amiss. The man even tussled the hair of Albert Sintes, the town dentist. The men left giggling comparing what they received. Charles caught the eye of the woman of the house. She wrinkled her nose at him, but nonetheless gave him a small wave.

"Onward Ho!"

Charles was dragged across the street to the next house.

"We gotta get you a costume Charlie! You're not gonna get any candy!"

This was madness. There were no children here, no women, only men non-ironically trick-or-treating. They were so excited that they didn't seemed bothered by the cold. However, when the wind blew, it bit deep into Charles's bones. He knew better than to complain. To the natives, the cold meant skating, snowmobiling, and hockey.

After ten houses, he estimated they had only worked down half the road. Fortunately, Marinere was the lone street here. It ran straight toward Kousaboo Lake before making a hard right following the water's edge for a few homes before ending in a cul-de-sac.

Charles stood back from each door, allowing his friends to get their candy and compliments on their costumes. He felt like a parent. Indeed, many of the elderly residents gave him knowing winks and nods as if he were in on the joke.

"Hey, Charlie, come here! Ms. Cardona wants to meet you!"

Charles approached the house reluctantly.

Frank spoke up, "Ms. Cardona, can you give Charlie a costume so he can join us? We just need a sheet, and we'll cut some eyeholes. Please!"

The old woman adjusted her thick bifocals to get a better view of the newcomer.

"Hmm, Charlie is it?" she asked.

"Charles, if you please."

He felt compelled to assert his name. He was starting to feel like a kid again in these strange circumstances. He refused to give in.

"You look cold, Charles. Why don't you come in."

The others parted. He had no choice but to walk up the steps to the front door. He could feel the warmth spilling from her house.

Ms. Cardona smiled kindly, a geriatric tremble in her top lip. Up close, she had the look of a warmhearted grandmother. Every one of her wrinkles and laugh lines were benign marks of a good life well lived.

"So, do you want a costume so you can join your friends, Charles?" the old woman asked.

Charles stopped breathing, seized with an inexplicable dread. His stomach soured, knees tingled, and blood thrummed loudly in his head. He could feel the heavy eyes of everyone on him, waiting for an answer. A part of him wanted to say yes, to lose himself under a ghostly sheet and join the carefree group. After all, he had relocated here determined to fit in. Every place had its customs, and surely, this was a most harmless one.

Or was it? Charles dizzied and his vision tunneled to the face of the old woman. He considered her wrinkles, yellow dentures, and snarls of white hair as props hiding something else underneath—some deep secret. Inexplicably, he felt this to be the most important question he had ever been asked, as if his destiny and very self depended on the answer.

"No, ma'am, I don't want to," he finally said.

Behind him rose a disappointed groan.

"Wrong choice, Chuck!"

"I told you he was no fun, eh."

"C'mon, there's still houses. Let's just ditch him."

The men ran down the street without him to the next house. Charles felt abandoned yet a weight was lifted off his shoulders. He caught his breath as his vision and balance returned. He felt silly for being so scared. There was nothing sinister here. This was only a lonely, old woman taking part in a bizarre, yet harmless ritual—the town letting off some steam before the long winter.

She pushed her basket of candy into his belly.

"Here. Answer the door if anyone knocks. And don't take any, Charles—they're not for you."

He had little choice but to take it. The chocolate bars that filled the black wicker basket were the large size like they used to give out when he was a kid. He would do as she asked and wouldn't take any. The candy wasn't particularly tempting to him anyway: he had lost his sweet tooth at some point over the years.

Ms. Cardona disappeared into another room as there came an obnoxious knocking. Charles opened the door and handed out candy to a group of giggling men. They barely acknowledged him as he dropped a chocolate bar into each of their half-filled bags.

No one else coming up the walkway, Charles shut the door glad seal off the cold. Finding himself alone, he examined the room. It reminded him of his grandmother's old home: drab colors, wainscoting, dust, and heavy floral drapes. There were figurines and sepia toned pictures clustered on every table and sill, remembrances collected over a lifetime. Many of the pictures were of skating. Charles assumed they had been taken on Kousaboo Lake. He looked closer trying to spot Ms. Cardona in her youth, rewinding her features for a match. He found a young woman with fair, reddish hair wearing a pair of thin rim glasses. However, he couldn't be sure if it was her.

"Excuse me, Charles."

She startled him, quietly sneaking up from behind. He wondered how long she had been watching him. However, she made no mention of his interest in her past handing him a heavy knee-length coat.

"Here, it was Mr. Cardona's. You take it. He won't be needing it anymore, God rest his soul. And you'll be joining him there if you continue to dress like that in these parts."

Charles mumbled a simultaneous sorry and thank you. The navy-blue coat was large enough that he put it over his own. Its thickness and the layering would keep him warm.

"Good, it fits you well. But take it off and join me for a cup of tea. Let's see if we can get some color back in those cheeks."

In no hurry to go back outside, Charles sat at the kitchen table while his host fussed over an electric stove. There came another knock at the door. Ms. Cardona hurried back into the front room to hand out candy to yet another party of tittering men. The old style kettle began to whistle and then scream. Charles made no effort to silence it. He didn't want to intrude here.

The old woman returned and took it off the heat.

"So, your first Halloween in Mersault. It's a lot to take in I suppose," she said while deftly preparing two cups.

Charles chuckled, "Do they really do this every year?"

"Oh, they're good boys. It's all good-natured fun. Truth is we don't get many visitors here. We enjoy it. It keeps us young in a way."

Charles felt guilty. He hadn't considered that this Halloween custom might be community outreach. The residents here were all long retired. With no job to provide structure or to be valued by the community, they must be especially lonely in this remote corner of town.

Charles engaged her in some airy conversation over the apple-scented tea. Ms. Cardona had served as the town's second grade teacher for many years. She had a funny story for each of the men with whom Charles had arrived. Surprisingly, he enjoyed her anecdotes. Despite the age difference, she was easy to talk to.

"Well, sounds like they were a lot to handle. Must have been tough given it had to be such an abnormally large class," he said.

"Large class? Why would you say that?"

"Oh, I just assumed. Seems like they're all the same age…at least they look to be," Charles said suddenly unsure.

"Well, time moves differently here." Ms. Cardona smiled and winked over her glasses.

Charles considered she could be right. There was much less stress here. The small-town living probably took ten years off everyone's appearance.

Rising from her seat with a crackle of joints, she cleared the two emptied teacups. Charles stood as well. Unfortunately, it was time to rejoin his so-called friends. He realized that no one had come to the door in a while. Hopefully, the men had made it to the end of the L-shaped street and were ready to return home.

He stepped back into the front room to put on his newly bequeathed coat. The tea having cleared his sinuses, he could smell the scent of cologne that clung to it. He didn't recognize the musky blend. He couldn't decide whether he liked it or not.

"Thanks for the tea, ma'am. I'll be heading out. Are you sure I can take the coat? I can drop it back off when we're ready to leave."

There was no answer. Ms. Cardona reemerged from a side hallway pulling on a pair of heavy mittens. She wore a heavy overcoat of her own.

"Nonsense, Charles, you keep the coat. You'll need it for the walk home. It's a long way around the lake."

Charles didn't know how to answer. Did she think his friends were going to ditch him because he wouldn't wear the stupid costume? However, she cut him off before he could protest.

"Come. Follow me."

She led him out of the house not bothering to lock the door. It made Charles feel good that there were still places in the world like this. It reminded him of the tightknit community where he grew up. It was one of the things he missed from his childhood. Maybe he had made the right choice moving up here after all.

The wind blew down from the north. It smelled clean, a fresh scent. There were no other cities or towns beyond Mersault, only untouched woods and snowcapped mountains.

Charles was led down the street towards the lake. Doors from the other homes opened, the elderly residents of Marinere Street joining them on the downhill march. Charles could hear the adolescent braggadocio and playful taunts of his friends ahead. However, they sounded far away, a trick of the wind.

Despite the abundance of streetlight, the fog hid Kousaboo Lake. It was here that Ms. Cardona steered him, taking a worn path between two houses that led to a weathered dock. He couldn't see how long it stretched, the end swallowed in the heavy fog. A number of hunched residents had already gathered at the shoreline. They seemed in high spirits despite the cold.

The trick-or-treaters were nowhere to be seen. However, their voices could still be heard past the jetty. Somehow, they were somewhere out on Kousaboo Lake. When the wind gusted hard enough to displace the fog, Charles caught a glimpse of the children on top of the ice. Through the billowing mist he watched the silhouettes, bulging bags in hand, triumphantly walking back home in their shortcut across the lake.

The wind stopped and he lost sight of the children in the reforming fog.

But there were no children here. Despite the immature behavior, they were men. The town's barber, butcher, high school principal, and mayor were out there on the thin ice. Charles squinted through the swirling fog. Another blast of wind revealed the trick-or-treaters again, this time as adults. They were a terrible sight, the men flailing in the icy water having broken through the thin ice. In stunned horror, Charles helplessly watched the panicked thrashing and suffered the frantic, mortal screams.

Charles wanted to cry out for help. However, when he turned to those gathered with him, they were calm. The elderly men and women exhibited such a lack of alarm that he second-guessed what he had seen. Hoping that the horror he witnessed may be a trick of the illusive fog, he scanned the lake again. However, the wind didn't gust hard enough and he could only catch brief, muddled hints of boys and men, diced laughter and screams. It was as if two distant radio stations overlapped, their disparate programming creating an unintelligible mess.

A hand stroked Charles's shoulder. A soft voice whispered close to his ear, "You could have joined them, but you didn't. This is our Halloween, the same every year. You'd be good to run home now, Charles. It's a long walk around the lake and it gets even colder after midnight."

He felt ill, the acute dread returning. He needed to be away from this place and its recurring tragic memory. He vowed that by first light he would be far away from Mersault never to return.

However, something kept him from running. He turned to Ms. Cardona, although the fog was so thick he couldn't see her.

"Why?"

Charles wasn't sure that that was even the right question. He especially wasn't sure if he wanted the answer.

"It's like I said, Charles…"

The old woman paused as if waiting for the next gust.

"…they keep us young."

A sudden, scentless wind plucked the words off her lips. Strands of auburn hair whipped across an easy, white smile, the streetlights dancing off her wire rim glasses. The smiling, merry neighbors circled around, standing tall and basking in the memories of the past.

The wind stilled and the fog resettled, shrouding everything once again.

Her hand slid down to the small of his back. She leaned against him, pressing her cheek to the lapel of his coat. Breathing deeply, she inhaled the musky fragrance trapped in the rough fibers. Charles could smell it too, and he sensed the memories it triggered. He decided he preferred the heavy scent, if for no other reason than because he knew she liked it.

"So what will you do, Charles?"

She pulled her cheek away from his chest although her arms were still wrapped around him. Charles realized that somehow his arms were around her too. He knew what he wanted and why he came here. He leaned in kissing her deeply. A weight was lifted off his shoulders.

He wouldn't be walking the long way home tonight. There was nowhere he would rather be than in this quiet, empty place. He realized that he hadn't moved all the way here for adventure, but for the lack of it. He cast off the anxiety of the present and the uncertainty of the future for those set, frozen memories of the past.

He would get used to them.

The residents of Marinere Street welcomed him in. Charles felt at peace with no regrets. He loved it here and it was time to stop running. He wasn't a kid anymore, and at some point over the years, he had lost his sweet tooth.

UNSEELIE THINGS
by Taylor Foreman-Niko

I.

One day, when he was a boy, he fired his BB gun at a wisp of reflected light in the garden of his family's estate. And it screamed.

Being a boy of six, he still possessed a childish need for wanton violence; his was a summer of stomping ants, de-winging butterflies, and ripping up anything green and good. He would come home, slathered in the detritus of his passing, and his parents would laugh and ruffle his hair and send him on his way.

The maid would strip him, bathe him, and pinch his nose. She smelled of flowers and when she neared he wanted to grab her white throat and see if she too would rip in his hands.

When, on his August birthday, he received a shiny black BB gun, he was elated. Yet on the estate, far from town, trips to market by the help occurred only once weekly and so, in his youthful exuberance, he was spent of BBs within a day. He did not cry nor moan when he found his bag empty, for he'd already shot a fair game, striking a robin from a tree and winging a passing hare. He had followed a trail of its trickled blood, wiped on bladed grass, to the forest at the edge of the estate before growing tired and retreating.

There would always be more hares.

When he reached home, he was faced with a dilemma: suffer an interminable four days without using his new toy or finding some other way to satiate his red desires.

The idea came to him as he passed Maddie, the maid, and the other servants eating in the parlor. Unlike the polished silver that he and his family slipped into their mouths, the servants' implements were thin, dark, crooked things that looked as likely to cut your tongue as they were to pierce or scoop food upon a plate. As they dispersed and Maddie began cleaning, he tip-toed past their table and sequestered two forks into the linen of his sleeve.

Next came the shears. Those he took from the garden shed as Wallace the Groundskeeper dozed. Wallace slept often and when he was awake, he appeared as if he should be sleeping, eyes red and face puffy. He smelled foul and the boy avoided him whenever possible.

The rest of supplies he came by easily enough and soon he was ready. Upstairs in his room, the boy reviewed his bounty: a pair of large sheers, two iron forks, a candle, a stack of cloth napkins, and a box of matches. He lit the candle with a match, gleeful at the spark and spit of fire as he dragged it across the sandpaper. Then he warmed a fork handle over the candle's flame. He held it there for a while, until the candle wax began to run, but the iron fork looked sadly unaffected. He daren't touch it, for fear of burning himself, but perhaps it was enough. He placed it carefully upon the stack of cloth napkins and grabbed the cutters. Using a cautious hand he placed the heated fork handle in between the shears' blades. Then he stepped back and put all his weight into squeezing the shears' handles. The blades sank into the fork, then snapped together and a piece of iron went skipping into the corner. Joy entered his chubby face and soon his pouch was refilled.

Which brings us to that day in the garden, where he shot a jagged bit of iron at a passing glare. A trick of the eye, surely, at which he fired for no particular reason. Surprisingly, the wisp let out a shrill cry and fell into the tall grass. Confused, the boy shouldered his rifle and walked to the source of the sound. A metallic liquid, like mercury, but lighter and more luminous, marked the grass where he'd seen the glare disappear and looking down—

He stumbled back, the BB gun clattering to the grass beside him. There on the ground lay a tiny woman, no bigger than one of his lead soldiers; she was long-limbed, pale of skin, and fair-faced. Her beauty was only marred by the metallic divot driven between her tiny, pink breasts. The shiny liquid seeped from there, dripping down her side. The boy watched as it spilled from her entirely and sank into the waiting earth.

A flower burst into life beneath it, pushing the body aside and rising above the grass, unfurling into a full, beautiful bloom. The boy stepped forward, eyes stinging with tears at the beauty he beheld. He placed his face into the odd folds of the flower's petals and inhaled.

It smelled like Maddie.

He smiled, then ripped it from the ground and walked back to his home. Later, when his mother asked him where he'd found so magnificent a Caladenia this late in the year, he told her he'd grown it himself.

II.

When he was a man and his parents were long in the ground and his darling Maddie was far from him, he became a horticulturist of much renown. With his vast inheritance, he moved to the city soon after the funeral and bought a charming home on the edge of town. It was situated in a nice neighborhood that was composed of respectable people and utterly intolerant of transients and foreigners.

He had chosen this particular flat because of its sizable garden and in this garden he had commissioned the construction of a greenhouse in the current style, but made of steel instead of iron. He was very particular on this point, so much so that he grew a reputation as an exacting, excitable client among the city's artisans. Fortunately for him, he was not frugal with his money and had a tongue that would have shamed the devil in its sharpness. After a few weeks of meetings, he chose an architect and the project began.

He said he wanted a structure to rival The Crystal Palace or perhaps even the majesty of the Glaspalast that he had seen with his parents on one of their trips to Munich. He would sit on his long chaise lounge in his parlor, as his poor, hunched architect showed him sketch after sketch of potential greenhouses. Hundreds were presented to him, yet each was imperfect in some small way: the ridge was too low, the roof spars too simple, the eaves inelegant. Then one caught his eye and stilled his tongue. He was so stricken by the brilliant simplicity of its form and the subtle splendor of its make that he knew he must have it.

And three months later, he did.

III.

He started with lettuce and basil, then moved onto eggplants and peppers. Simple, edible things, requiring little skill to grow. Yet he delighted when he cooked, popping herb-sprinkled pasta into his mouth or sinking his teeth into the flesh of a cooked summer squash. He had made something, consumed it and, in doing so, had transferred its essence into him as something new, transformed.

Within a year, he had moved on from edibles to flowers. First generalities: roses, tulips, the odd lilac here and there. Then to rarer fare: a star-faced flower from the windswept faces of the Himalayas, blue as a mountain stream; a vine of claw-shaped green petals, looking like chips of jade hanging in an upside-down bouquet; a trio of orchids that smelled of vanilla, their petals a rich, dark brown.

The crown jewel of his collection sat at the end of the greenhouse, in a pot upon a simple stand: an orchid from savage Africa, transported to the homeland with greatest care. No one quite knew what made it bloom, so though it sat amongst the great wealth of his collection, wilted and sad, its true beauty lay in its potential.

Sometimes he would sit in his greenhouse and bask in the achievement of his works, weeping at their insurmountable loveliness. It was almost too much for his heart to bear. But he knew that their perfection would fade with the seasons and leave him to languish in ugliness until they bloomed again.

That was something he could not abide.

IV.

The first one was more difficult than he had imagined.

He had bought the house with a specific purpose in mind. It sat at the quiet fringe of the city, flanked by the remnants of a once massive forest. On morning walks he saw them, looking like wisps of moisture, caught in the light between the trees. They called to him, stirring a primal need within. *Come. Come. Come.* He knew better.

The forests were dying. As the inexorable machine of industry marched across the countryside, the haunts of the forest folk grew ever smaller. Long had there been reports of mischief in the neighborhood: shoelaces tied together, car tires slashed, morning milk spilled across welcome mats. That he had a greenhouse filled with beautiful things, it was only a matter of time before he attracted attention.

The first came in the night: a squat, dusky-skinned fellow, with thick features and a stringy beard. He was clad in a filthy woolen coat and holey boots of leather. The man invited this imposter in without asking his name and together they shared a quiet meal of carrots, onions, and baked haddock. After supping, he gave the squat fellow (which he had surmised was a boggart in disguise) a tour of his home, ending in the greenhouse. The boggart was entranced by his collection of tended wonders.

"This one here," the man said, gesturing to a regal looking bloom sat upon a high shelf, "is from the Orient. Smell it. The aroma is quite pleasing." The boggart grunted and leaned over a planter to reach the bloom. The man withdrew an iron straight razor from his sleeve and drew it across the boggart's throat.

The boggart gave a sharp inhalation and panic spread across its ugly features, beady eyes glowing with malice. It pounced upon him and there in the greenhouse they struggled mightily, spraying luminous, mercurial blood across the floors and windows. The man struggled to keep the flailing thing from upending shelves and knocking over his potted plants. He winced as a rare Swedish carnation crashed to the floor, soil exploding across the tiles. It was only after he jabbed the boggart in the chest that its weight did sag.

After, he worked quickly. He tied a rope around the thing's ankles and lifted it onto a hook that he lowered from a pulley secured at the center of the greenhouse's roof. He hauled on the rope, lifting the limp weight of the boggart until its hands no longer dragged on the floor. Panting and dripping with sweat, he pushed a metallic tub beneath its still form and fell to the tiles, exhausted. Only then did he catch sight of one of the blood-speck-led planters. It was overgrown with flowers, so bright and vibrant that his breath caught in his throat. He laughed that such beauty had been so easily gained, then stood and retrieved his saw from within his garden's toolshed.

He cut off the boggart's head and hands to hasten the draining process, then retreated into his home for a cup of tea.

That year he won the Horticultural Society's highest honor.

V.

In time he learned that boggarts were easy. Dull, stupid creatures whose only drive was to satisfy their base desires: hunger, shelter, etc. Red Caps were infinitely more difficult to handle. Driven to starvation by the destruction of their castle homes in the country, they swept into the suburbs, appearing mostly as drug-addled young men with long fingernails and bloodshot eyes, wearing dirtied brown hats. He dined them upon raw meat and waited until they began choking on the bread that he'd hidden in the meat's center before accosting them with his straight razor. The first one broke his mother's china in its death throes, but he gained another pail of ambrosial blood.

Unfortunately, the elixir did not keep. Nor did the bodies. He had stashed the first boggart's body in his kitchen's spacious freezer, deter-mined to study the corpse in order to find other uses for it. In the morn-ing he had discovered only a pile of gelatinous entrails that sloughed into nothingness at his touch. The iced blood in the metal tub was likewise evaporated to a tacky reduction with no discernible application. He would have to make his horticultural endeavor a year round exercise.

And so he did.

VI.

He planted a thorn tree beside his house. He hung the door with posies, picked daily. Brambles and twigs adorned the edges of his front door. He allowed birds to roost in the eaves of his roof and kept the bits and pieces of animals that stray cats gifted him, displaying them proudly upon his porch where they moldered, revealing bone. Furniture hewn from Rowan wood (imported from far off Himalaya) filled his home: chairs, end tables, dressers, and armoires. His iron utensils were put in a drawer for safe keep-ing, replaced with copper ones he'd fashioned himself using a makeshift forge he'd constructed next to the greenhouse.

He saw neighbors only fleetingly and kept to himself. He kept the Neighborhood Council at bay through generous donations, delivered monthly, that allowed them to erect a gate and repave the road among other things. Though passersby gave him furtive glances of judgment, he knew they took part in his great wealth and their hypocrisy he found humorous. He had become something of a neighborhood eccentric and that pleased him. His strangeness made him distinct in a colorless world: he was not them and they could not fathom his work. He had his garden and in that he was fulfilled.

VII.

Brownies came to him in the night disguised as children looking for work. He twisted their heads off and watered his rhododendrons with their blood. Next, a water hag in a rainstorm, looking like a shriveled grandmother. He parted the hanging, turkey folds of her gray neck and held her over his planter while she gargled and kicked.

His hoard of wonders grew. Stalks lengthened and bushels engorged, bearing fat fruit that gleamed, moist and ever-ripe. Squash the size of newborn sews lined the tiled floor, alongside pumpkins as large as elephant heads, heart-sized tomatoes, and cucumbers bigger than his arm. The flowers unfurled, unnatural in their size, their smell potent, and heady; so fresh it made him dizzy.

The Horticultural Society's judges reveled in the results of his work each year, thinking him a deific green thumb. They asked him what his secret was.

He said to divulge such things would be, "unseemly."

VIII.

Yet despite his success and the collection of silver plates and golden plaques that climbed up the shelves of his study, he was unsatisfied. For at the end of his greenhouse, nestled between the teeming petals and thick stalks, sat the orchid from the deep-dark of savage Africa. Where other flowers had taken a drop of fairy blood to burst into life, the whole of a boggart's lifeblood had done nothing to coax it into bloom. It sat, as ever, withered and wilted, pale and bruised as dead flesh.

IX.

The years passed and his body began to sag and weaken until one night, as he looked down at a sprite that struggled beneath his weight, he was struck by an epiphany. He leaned down and bit her hard upon the neck. She snarled and bared her sharp teeth at him, but he was too strong and only grew stronger as his mouth filled with a warm, sweet milk. He sucked hard and she cried out. Her diaphanous shift tore beneath his groping hands and he was renewed.

X.

The world changed, yet he persisted. Young and strong in his solitude. The thorn tree now reached higher than the rooftop of his house and new neighbors had moved in around him, changing the neighborhood to fit their dull sensibilities one building at a time. They waved at him on occasion. Foreigners in foreign clothing. He watched them pass without acknowledgment. His work continued in secrecy and his garden flourished until

XI.

one night, she appeared at his doorstep. As with any night, he was prepared for company, dressed in an expensive suit (the Fay folk despise tawdriness). She was tall as he, slim-shouldered, and statuesque; slender in a powerful way that made him want to grab her and force himself against her flesh.

"Hello, Miss," he said. In the dim light of his porch lantern, his skin shone luminous and healthy. "Are you lost?"

"I am afraid so, Sir," she said, voice light and breathy; he imagined it was what the wind would sound like if given the power of speech.

He ushered her into the foyer and closed the door. She turned to him, now fully illumined, and his breath caught in his throat. He'd had sprites and pixies before (he enjoyed pinching their pale skin and watching it pink and redden beneath his prodding), but never like this. There was something immediately regal about her. High cheekbones, eyes the color of dark wood, hair an ebon black. She was pale and freckled, her nose rouged by the cold. She wore a dress of white fabric, dyed purple, tied at the waist by a belt made of reeds.

"You're cold," he said. He turned to the coat rack beside the door and grabbed one of his fur coats. He draped it about her shoulders and she thanked him, her enormous eyes tinged with curiosity and something else he could not discern. Her slender fingers twisted through the fur, caressing it. "Let's warm you up."

They sipped at bowls of steaming, fire-red soup in the dining room, separated by a table of polished oak and warmed by the fireplace set into the wall beside it. A line of candles burned low between them, their bases beset with brambles, herbs, and twigs. Bowls of fruit were scattered across the table, alongside a cooked pheasant.

He watched her as she ate. He had elected to forgo poisoning her with bread and had sequestered his iron utensils even farther into the freezer, save for an iron dagger that he kept within a copper sheathe tucked into the back of his waistband. His guest spooned the piping liquid into her mouth, slurping loudly; insatiable. He only hoped that she would be as enthusiastic later.

"This is delicious," she said, stretching each word; they sounded odd and unnatural upon her pale, purple tongue.

"Indeed. It is made from fresh tomatoes, from my garden."

Her eyes grew large and soup dribbled down her chin. She raised a hand to her face and wiped it away, laughing in embarrassment. The purity of the noise, like silver chimes, sent a thrill through him, warming him where the soup could not reach.

"You grow?"

"Yes," he tipped a glass of wine to his mouth. She mimicked him. When she lowered her glass, the wine stained her colorless lips, wetting them the color of blood. He ached.

"Would you like to see?" he said.

"Yes, but why not delay for a moment, I wish to eat more before the merrymaking."

He nodded to her, nearly staggered by her forwardness, unable to stop the grin that spread upon his face. Yet caution burned low in the back of his mind. There was something cruel and predatory in her coal-black eyes. Was it lust or—

He reached forward and grabbed a stick of cinnamon that stuck from the brambles adorning the base of the candles at the center of the table. He crushed it in his palm and lowered his head slightly, letting the aroma fill his nostrils and clear his mind. He looked up.

She had finished the soup and now sat hunched over a bowl of grapes, splitting each in half with her teeth rather than placing them whole into her mouth. She bit and the juices splashed down her chin, trailing down her slender neck, and between the fullness of her breasts.

"Have you lived here long?" she asked, still chewing. Her other arm scooped the plated pheasant towards her. She dropped the bowl of grapes and began dismembering the bird. A wing came off in one hand and she snapped it with ease, suckling greedily at the marrow within its knobbed end.

"A span of years," he said, attempting to conceal the desire that burned in his chest. Blood pounded in his head as he envisioned the violent ravishments he would visit upon her. "And hopefully some years more."

"You are still in your prime," she said, her eyes meeting his, a strip of charred skin slinking up into her mouth. "Made smooth as river stone."

"I am young still," he said. She looked at him as she crunched a leg bone between her perfect teeth. She did not blink. "And what purpose brought you to my doorstep this night?" he said, the words coming unbidden. He never asked of their purposes. He much preferred the music of their muffled screams to the awkward stilting speech that plagued most of the Fay.

Yet she was different.

"I have been on a long journey, Sir, from Court to Court in search of knowledge about a fell thing."

"Indeed? And have you come to your journey's end?"

Her tongue darted out, roving around her full lips.

"Nearly."

Nearly, a voice whispered in his mind. *Come.*

He could not contain himself any longer. He stood and walked across the room. He stopped beside her. She looked up, her chin slick with grease.

"Come with me. Please. I must show you the garden," he said, struggling to keep the dire need from his voice.

She nodded once and dropped the remains of the cooked pheasant to the table and stood, wiping her face and hands upon her dress. So pure were her actions, unburdened by formality or propriety. He would take her upon the tiled floor and fill his mouth with the taste of her.

Her hand grasped his lightly and burned like someone with fever. He wanted to share in her warmth. He led her to the greenhouse. He reached forward and opened the glass door, looking back at her, watching for the revelatory moment.

The light of the greenhouse bathed her face and lit it with dismay. They entered and she looked about, tears springing into her enormous eyes, her mouth falling open. He loved that mouth already, loved the possibility that existed within there.

She walked into the center of the greenhouse and stood in silence. The flowers seemed to shift towards her as if they looked upon the sun, but he didn't care. She was a sun in her own right; a star, luminous, and fiery. Tonight at least, she would be the center of his solar system. She turned towards him and there was fire in her eyes and he knew.

He swept forward and took her in his arms, pressing his mouth to hers and ripping the fur coat from her shoulders; she met him in his violence. She seized him by the hair and sank her teeth into his lower lip and crushed her face to his. Their bodies writhed together, questing, hungry.

And then she pulled back and looked him in the eyes. Tears stained her face, wetness streamed from her nose, her black hair tousled and wild. His hand reached back, fingers settling about the wrapped-leather handled of his iron dagger.

"Which one is your favorite?" she whispered, sounding like a girl in her curiosity, inflaming him further. "Show me." *Show me.*

He stepped back from her, one hand still pressed to the small of her back. Part of him screamed within his mind, but he did not know what for. Her puffy eyes stared at him, waiting, expectant. He could not displease those eyes. His head turned and his gaze found the blue face of the Himalayan flower.

He reached towards it with his free hand, stooping towards the pot in which it was planted. And then there was a weight upon the back of his neck and confusion in his eyes.

Pain. White hot and flaring, it struck across his throat and he stumbled, looking up to see the woman, holding his knife. It fizzled and whined in her hand, but she did not drop it. In his tear-blurred eyes a crown of bone and berries swam into being upon her head, but she seized his neck and forced him to stand, obscuring his view of her, spinning him around in a parody of a lover's embrace, spraying his blood about his life's work just as he'd done with the blood of her people. And as his eyes grew heavy and he slunk to the floor her visage did change as well as her form; her breasts shrank into her torso, her hips narrowed, her face grew young and masculine. The dress lengthened and tightened into a suit.

As his world darkened, it was as if he looked up at a mirror, that strange face that was his and not his, marred by both pleasure and pain.

Is this what I had wrought all those long years?

The words passed through his mind just as his heart pumped once more and consciousness fled from him and all was dark.

XII.

The morning after, the judges for the Horticultural Society appeared at the house's doorstep. When the head judge went to knock, the door swung open. The host greeted them at the door and led them to the greenhouse. There the judges screamed and screamed and died.

When the police investigated the premises due to a noise complaint, they found the bodies of the house's owner as well as the Horticultural judges spilled open upon the tiles of the greenhouse amid a deafening cloud of flies. Their fluids had painted the walls and coated the plants, spoiling the vegetables, drowning the fruits, and choking the priceless, rare flowers.

Yet at the end of the greenhouse, nestled amongst the fetid, dead plants and bubbling egg sacs, stood a single pedestal upon which sat a lone pot. Within its blood-soaked soil, an orchid from darkest Africa stood, unfurled and perfect.

✗

THE VENERATION OF EVIL IN THE KINGDOM OF ANCIENT LIES

by John R. Fultz

A poet's life was never easy, but occasionally it offered certain unique benefits. For instance, one never knew when he might be whisked away on a flying carpet to sip wine on a wizard's veranda. In the back of his mind Magtone was already composing a sonnet to mark this spectacular day. The wind whipped at his braids as evening stars winked to life.

The carpet had arrived at a particularly expedient moment. Magtone was fleeing three mailed guardsmen after filching six coins from the pocket of a silk merchant. The fool's loss was his own fault; he sold sub-par merchandise at outrageous prices. Yet the constables had not agreed with Magtone's justification. They threatened him with broad-bladed swords. Magtone did the only thing a clever poet could do in such a circumstance.

He ran.

Hoping to lose his pursuers in the Spider's Den, he raced up the spiral stairwell that connected its four floors. The swordsmen followed him, cursing and knocking drunk patrons out of the way, never even pausing to gape at the dancing girls. Along the high outer balcony Magtone leaped on a table and grabbed the eaves of the building's roof. He was pulling himself over the cornice when the guardsmen burst through the crowd on the balcony. He would have fallen to his death when a roof tile came loose in his hand, but instead of plummeting into the mud-spackled alley below, he landed on the flying carpet. Soft as a cloud it raced across the city while Magtone looked back and laughed at the sword-waving guardsmen. He shook a crimson handkerchief at them and settled into a cross-legged position for the ride. The trip had been arranged hours earlier, so he knew exactly where it was taking him.

Karakutas lay inside the bowl of an extinct volcano, a collection of stone towers, sculpted terraces, and ripe orchards. For three thousand years the city stood impershable, thanks to the Thirty-Seven Adepts of Zukario. Only once had a foreign power attempted to invade Karakutas—the mighty Aeolic Host was destroyed in less than a day by the power of the Adepts.

The wizards were immortal by virtue of their odd sorceries, and there was no city in the world that could match the ancient grandeur of Karakutas, not even Odaza, City of Walking Gods. Even Great Odaza was only half as old as Karakutas, and still half as populated. It lay far across the world, connected to Karakutas only by lengthy and precarious trading routes. The gods of Odaza might still walk in the daylight, but they seldom left that holy city, and they never dared to confront the Thirty-Seven Adepts of Zukario.

Ogmandolin was one of those Adepts—the one who had invited Magtone to his palace. Magtone had no idea why, but his mind boggled at the possibilities. Here was opportunity the likes of which most men never saw in their entire lives.

After the carpet ride he sat among trellised vines ripe with clusters of grapes, staring across the green bowl of the city. Eight central precincts lay in the center of the volcanic basin, but its verdant slopes were dominated by the great estates of the Adepts. Thirty-Seven palatial abodes, walled and gated, adorned with basalt gargoyles and angels of green marble. The only edifice to rival the splendor of these estates was the golden pyramid of the Royal Palace at the city's heart. Yet even the King and Queen of Karakutas bowed to the wizards who preserved their kingdom.

Magtone considered the mansion at his back while his eyes scanned the cityscape. What glories, what treasures—what horrid secrets—lay within the House of Ogmandolin? What precious trinkets might a nimble-fingered poet find to drop in the pockets of his waistcoat? The carpet had delivered him to this high veranda, but he would have to find a good reason for the wizard to invite him inside. It would be impossible to rob Ogmandolin from out here among the grapevines.

"Enjoying the wine?"

The voice was old but not tired, deep and resonant with restrained power. Magtone turned to face his host and bowed from the waist. Ogmandolin was tall and his limbs were draped in yellow and purple silks. A rainbow of exquisite stones glittered on his fingers. At his neck a chain of blue diamonds caught the sunset's flame and threw it into the poet's eyes. The wizard's beard was silver-grey and he was meticulously groomed. Ogmandolin might pass for a middle-aged nobleman if he visited the king's palace, but that was something he never did. Occasionally the king would visit the Adepts, but the Adepts did not visit the king.

"My Lord, your hospitality is overwhelming," Magtone said. "As is the quality of this fine vintage." He sniffed at the cup he had nursed while waiting. "Springtime and elderberries...from your own vineyard?"

"Where else?" said the wizard, and his smile was a charming mask. "Thank you for coming." He took a cup from the veranda table and sat himself in one of the cushioned chairs. With a second bow and a practiced flourish, Magtone joined him. The chair was soft, but not half as soft as the flying carpet. Already he missed the thrill of it. He stared again across the great bowl of Karakutas.

"Quite a view you have here, My Lord," Magtone said.

"Please, call me Og," said the Adept.

"As you wish Lor—Og." They shared a drink and a moment of contemplation, admiring the sunset. Graystone towers took on the scarlet hues of dusk. People looked like ants scurrying through the maze of alleys, streets, and plazas.

"I must confess," said Magtone, "I was astonished to recieve your invitation."

"Most men would be," said Ogmandolin. His deepset eyes scanned the city as if its secrets were revealing themselves to him. Perhaps they were.

"You wonder why an Adept would even take notice of a starveling poet," said the wizard. "Or why he would summon a man widely known for his acts of larceny."

"On the contrary, Lord. I have never—"

Ogmandolin stopped him with a raised index finger. "Please. No use lying to me. I know who you are, and I know what you are."

Magtone drained the last of his wine and immediately wished for another cup.

"You…you've read my work then?" he asked.

The wizard grimaced. His eyes turned from the darkening city to Magtone. His face lowered as he met his guest's eyes.

"I have indeed," Ogmandolin said. "I was greatly impressed by it. The quality of your imagination, your skill at word and phrase…these are the reasons you are here today."

Magtone's eyebrows lifted. "Do you wish to become my patron?" This could be the luckiest day of his life.

"Of a sort," said Ogmandolin. "I need your skills. I need you to be my hands in chronicling the details and justifications for what is to come."

"Ah, you wish me to write your biography…" Magtone smiled. He could charge a fortune for such a work. It would set him up for years.

"No," said Ogmandolin. "This work will be a historical record."

"Historical? Pardon me, Lord Og, but…a record of what exactly?"

"The end," said the wizard.

"The end of what?"

The wizard waved his hands to indicate the twilight city.

"All of this," said the Adpet. "You must record the Fall of Karakutas."

Magtone's stomach churned.

"Are you serious, Lord?"

The wizard cocked his head. "I am always serious. All of this is coming to an end, Karakutas and its ancient lies are about to perish. However, it is essential that future generations have a factual record of how and why this occurred. That's where you come in. You will be greatly rewarded for this service, beginning first and foremost with your escape from the coming destruction."

Magtone's cup had somehow refilled itself at a wave of the wizard's hand. He drained most of it in a single gulp. Some went down the wrong way and he coughed. He wiped his lips with the back of his hand.

"Before I give you my answer," Magtone said, "tell me this: Karakutas is the mightiest city-state in all of history. What could possibly destroy it?"

"I can," said Ogmandolin. "I will destroy it myself. All of it."

Magtone swallowed. "But the Adepts have always protected the city."

"The Adepts built the city," the wizard said, "and we have sheltered it from outsiders. But who is there to protect Karakutas from what has become of Zukario's Disciples? No one." He sighed. "No one but me."

"I don't quite understand, Lord," said the poet.

"No one does," said the wizard. "Not yet. Your chronicle will make the outside world understand. This will be your greatest achievement, a tale that will spread across the entirety of creation when this city is dust. A legend kept alive for eternity by the words you'll write at my insistence."

Magtone took a deep breath. He had little choice. The wizard could be entirely mad, out of his head with prophecies of doom. Yet he could easily murder Magtone with some dreadful spell if the offer was declined. Mad or not, Ogmandolin was exceedingly rich. The rewards to be gained from this arrangement were very real. A poet must learn to make the best of every bad situation, a talent at which Magtone excelled.

"Although it fills me with dread and awe," Magtone said. "I accept your commission."

Ogmandolin nodded, as if he'd already known how Magtone would answer.

"Of course you do. I have prepared parchment and quills for you. Shall we go inside?"

Magtone smiled. If Karakutas was truly doomed, who was he to prevent it? This was his lucky break. Crisis always breeds opportunity.

He followed the Adept through corridors lined with tasteful treasures.

* * * *

The wizard's laboratory was messy but comfortable. Ogmandolin had arranged a table of dark wood and a pair of padded chairs. On the table lay a stack of blank parchments surrounded by jars of ink and the finest peacock quills money could buy. Magtone held his composure as a smiling ghost girl brought him wine and a tray of flaky biscuits.

Ogmandolin lit a pipe while checking a few of the valves on his alchemic network of beakers, tubes, and electrochemical contraptions. Eventually he came to sit at the table, blowing purple smoke from his lips and nostrils. The smoke did not bother Magtone, but he did not like the other smells of the laboratory: the faint stench of invisible vapors wafting from glassworks to skylight. The place stank of sulfur, coppery blood, and unnameable things. Of course the Adept must be used to the stink, as the pig farmer gets used to the smell of pigshit. Magtone drank the potent wine and tried his best to ignore the reek of alchemy. There was also the faint scent of rotting paper, a product of the ancient library overstuffing the room's many shelves.

"Are you ready?" the wizard asked. The end of his pipe sat between clenched teeth.

Magtone drained his cup dry and held it up for the ghost wench to refill. She responded almost immediately. "Ready as I'll ever be," he said, flourishing a chromatic quill.

"Good. Now write down every word I say, exactly as I say it."

"Excuse me?" Magtone sat down his cup and his fingers almost snapped the delicate quill in half.

The wizard focused his ageless eyes.

"I said write down every word I say, exactly as I say it."

Magtone put down the quill. He pressed the tips of his fingers together and propped his elbows on the armrests of his chair.

"I'm sorry, Lord Og," he said, "but I am not a ghost maiden."

"What do you mean?"

"If I am here only to transcribe your every word, then you could easily have one of your tray-toting spirits do the job. Or better yet: Take up the quill and write your own memoir. You don't need a poet, Lord, you need a scribe."

The wizard stared across the table, chromatic fires dancing inside his pupils. Magtone feared for a moment that he had gone too far, but his casual posture disguised fear as arrogance. Finally, Ogmandolin smiled at him.

"I see," he said. "The great poet's ego supersedes all."

Magtone blinked and returned the Adept's grin.

"What do you propose?" Ogmandolin asked. He blew a cloud of smoke that coiled like a serpent about his gray head.

"Tell me everything in your accustomed manner," Magtone said. "And I will take notes. When you are finished, give me seven days to write the tale in suitable verse of my own style."

"Agreed. As long as you tell the truth and nothing else. No mingling your romantic fantasies into the narrative."

"I wouldn't dream of it," Magtone said.

He dipped a quill into the nearest inkpot and cleared his throat.

"Now then, My Lord. Tell me why you want to destroy the city."

For awhile Ogmandolin said nothing, wisps of smoke rising from his nostrils. Then he began to talk, and Magtone listened, making notations, jotting down important details as necessary. Once he had all the facts, knew the shape of the story, he would spin it into a masterwork that would enshrine his name in the librarium vaults of history. His legend would grow alongside that of doomed Karakutas.

Ogmandolin talked and smoked. The first thousand years of history was a Golden Age, he said. In that era Zukario lived among his disciples and fostered their magic. As their wisdom grew, so did the size of the city they had founded. Karakutas knew peace and prosperity in the shadow of Zukario's temple. That innocent age died when Zukario's long-postponed mortality finally caught up to him. Terrestrial life can only be extended for so long, even if you're the most powerful mage in history. After Zukario's funeral and the Sunless Year of mourning, the Thirty-Seven Adepts began to build their individual estates on the upper slopes of the bowl-city.

"When we abandoned the temple where we had lived for centuries learning Zukario's secrets, we abandoned ourselves. Once physically apart, we began to lose the cohesion of thought and action that defined us and made us invincible. Then came the Aeolic invasion, and we reunited to drive out the invaders. Then we created the Royal Family to take over the day-to-day ruling of the city, automatons to pose as each successive generation of the same lineage."

Magtone raised his quill.

"Are you telling me the king isn't human? That he's some kind of..."

"Machine, yes," Ogmandolin said. "As is the entire set of royals."

"From the very beginning?"

"Weren't you listening? Perhaps you should take more notes."

Magtone jotted down the impossible secret. The King of Karakutas was a magical automaton. The entire Royal Family were puppet-creations of the Adepts. The power of the Adepts wasn't there to back up the throne; the throne had been invented to serve the Adepts.

Magtone swallowed another cup of wine. Some secrets were worth more than jewels.

"Please, resume..." Magtone said.

Ogmandolin sighed and pulled the pipe stem out from between his teeth.

"Our restored unity did not last. Freed from the responsibility of ruling the city, we sank deeper into our own private obsessions and magical studies. The city thrived under its line of puppet-kings, and we stayed locked in our palaces, lost in the depths of supernatural curiosity. Walking the Path of Eternity into mysteries we could never abandon or deny…"

The Adept's hands spread wide to indicate the laboratory behind him. Somewhere a viscous fluid bubbled and steamed in the glassworks. A bolt of blue energy danced between a series of golden rods. The smell of sulfur and roses emerged from the lingering melange of odors. Ogmandolin explained how the end of the Second Age marked a series of wars and disasters that decimated the nations outside the realm of Karakutas. Yet the city founded on Zukario's wisdom endured.

"By this time factions had begun to form. The elementalists began it with their secret pact, soon exposed by the enchanters and their ethereal allies. The third faction to arise was not a discipline, but a cult. The Order of the Great Malignancy. Their powers expanded beyond all others when they received the blessing of the universal daemon, the One Beyond All, the sentient entropy that lurks behind space and time, forever gnawing away at biological existence. We should have banded together then, in that first decade of their corruption, and destroyed them all. Even the necromancers denounced their evil."

Ogmandolin grew silent and misty-eyed. He refilled his pipe's bowl with pinches from a vial of enchanted herbs. Magtone took a swift drink and re-dipped his quill.

"Why didn't you?" he asked. "Come together and confront this cult?"

Lord Og looked up, as if suddenly remembering Magtone was there. He blinked and his eyes glowed like amber flames. He exhaled a cloud of glittering smoke and gave his answer.

"We were fooled," he said. "The Order saved us all from a horde of deadly beasts spewing through a fissure between the worlds. But it was a lie. I learned a few years ago it was the Order themselves who had opened the fissure—so they could publicly seal it and claim to save the city. To justify their continued existence. This gambit converted even more Adepts to their ranks."

Ogmandolin described how the Order's practices were gradually absorbed into the daily life of Karakutas. The Order constructed new temples and shrines to the Great Malignancy in every part of the city. In less than a century their rituals and ceremonies, their red-handed priests, controlled the population. Monthly human sacrifices were now the norm, with each deluded victim marching gleefully to his or her death. The highest honor in the city was to have your heart carved out as a burnt offering for the One Beyond All.

Magtone's uncle had won the honor ten years ago. The party to celebrate his luck had been a grand affair, appropriately decadent and gloriously obscene. At the time even Magtone himself had envied the man. Everyone knew that wealth and prosperity came to the families of sacrifices. They were the Heroes of Karakutas, who died for the benefit of others. Men stood outside the temples every day begging to be the next victim. Despite prevailing beliefs, Magtone had not benefited in any way from his uncle's holy death. He was the only one of his brood still alive, yet his fortunes hadn't improved at all. No wealth, no prosperity. He still made his living with quick fingers and sharp ears, stealing what he needed to keep himself and his verse alive.

Now it occurred to him: Could this assignment, this chronicling of a mad wizard's confession and its inevitable rewards, be the delayed blessing from his uncle's sacrifice? If so, why had it taken ten years to materialize?

"The truth is that for five hundred years now the people of Karakutas have been giving up their lives for an unknown purpose," Lord Og said. He puffed on the pipe and closed his eyes.

"Sacrifices are meant to placate the One Beyond All," Magtone said. "To gain his favor. Blood magic to enrich the lives of the living. If you believe such things."

"Blood magic, yes," said Og. "But one that will only lead to ruin. A greater destruction than this world has ever seen."

"I'm afraid I don't follow, Lord."

"Then I'll put it simply: The Order is about to complete a centuries-long ritual that will tear open our universe, as well as several adjoining dimensions, letting the Great Malignancy come spilling through like an ocean of plagues. It is a timeless corrupter of realities, an cataract of suffering and evil. The carnivorous antithesis of biological life as a concept. It will infest all the flesh in this city, blending rotten bodies like pigments in a pot, all to create a massive and horrible form for itself in our world. Then it will begin to feed…"

Magtone rubbed his eyes.

"So the Order is going to destroy the city? I thought you were going to do that."

"You think too small," said Og. "Once the Order's god-beast is loosed it will consume Karakutas and swell to consume the continents, the oceans, and eventually the entire world. Perhaps our entire universe."

"Why would the Order want that?"

"They wish to become one with their timeless god. They believe it will be so."

"And will they?"

"What does it matter?" Og said. "The Great Malignancy still ends our world."

Magtone lay down the quill and rubbed his fingers. His wrist ached. He had been writing feverishly for quite some time.

"I understand now," he said. "You would destroy the city to save the world."

Ogmandolin smiled at him again. His eyes flashed like minature torches.

"You're a clever one," he said. "I knew I had chosen the right man for this job."

"Wait," Magtone said. "What about the people?"

"What people?"

"The people of Karakutas," Magtone said. "Surely at least some of them deserve to survive."

Ogmandolin shrugged. "Why?"

"Well, they're..." Magtone struggled to find the right words. "They're..."

"Innocent?"

"Yes! Innocent."

Lord Og laughed, and a silver flame shot from his right nostril.

"Perhaps it's true what they say. All poets are fools."

"Lord?"

"My boy, no one in this city is innocent. Every living being here is enmeshed in the matrix of the Order's long ritual. The cord it has used to strangle history must be cut. Yet the city's death will be the ultimate sacrifice. Do you see the poetic justice of it? The irony?"

Magtone considered it. "Yes I..." His mouth clamped shut. "No. It doesn't hold. What about the children? Surely they deserve to escape this doom?"

"You're not listening, Magtone." Og said. "Nobody escapes. They're already caught in the spell. Everyone here must die so the world outside can live. Everyone except you."

"Why me?"

"Because I hired you."

"Yes, but aren't I part of this spell-matrix too? I'm part of the city."

"Indeed. It has taken many great spells to unravel your fate from the grand skein that binds the rest of us together. But I've done it. You now stand outside of history so that you may observe and record it."

Magtone held his empty cup in the air, but the ghost wench did not return this time. He sat lost amid a rushing of thoughts, hand in the air for awhile. The wizard puffed quietly beside him. The skylight sparkled with stars.

This was either the ultimate heist—saving himself from cosmic destruction, or the ultimate crime—turning his back on a hundred thousand living souls. The iron-jawed soldiers and guardsmen with their penchant for public lynchings, the drug dealers and their gangs of throat-cutters, the wicked priests claiming lives in the name of grace, the harlots in their dens of iniquity, the public torture parlors where slaves endured torments beyond description, the sweat-stained laborers and dirt-fingered farmers, thousands more who kept the city alive every day.

Magtone's head swam with visions born of guilt and memory: Oblivious nobles in lizard-drawn carriages. The dank prison where he'd spent two years for offending a constable with a particularly vicious poem. The alley where his mother had died when he was six years old, stabbed and bleeding into the gutter as he watched. The graveyard with his father's engraved stone. His cousins, all of them dead before the age of twenty. Every woman or girl who had won his heart and then returned it. Maricia. Nayeli. *Angelita*. Every word he had written in every poem since the day he first set pen to paper, a waterfall of phrase and stanza.

It was all Karakutas. It would all survive in his masterwork.

"How long do we have?" he asked.

Ogmandolin consulted a scroll and checked a mystic chart on the wall. "One month and three days until the Great Malignancy arrives," he said. "Yet I will act pre-emptively. Karakutas must be annihilated well before that day comes."

"When will you do it, Lord?"

"As soon as your manuscript is finished," Og said.

"And...how? How will you do it?"

"I have contracted a legion of fire spirits deep within the earth," Og said. "When I pronounce a final incantation, they will re-ignite the extinct volcanic chambers beneath us. The resulting eruption will be more powerful than you can imagine. You must be far from here when I speak those final runes."

"I have one more thing to ask," Magtone said.

Ogmandolin tilted his head.

"Can I keep the flying carpet?"

The Adept removed his pipe and smiled. "Indeed. You'll need it."

Lord Og stood up and gathered his voluminous robes. "Now get to work. You have seven days to write it down and make it sing, or whatever it is your poetic soul demands. Remember your charge: Stick to the truth."

"Truth is the blood that flows in the veins of all poets," Magtone said.

"Is that right?" Og said. "I would have guessed it to be wine."

The Adept disappeared into the far shadows of his mansion. Eventually the ghost returned, bringing more wine and a tray of fruits, some piping-hot bread, and a pot of black tea. Magtone stared at the skylight for awhile. The stars shimmered beyond its panes, as if they were floating in some dark underwater void. On a fresh page he began to write, forgetting all about wine and tea.

The Fall of Karakutas would be his greatest epic. He wrote long into the night and well into the next day. Sometimes he passed out for an hour or two, rising only to gulp down tea and bread before returning to the parchment. This cycle of rabid creation repeated itself again and again. Sometimes Magtone paused to consult volumes of history, looking for precise details. Other times he meditated until the narrative reached full ripeness, and words spilled across the page like rain in springtime.

Ogmandolin tried to speak with him once or twice, but the spell of creativity prevented Magtone from hearing any more of the Adept's words. He was done listening now. The act of creation was his own ritual, his all-consuming act of magic. A spell that blended truth and beauty. A tale that spanned three thousand years and touched a billion souls living, dead, and not-yet-born. And so it went: Magtone wrote while the wizard waited.

* * * *

After six restless days and nights the work was done.

Magtone wrote the final line of the final verse, put down his quill, and lay back in his chair. His head spun with that peculiar vertigo he always endured after finishing a major piece. He kept the folio open so the freshly inked page could dry as he downed a sobering cup of tea. He staggered to the pile of books and blankets he had been using as a cot and lay himself down. The sleep that came then was deep and dark and dreamless.

The peace of sleepful oblivion was destroyed by a sudden crack of thunder. Magtone's eyes sprang open and his head throbbed with a pain born of weariness. Again the thunder roared, and the laboratory shook, glass implements falling from tables to shattered across the floor. Dust fell from cracks in the ceiling. Magtone forced himself to stand, wrapped a woolen blanket about his shoulders like a cloak, and staggered toward the writing table

Ogmandolin rushed into the room, his fine robes blackened and tattered. Strips of his flesh also hung in tatters, exposing his naked white bones. He dripped a trail of blood across the laboratory. Part of his skull-bone peeked out from beneath his ruddy left eye. His mouth was a grimace of agony, but a terrible inner strength made him snarl like a gladiator entering the pit.

"What's happening?" Magtone asked. Morning sun flowed bright and painful through the skylight. He'd only slept two or three hours since finishing his masterwork. He stood between the bleeding wizard and the completed manuscript, as if he would somehow guard it. In truth, he was wholly at the mercy of Ogmandolin's power. Lord Og opened his mouth to speak, but the wall behind him exploded. Bricks flew into tables heavy with glassworks, and slivers of glass filled the air like a driving rain. Og fell to the floor, blood spattering from his open wounds. Magtone leaped for the folio, sheltering the manuscript from the raining shards with his own body. The blanket and his distance from the glassworks saved him from any deep cuts. He closed the folio and clutched the unbound book to his chest. The wizard rose with his back to Magtone as three figures floated toward him through the smoke and dust. They were wrapped in white robes like shrouds, their faces scarred to obscenity by ritual mutilations, their eyes alive with dark light. Their mouths displayed teeth carved into points, and frog-like tongues quivered between their jaws. As one they raised their pale hands, fingers tipped by golden claws.

The Order had come for its greatest enemy.

Ogmandolin did not turn his head, but Magtone heard his words clearly.

"Run! Take the book and go!"

Spirals of radiant darkness flowed from the trio's claws. Ogmandolin raised his arms to ensnare the black energy, whipping it about himself like whirlwind and casting it back toward the assassins. They hung in the air spazming and twitching, captives of their own magics, at least for the moment.

Magtone's fascination broke and he ran toward the window. The carpet was already waiting for him. It rose to meet his feet as he leaped. His bottom hit the fabric as if he'd landed on a dense cloud. Once again thunder broke inside the mansion, filling the laboratory with chaos as Magtone shot through the open window. He looked back to see flames engulf the Adept's palace. Lord Og's laboratory was the heart of an inferno now.

The city awoke in its verdant bowl as the light of dawn filled the sky. The carpet had its own will, its own set of instructions from Ogmandolin. It glided above the high towers and the smoking streets, gaining speed as it raced toward the city's far edge. Beyond the rim of the volcanic wall, the sky gleamed bright blue: the color of freedom. Magtone's heart beat like a savage drum in his chest and his eyes welled with tears. This would be the last time he saw Karakutas. There was no telling what strange land the carpet might deliver him to—or what kind of life awaited him there. He reminded himself that any kind of life was preferable to death, and in that moment he truly believed it.

Yet he couldn't just abandon the city. He had to tell someone about the coming destruction, and this would be his only chance. He believed now that the city was doomed, that the Adepts had been corrupted by madness, but maybe he could save *somebody*. Even a handful of traveling companions would ease his terrible burden. Ogmandolin had insisted the entire population was tied into the matrix of the Order's apocalyptic spell. That might prove to be true, but could the wizard have lied? If Magtone carried one or two people away from the city before it died, would Ogmandolin or the Order ever know the difference? If Magtone didn't at least try, he would never be able to live with himself. He had to see Angelita. Now

If he could overpower the carpet to change its direction, maybe he could change something else. Maybe he could save Angelita and her two little girls. Take a family with him into the outside world. He mustered his willpower, clutched the folio tight in one arm, and pointed to where the Spider's Den stood above a maze of squalid streets. To his surprise the carpet immediately arced and sped downward. It was taking him where he wanted to go. Lord Og may have given it the command to get Magtone out of the city, but the carpet's rider had final command over its magic.

He looked back across Karakutas toward Ogmandolin's estate, but there was no sign of flames or the sorcerous battle waging there. A screen of illusion kept up the appearance that Og's palace was undisturbed. The city's high towers raced by Magtone on either side as the carpet brought him to the roof of the Spider's Den. He ordered it to wrap itself around the folio-book like a satchel, and hid it next to the building's chimney. Slipping over the side of the roof, he slid onto a balcony that was still completely empty this early in the day. He prowled about the exterior until he found Angelita's window, then used his curved dagger to pry open the latch.

She heard him coming through the window and rose from her bed, clutching a sheet to partially hide her naked body. Magtone put his feet on the floor and smiled. Her hair was long and dark with wild curls. A snoring soldier lay in the bed, exhausted from a night of romantic exertions. Angelita's kids always slept in the room down the hall when she was doing business.

She glared at Magtone with murder in her eyes.

Such beautiful eyes that he didn't mind.

"What are you doing here?" An angry whisper.

Magtone reached into his belt for an expensive jewel he had pocketed in the wizard's mansion. He offered it to her on his open palm. He said nothing until she accepted it, her teeth gritted at him. She might have torn open his throat with those teeth if she weren't trying to avoid waking the man on the bed.

"Get out of here, Mag!" she whispered. "I told you. It's over."

Magtone lost his smile. "Listen to me," he whispered. "We have to leave the city. The Adepts are going to destroy it. Well, one Adept actually...he's going to do it before the rest of them can. Everybody and everything here is going to die. Get your girls and come with me. It's your only chance."

"You've lost your mind," Angelita said. Her lover groaned and turned on his side, showing his hairy back. The man must have been very drunk, or he would surely have roused by now.

"I swear on my mother's own soul," Magtone said. "You have to trust me."

"Why?" she indulged him. He knew her look.

"I love you," he said. "You know this."

"Yes, you've written many poems about it. But you don't love me, Mag."

"Isn't this proof of it?" he said. His whisper rose into a harsh growl. "I'm trying to save you when I should be on my way to freedom. You don't have to believe that I love you, but you must believe me: Karakutas is about to die in a torrent of blood and fire. Or worse."

"How do you know all of this?"

"I've been working for Ogmandolin."

"You mean stealing from him?"

"Well, yes, but that's not the point. I've written the whole thing down. Come with me now and I'll tell you everything. Please…we have to go."

Angelita laughed, and the man on the bed woke up. He yawned and stretched, slowly taking note of the unwelcome visitor in the room.

"You really think I'd run off with you on a moment's notice?" Angelita's voice rose now. It took on that cutthroat quality that always preceded an act of violence. "Leave behind everything I've ever known? On the word of a broke-down poet with delusions of grandeur? Crawl back through that window right now and you won't get hurt."

"*Angelita…*"

She turned to the man on the bed. His corded muscles flexed as he threw back the covers. "Kill this fool," she said. The man reached for a sword lying next to the bed. An off-duty guardsman.

"If you stay here you will die," Magtone said. "So will your girls."

"No, you will," Angelita said. She wouldn't look at him anymore.

The naked brute bounded across the floor with blade gleaming. Magtone sidestepped the swing and slammed his elbow into the swordsman's jaw. The man staggered and blinked as Magtone leaped out the window. He didn't follow when Magtone climbed to the roof.

Retrieving his carpet, he was in the air again, wiping hot tears from his eyes and damning himself for a fool. He clutched the book to his chest and the carpet sped toward the city's edge. *At least I tried*, he told himself. The carpet flew above a market plaza where thousands of people engaged in the commerce of the day. Fruit and vegetable vendors pulled carts toward open booths, blacksmiths hammered at their forges, slaves carried buckets of water from public wells, and lizard-borne palanquins carried noble families through the crowd. The smells of roasting pork, baking bread, and orchard blossoms filled the air. Soon it would be filled with nothing but flame and magma and the ashes of a dead race.

Magtone pointed to the crowd and the carpet obeyed him. It brought him down low to hover above their heads. Faces stared up at him, some filled with wonder, some with annoyance, others with blank curiosity. Even the slaves ceased their labor to watch the spectacle. Magtone stood on the floating rug, still clutching his book, and shouted at the crowd. He told them what he had told Angelita: The Adepts were going to destroy the city. Everybody would die unless they fled right now. There was no time to spare, they must all leave now or perish in fire.

"Flee!" he told them. "Flee for your lives!"

Soon they began to laugh at him. Men called him "fool" or "clown." Women exchanged glances of concern that turned to wicked amusement. Children stared, uncomprehending, entirely dependent on the decisions of their parents. Magtone tried his best to make them listen. He repeated his warning again and again, drifting about the plaza like a slow-moving cloud. Always his eyes glanced back toward Ogmandolin's estate, as if he could sense doom approaching from that direction. But he saw nothing unusual. If the Adept had survived the Order's attack, he must be preparing to cast his ultimate spell even now. How many precious seconds of life were left for these people?

Someone threw a stone. It struck Magtone in the side of the head, spoiling his balance. Clutching his book, he fell into a mass of people who were already cursing his presence.

"Leave us alone!" The words had come a split-second after the flying stone.

His body struck the pavement, and the manuscript fell from his hands to lay on the flagstones beside him. His eyes were fixed on the carpet's intricate weave-patterns while it hovered still above the crowd. Sandalled feet kicked at him, and calloused hands grabbed him by the shirt. Someone punched his face while someone else kicked him in the groin. They spat on him, calling him "heretic" and "assmonger" as they beat him senseless. Behind a blur of fists and legs, he saw them reaching for his manuscript.

"No!" He screamed for mercy, but it was too late.

Six men held and pummeled him while two others opened his folio. Unable or unwilling to read its contents, they tore the pages to bits one by one, flinging them into the air like parade petals.

"Kill the fool!" someone shouted.

"Spike his head on the temple gate!"

Magtone curled himself into a ball as they thumped the life out of him. Someone started on his back with a club, sparking cheers from the others. Someone else pulled Magtone's own dagger and raised it high. His confederates leaned backward to let the dagger-man do his work. Magtone's right eye had swollen shut, but his left eye watched the destruction of his manuscript. The loss of it pained him more than his flesh wounds.

So be it, he decided. *No one will ever know what happened to Karakutas.*

The man with the dagger split in half. The left and right sides of his body fell in opposite directions. Blood and guts spilled across the pavement, as if someone had overturned a butcher's bucket. Ogmandolin floated in the air next to the carpet. His hands were thin and skeletal, gleaming with deadly magics. His wounds no longer bled, but none of them had healed. The crowd fled in fear from the presence of an immortal Adept in all his murderous glory.

"Poets are fools," Lord Og said. He sank to earth and offered Magtone a bony, glowing hand. "I told you they're all trapped here. You've been freed of destiny, but they have not. You cannot persuade anyone to leave this place. You should have listened to me and spared yourself all this pain."

Magtone stared at the stained and muddy shreds of his masterpiece. He spat blood.

"They tore it apart…" he said. "There's no book…nothing left." He lay back on the pavement, ready to die with the rest of the city. The pain of losing all his hard work of the last week was too much. Let flame and sorcery cleanse this evil place. Let Karakutas get what it deserved. *Let us all die and be forgotten.*

Ogmandolin looked toward the shredded manuscript. He waved his hands, muttered an incantation. Torn scraps of paper rose into the air like a flock of butterflies. They whirled and gleamed and turned to motes of swirling light.

"Open your mouth," Lord Og said.

Magtone wiped his bloody lips and did so. He wasn't exactly sure why he did it.

Maybe he wasn't quite ready to die after all.

"A bit wider if you please," said the wizard.

Magtone opened wide, his bruised and split lips shooting with pain.

The whirling motes rushed at his face and flew straight into his mouth. He didn't even need to swallow as the luminous flood poured down his throat into his belly. A strange warmth filled his middle, and his brain raced with the effects of digesting sorcery. The pain of his wounds was not gone, but somehow it no longer bothered him.

"Now *you* are the chronicle," said Ogmandolin. "The time is short. Go."

The carpet lowered itself and Magtone climbed aboard. The words of his lost epic swam in his head like the effect of a strong wine. Each and every word was there. The entire manuscript, every line of every verse, clear and persistent in his memory. The book was gone, but the story lived on.

"Quickly," Lord Og said. "They're coming."

Magtone had no time to say farewell. The carpet soared fast as a hawk, sailing between the tower-tops and out of the city. Magtone turned as it flew, looking back at the plaza. The people of Karakutas gathered in its far corners or hid behind merchant stalls as a great wind rushed into the marketplace. Ogmandolin floated in the air, arms outstretched, singing the words of his ultimate spell. Twelve white-robed fiends fell toward him like burning meteors.

The carpet sped past the outer wall of the city-bowl. Ogmandolin's spell exploded like a shockwave across the city. The earth trembled and roared as stone towers crumbled. Already people were dying as the Order assailed Lord Og's magical defenses. Yet his great spell had been cast. Fire elementals raged deep inside the earth and fulfilled their pact. The volcano woke from its long sleep. It woke angry, spewing liquid fire.

Far behind Magtone the earth exploded in a column of red flame and black smoke. Colossal chunks of stone hurled through the sky in all directions. The carpet veered left, then right, threading between a rain of blazing boulders. Magtone looked back as a sea of orange lava overflowed the volcano's rim, and the debris of Karakutas pounded the earth of the surrounding lands. A cloud of ash rose into the sky, expanding until Magtone found himself flying through the darkness of an early night. The carpet soared even faster, until it broke free of the overcast lands and emerged into fresh sunlight.

A yellow desert lay far below, and the sky was deep blue. The color of freedom.

Sudden loneliness fell upon Magtone like a sickness, but the warm wind dried his tears and the blood on his face. He flew on across seas, mountains, and forests. He flew over plains thick with golden wheat, the crumbled watchtowers of lost empires, and river valleys full of battling serpents. Somewhere ahead must lie a town or a city, some bulwark against the constant wilderness. Someplace where people lived and loved, perhaps a city where poets dared to dream out loud. A place to tell his story.

"Where are you taking me?" he asked the carpet.

It gave no answer.

LIVINGSTONE
by Cody Goodfellow

An hour later, Harley was still nursing a bad case of butthurt about shooting the looters.

Vic never stopped riding him about it. "You don't see me cryin', and they could've been my cousins. Harden the fuck up, *mijo*. This is how we roll in the real world." He winked at Troy and Mitch, and the subject died.

Troy had only been with Eris Security Solutions eight months, but he already knew how to shake down peasants in four languages. Mitch was new, but he got bounced out of the Army for a shady engagement that killed civilians, so he was already like family.

Harley seemed hard enough already. Squeeze him any harder and tears would squirt out his ears.

Troy could almost relate, but he kept a lid on it. His great-grandfather came down here with the Marines in the 30's to quell a strike. Said they were the nicest people he ever had to kill. After two tours in Iraq, it felt good to be out in the rain. Even better that the people they shot at never shot back.

"Seriously, dude," Vic went on, "it was a righteous fight. They should've evacced a week ago. I *told* them to drop the shit. *You* fired a warning shot. By disobeying a direct order, they as good as committed suicide. You should be mad at *them*, man. They used us to off themselves."

Harley didn't answer, ran the motor up louder. He didn't seem to want to touch his gun. The big sixty had cut two men and a woman down as they struggled through waist-deep floodwater, pushing a canoe filled with bottled water and canned fruit. After Harley lit them up, the canoe floated away.

"That really how it is?" Troy asked.

Vic spat in the flood and nodded. "Same as in the sand, but we play big boy rules all day, out here. God's not watching."

A fleet of gigantic gray thunderheads still hung over the coastline, dumping sheets of blood-warm rain, but the flood had begun to drain out of the city, laying bare the brown, slimy ruins of Puerto Barrios.

They zipped around the drowned coastal slums for another hour without seeing any action, then stopped at the rally and resupply point on the old United Fruit railhead. Eris had a couple dozen teams training the Guatemalan *federales* in counterterror maneuvers in the mountains when the storm hit. They came down to help evac the towns, but with the mission all but over, the boys had broken out the Jet Skis and spear guns to go shark hunting. Vic's team pulled the long straw. Orders were to patrol the mouth of the river, "secure property and locate survivors" and "escort them to the nearest relocation staging area," if they felt like doing paperwork.

The nameless tropical storm had budded and spun off Hurricane Aloysius and turned south at Cuba. It carved a meandering trench down the Caribbean coast, rearranging hundreds of miles of hellish Honduran swampland before creaming Bahia De Amatique. The storm broke, Lago De Izabal flooded, and the black river that poured into the bay rose up and swallowed half of Puerto Barrios—the poor half, known as Livingstone.

The forty thousand Afro-Carib and Maya citizens of Puerto Barrios would never rate the kind of protection Eris offered its clients, but Dole and Del Monte still shipped out of the port, and the bustling community of American retirees on the hills would sleep safer in their beds knowing somebody with heavy automatic weapons stood between them and the soggy, starving natives. They'd sleep even better, knowing they would soon have a new golfcourse.

At the mouth of the river, Troy could see only the jumbled rooftops of the fishing village of Livingstone, sticking out above the brown wavelets from the bay. Place was named for some white guy who helped Guatemala become a country, but it'd been here for centuries before that, without amounting to much. No city government, no cemetery, none of the roots that bound a community. All of the surviving residents had been evacuated. Vic's team had the duty of shooting anyone who tried to come back.

Out of disaster would come progress. From an unsightly beachfront slum to a string of luxury time-shares, a four-star Masters-grade course, and a massive levee so this would never happen again.

Harley steered them into the straits between the old Spanish fort and the reefs of sunken houses. Most of the palm-thatched shacks and jetsam cottages had washed away, but a hazardous maze of cinderblock walls and satellite dishes jutted out of the black water, and a few multistory houses and somebody's half-ass idea of a church leaned crookedly above the oily flood, which came alive like stained glass in a cathedral under their halogen searchlights.

At least down here, they didn't have to worry about looters. There was nothing worth stealing down here *before* the flood.

"You still bent out of shape, dude?" Vic asked.

"We're supposed to be *helping* people, man," Harley said.

Vic spat in the water. "We are so *not* here to help. We're here to restore order and secure property. And I thought we did *commendably*. You guys think we did anything wrong?"

Troy and Mitch shook their heads.

"What if that guy *was* the storeowner?" Harley brayed. "What if the only way for him to survive was locked up in those stores? What would you do, if it was *your* family, out here?"

"Those people don't own anything, which is why they let it go to shit. In case you didn't notice, *my* ancestors didn't come here on the Mayflower, and you don't see *me* crying."

Troy could have said something. Vic had seniority on him, but not rank. He didn't say anything because it scared him, being able to relate to the people of Livingstone.

Troy grew up in the 9th Ward of New Orleans. He was a Ranger living in Saddam's palace in Tikrit when the levees broke. For a year after, his grandmother and aunt lived in a shitty trailer, eating canned cat food and breathing formaldehyde fumes. He had not joined the Army to be anyone's hero; it was just the only employer that was hiring. His country couldn't protect his family while he was away, so he went across the street.

Since coming to Eris, Troy had worked in three failed states and "free market zones." His grandmother and aunt had a nice condo in Shreveport, far from the toxic ghost town their old neighborhood had become. Nobody looked out for him and his, or gave them a dime when their home washed away. He supposed these people would make out alright too, if they were worth a shit.

The water was like motor oil, which mercifully hid most of the things drowned in it. The surface was a dazzling oilslick swirl of unholy rainbow hues, broken here and there by phantom ripples. A dead dog bobbed up in their wake, swelled up like a sausage casing. Apparently, the evacuation hadn't been as thorough as advertised.

"Up there!" Harley pointed at a second-story balcony, with a warped cast-iron railing. The balcony was a boat landing, now, only inches above the lapping black water.

Troy had seen something, too. A pale oval between the curtains, but he didn't say anything.

"Go on in, boys. Make Harley feel better. *Help somebody…*"

Mitch reached out and grabbed the railing. The rusted iron broke off in his hand. He almost fell in, but Vic shoved him, and he gamely jumped onto the balcony. Troy jumped after him before Vic could push.

Mitch looked in the window, smashed the glass with the butt of his rifle. "There's nobody in there, man."

Troy climbed over the windowsill. His foot sank into rotten floor-boards, pulpy like wet bread. He had seen the girl, too. He didn't want to stick his head out. If they found nothing, they could keep moving. When you tried to help people like this, half the time, somebody ended up dead. They weren't here to save anyone or protect anything but equity.

Something squirmed and screamed under his boot. Jerking back, Troy swept the floor with the flashlight taped to his gun barrel.

A pale, bloated body lay across a futon by his foot, seeming to jerk and toss as if trying to get up and cover its nakedness. Troy reached out for her hand and took hold of it, then dropped it and wiped off the putrid skin that'd sloughed on him.

She wasn't moving. Sleek gray and black bodies ripped into her and dragged her limp limbs back and forth across the mattress in a hideous tug of war, pouring out the hole in her face.

Rats. The room was filled with them. He turned and swept the room for another girl. There might have been furniture under the rats, but every rodent in Livingstone was holed up in this shitbox apartment. Stairs went down a hole in the corner of the room. The water that filled the stairwell rolled and smacked like lips chewing food. He thought he saw something pale and slim bob on the surface, and then a gray, filthy wave broke over his feet.

Troy opened fire and raked the floor as he backed up. They were coming up his legs, chewing holes in his pants. He felt little claws like hordes of needles pricking him all over. He leapt over the windowsill and dove into the raft. Mitch shoved off.

A river of rats flowed out after him. The water churned with their shrieking, frenzied bodies.

"Where's the girl?" Harley asked. "What's in there?"

Hyperventilating, Troy racked a phosphorus grenade into the launcher. "Nothing," he said, and blooped the grenade through the open window.

Vic punched the motor and dropped the prop into the rat soup, set it to puree. Severed tails and filleted furry carcasses flew in their crimson wake.

The house popped like a balloon and sagged beneath the smoking water.

"No girl," Troy gasped. "Nobody alive in there… Just…oh God…" His crotch wriggled. Troy moaned and ripped open his zipper to let a rat the size of a kitten scurry out.

Mitch punched Troy's shoulder. "No fucking way! You're hardcore, bro."

"If the rest of you see any survivors," Vic said, "keep it to your selves."

* * * *

But Vic saw the next one.

She stood ankle-deep in the water at the end of the main drag. Her tattered cotton shift was the color of mud. Her long black hair fluttered in the wind-driven rain, covering her face. She waved and reached out her arms, and called out to them in a language with too many x's in it to be Spanish.

"God damn it," Vic said. "How do these fucking fugees keep breaching our fucking perimeter?"

"Maybe they never left," Harley said. "Like I told you, this is their home, they never completely evac…"

"Can't believe this shit," Vic growled, but he killed the motor and set them gliding closer.

She stood on a stone monument—a cenotaph, Troy recalled. They had them in New Orleans, and anywhere else people went to sea and never came back. The flaky limestone pillar was carved up with crude names and symbols and shapes.

"C'mere, sweetheart," Harley said, "I won't hurt you." He put out a hand, but she shrank away. Harley stepped out of the boat, putting a foot on the cenotaph. It crumbled under his boot.

Harley said, "Fuck," and fell into the water.

The girl came closer, weeping through her curtain of waving black hair, waving like something under the sea. Her tears were mud. She was standing on the surface of the flood.

Troy reached down for Harley. He couldn't see an inch into it, felt the water itself pushing against him, like millions of drowning earthworms wriggling against his hand. He chopped at it, searching for Harley's head or hands, but he couldn't find anything.

Vic raised his gun and shot the girl in the belly. She didn't make a sound, just bent over with the impact of the slugs.

Gouts of thick black slime splashed between her toes. Black, slimy mud spilled out of her instead of blood. The stream of mud twisted in the air and reached out—not like fluid escaping a wound under pressure, but like something alive, seeking to escape, or attack. And then she simply came apart like a cake in the rain and sank out of sight.

Troy recoiled from the water—fuck Harley, he wasn't coming up.

"Did you see that, man?" Mitch kept screaming. "Oh shit, did you see that?"

Vic slapped him so hard he fell down in the drifting raft. "Get us under way."

Troy stared hard into the flood, but he wasn't going to touch it again. "I don't see Harley…"

"He's gone," Vic said, "and so are we." Hauling on the starter, he snapped, "Call it in. We're under attack."

From what? Troy got out his phone. It wasn't waterproofed, so he kept it in a Zip-Loc bag. His fingers were slimy with that viscous black shit. It didn't smell like mud. It smelled like sweat. It tasted like tears.

He thumbed the 911 button and shouted, "Franchise One, this is Drive-Thru One-Two, we have a man down in Sector 3…"

Crackling like a campfire, the voice of the front office sounded beyond pissed. "...got real *problems here, so spit on it for now, 'kay? Thanks, and stay off the fucking commo lines—*"

The phone squirted right out of his hand like soap in the shower, disappeared in the black. He was about to throw it anyway.

"Why aren't we moving?" Vic demanded.

"We're fouled up in something, I don't know…" Mitch leaned over the side. "Oh God…"

"Cut us free!"

"I can't, dude… I—oh Jesus, no…" Mitch dropped the knife in the water.

Whatever he saw went unsaid, preempted by the repeat appearance of his breakfast.

Troy leaned over the stern and took hold of the snarls of black weed wrapped around the props, but it wasn't weed, or wire, or fishing net. It was human hair, yards and yards of it braided around the propeller.

As he tugged at it, her head came bobbing up like an anchor.

"Fuck this shit!" Vic shoved Troy aside and stabbed frantically at the bobbing body. Gelatinous flesh came off the bone like something marinated far too long. She was full of mud. She was made of mud. Black pseudopods of it engulfed Vic's arm, nearly pulling him out of the raft. "Get off, get off!" Vic screamed, totally losing it.

Troy heard a splash and looked up. "They said they evacced everybody," he said, quite suddenly and blissfully detached from the reality of the moment.

One moment, the street was a river; the next, the smooth black ooze bubbled and ruptured like a mother's water breaking. The flood was a bubbling black gumbo of bobbing, bloated corpses.

Mitch saw it, too. He started crying. Before Troy could point this out to Vic, they all sat up.

They'd been at the bottom for days, shot in the gut and weighted with rocks so they wouldn't float up when they decayed and filled with gas. The crabs and fish had been at their eyes, but they could clearly see. Wiggling tendrils of black slime thrust out of their empty sockets and every other orifice, tasting the air and trembling in sympathy with the screaming.

"Vic, they never evacced the indigs, did they?"

Vic didn't answer, cussing and chopping the wads of human hair out of the props.

There were dozens, but most were older than the flood. Little more than bones animated by the mud itself, they lurched up out of the mud and closed ranks until the raft rocked in their arms.

Something deeper than death had seeped up out of the soil of Livingstone, and fused with the oil and PCB's and industrial runoff and city filth. Something in the dust and the breath of this place, the angry undead memory of it, had turned the soil and the water to weapons. Worst of all, they had killed everything that lived in this place, and now the place demanded…

"What do you want from us?"

Mitch hit him and shrieked, "Get some!" They strafed the soup of waterlogged bodies like putting out a fire. The tumbling hollow-point rounds splashed through them, ripping them apart, but not stopping them. Troy popped off his last grenades when his clip ran dry, shouted every slur and curse he knew when he ran out of those.

Fuck off and lie down and die. The game is over, and you lost. The great game that started with Columbus and ended with Coca Cola was the only game that mattered, and this was not how it was played. Home was just a place, until you lost it. You didn't get killed to keep a shitty fishing village or a rundown, flooded ghetto; when times got tough, you took care of your own and moved on, and maybe someday got a job doing the same to dirtier, poorer people, somewhere worse, so it all evened out.

But he didn't think they'd understand. They sure didn't understand bullets. Mitch slapped his last clip into his MP5. He couldn't stop giggling.

Vic gunned the motor and the raft bolted into a cresting wave of bodies, jolted upright as something stood up under it.

Mitch was flung over Troy's head as he slid backwards on top of Vic, who drew his sidearm and fired through the floor of the raft.

Troy hit the water and went blind. Cold, but it burned his skin and it was so much thicker than water…more like rancid, curdled blood. He kicked and fought to keep his head above it. He felt it trying to get into his mouth and nostrils, probing his eyelids like blind fingers.

He caught a pontoon and threw himself onto it, but something grabbed his web belt and snatched him back. He whipped around and found Harley.

"Xaaaa…" Harley said. His eyes burst and curious worms of black slime thrust out at Troy's screaming face. His jaw dropped and came unhinged, overstuffed with flapping black tongues.

Vic wedged his arm between them and put his gun under Harley's jaw. "It's not Harley," he said. Christ, was he asking permission?

Harley dunked Troy. Something grabbed his thrashing ankles with a grip like bony scissors.

Vic pulled the trigger. The top of Harley's head blew off in a fountain of black slush. Vic shoved the barrel of his automatic into Harley's eye and shot him again and again, until he'd whittled Harley's head completely off.

Vic dragged Troy back into the raft. "Time-and-a-half, my ass," he grumbled. "This shit is… Ah, *madre de putas*…"

Troy was shivering and numb. All he could do was watch when Harley's headless mud-puppet sprang out of the water and wrapped its arms around Vic's legs.

Mitch shot Harley four times, hit Vic twice in his chest before he went under.

The street was a lazy river again. The water slurped and sucked at itself, but nothing stood up. The flood had made its point. Troy jumped for the throttle and steered the boat out of Livingstone.

They drifted in the channel. The wind picked up, driving fat raindrops in their faces.

"Yo, Mitch. We got to get our story straight."

Mitch dry-heaved over the side and prayed to Jesus to forgive him.

Troy told him to shut up and get Harley's heavy machinegun. "There's more of them, on our nine."

About a hundred yards out across the river channel, they stood on the surface of the rain-dappled water in a defiant, beckoning line. And these ones were armed.

They pointed something at the raft, something big and shoulder-mounted. Troy ducked down and shouted at Mitch. The kid took up Harley's SAW and raked them until they all fell down and merged with the flood.

Troy brought them closer, wiping the slime out of his eyes. The raft ran aground and jerked to a halt on a sandbar.

The adrenaline and terror turned to poison in his veins.

Mitch danced around the bodies. "*Yeah, motherfuckers!* This is our house, now!" Maybe he didn't see them. Maybe he couldn't see anything, anymore.

Troy looked around for more mud-people, but the lights from the railhead hit him full in the face, washing the scene with unwelcome color.

The dead were armed with cameras. The CNN logo on the big live uplink camera sank out of sight just before the red light on the viewfinder blinked and went black. The famous reporter in a snazzy hooded camouflage poncho blew black bubbles as the current pulled him seaward.

Troy threw down his gun. They would use any excuse not to take him alive. There could be no witnesses, now, to whatever happened next.

In the end, he could take comfort in knowing he'd fought for the winning side. And whatever happened to him, Puerto Barrios was going to get a beautiful golf course.

✗

NOW WE ARE JOINED
by Darrell Schweitzer

Now we are joined in the dance of death,
just like in that movie, The Seventh Seal,
hands together, somebody up front
actually clinging to the robe
of the tall guy with the scythe and hourglass,
the chill passing back through the rest
like negative electricity, all strength, all will
drained away as we weave
up and down the gray hills,
as insubstantial as a curtain of rain.
I try to think of the Stoic epitaph:
I was not, I was, I am not, I don't care.
But it's no good: from up ahead I hear sounds,
not the shrieks or crackling flames you'd expect,
but babbling voices, traffic noise, trashcans banged together,
the roar of some engine.
Does it go on forever, as an adventure,
or is this where the horror begins?

TATTERED LIVERY
by Kyla Lee Ward

A paradox awaits their eyes:
a courtier in beggar's guise!
A ragged, jagged, mad array
and yet suggestive of the day
when I, perhaps, was much like them.
A most ingenious stratagem!
For many holding this belief
will offer tokens of relief
to turn their own ill luck aside.
What fallacy, what foolish pride
left this young fellow so bereaved?
But in this, they are all deceived.
There is a glory in my dress
surpassing all they might possess!
There is a river, dark and strong,
that carries all who dream along
and, drifting, I could not resist
a pale meander, thick with mist,
so found the lake that never can
reflect the face of star or man.
Instead, the captive of the stream
beholds the phosphorescent gleam
of sunken, lost and ruined things
enshrouded by their sails and wings,
and floating hair. As life recedes,
flavescent, a corona bleeds
from all who die in hate and fear,
and all in time are gathered here
where he who lifts his gaze will see
black towers rising endlessly.
In bravery, catastrophe!
And he who grants me charity
dips hand into the river, he
will feel it cold and shivery,
I wear my tattered livery
and serve a tattered king.

* * * *

A branch the drowning man reprieves:
a tree with needles for its leaves
and lightest touch of naked skin
conducts these slivers deep within.
Beside this tree, the stairs of stone
admit such supplicants alone.
A thousand steps, eroded by
a thousand, thousand such as I.
A thousand steps above the falls
to enter the tenebral halls
wherein the ever-moving feast
leaves ashes strewn and platters greased,
and there the prints, in ichor sweet,
of hooves and claws, and dancing feet.
The catch of laughter, trill of strings,
the raucous echoes screaming brings:
so he may wander, night on night
before he sees the fulvous light,
before he hears the silken voice
and understands how every choice
was none at all: no prize to gain,
the wearisome annular chain
has brought him here, already bound,
a fitting task already found.
To see one's soul turn crystalline
within that hand, and so resign!
To see it join the lucent drape
of all who in this way escape
the ache of their autonomy,
suspended for eternity.
In slavery lies ecstasy!
And all who lay their hands on me
suspecting fraud or thievery,
by proxy touch the sliver-tree!
I wear my tattered livery
and serve a tattered king.

* * * *

And as the pangs of day replace
the shrilling pipe and barbed embrace,
I tread through streets no longer known,
for all their former sense has flown.
These soaring spires and tiny greens!
Whole lives compacted into screens!
I seek out those I knew before
and mark the Sign above their door:

the ones who scorned, the ones who stole,
and these His hunger swallows whole.
But one remains whose love was true,
I seek her out and peering through
a winter crevice, see her stand
before an easel, brush in hand.
Remember that I once stood there,
before the doubt, before despair,
before I knelt before the throne,
had visions that were all my own.
Believed it was my task to show
the world to all who did not know
the precious piece of cosmic art
of which they are themselves a part!
So vulnerable she seems, and slight,
and yet before her inner light
I am a mummy: gutted, dried,
with only darkness left inside.
But I do not resent the time
she has to draw and dance, and rhyme.
I watch and wait, until I see
the world reward its devotee
with poverty and mockery!
And when she reaches out to me,
my darkness I shall give her free;
her deepest heart a-quiver, she
shall share this tattered livery
and love our tattered king.

THE DEATH AND BURIAL OF POOR CRACK ROBIN

by Abdul-Qaadir Taariq Bakari-Muhammad

Woe our hero is dead.
We have but one question.
Who killed Crack Robin?

It was I, said Mr. Herring Sparrow.
With a sharpen decision and pen like arrow.
I killed Crack Robin.

Who saw him die?
I, said the Fly, his most hated villain with my cop cam eyes,
I set the aperture to extinction to make sure he would fry,
I saw him die.

Who caught his blood?
I, said the Fish,
To examine the source of his power was my life long wish,
I caught his blood.

Who'll make his shroud?
I, said the Divine Beetle,
After all I possessed his veins by supplying his needles,
I'll make his shroud.

Who'll dig his grave?
I, said the Owl,
He denied my warnings and painfully ran afoul.
I'll dig his grave.

Who'll bear the pall?
We, said the Wren,
His brother, sons, and dearest friends,
We'll bear the pall.

Who'll carry him to the grave?
I, said the Kite,

May the eyes of Ausar grant him with sight.
I'll carry him to the grave.

Who'll be the Parson?
I, said the Rook,
Even though he's already burning in hell according to my book.
I'll be the Parson.

Who'll sing a Psalm?
I, said the Thrush,
Pity a bag of rocks was his God in Trust,
I'll sing the Psalm.

Who'll be the Clerk?
I, said the Lark,
But only after dark, souls of the dead wail until sunrise spark,
I'll be the Clerk.

Who'll be Chief Mourner?
I, said the Dove,
He was my husband,
 And my heart that I will always love.
I'll be Chief Mourner.

Who'll carry the Link?
I, said the Linnet,
And may the steps of heaven be his harpsichord spinet,
I'll carry the Link.

Who'll toll the bell?
I, said the Bull,
Full with muscle and tone,
I tried leave but he hated being alone,
He called to me only when habits he couldn't denounce,
At age 40 with me in hand dead he was pronounced.
I'll toll the bell.
Throughout the world of tv land many people sighed and sobbed
        in due course,
The life of their hero halted without remorse,
In given notice the writing was on the wall,
Poor Crack Robin would not debut any season…none ever at all.

The next day Mr. Herring Sparrow had this to say.
"The networks would have hung me by the neck.
A lead black male super hero? Ha! That you can forget!

Drug addict, drunkard, from rags to riches?
Nonsense give me a script about one pulling up his britches.
Until then don't ever talk to me about diversity.
Poor Crack Robin sounds more like perversity."

He laughed the cruel producer Mr. Herring Sparrow,
The name they called him out of spoof.
During sweeps week he was found thrown from his penthouse
    roof.

CAUGHT IN DIMENSION
by Denny Marshall

Travel to other dimension only to find.
Strange forms engaged beneath an unfamiliar tree.
All thoughts marked out of date, inside expanding mind.
While all around spiral-like shapes and spheres swim free.

Package will not wrap bow between inside or out.
With light and darkness, taking turns at trading places.
Sounds bond from altered corners as they speak and shout.
Move in all directions with fluctuating faces.

Buildings stir and transform, depending on the day.
Colors shift opposite and turn different shades.
Mountains dance across the land, engaging in play.
As sky turns up volume or down until it fades.

Labyrinth paths at uncommon levels and heights.
Paintbrush of the unusual count away the nights.

Made in the USA
Columbia, SC
23 December 2017